The Case of the Grudge Tiger

by

Judith Fournie Helms

Cover Art by *Teddi Black*

The Wild Rose Press, Inc.
PO Box 708
Adams Basin, NY 14410-0708
Visit us at www.thewildrosepress.com

Publishing History
First Edition, 2026
Trade Paperback Print ISBN 978-1-5092-6437-7
Digital ISBN 978-1-5092-6438-4

Previously published 2021 TouchPoint Press
Published in the United States of America

Dedication

In memory of Susan, who loved her cats and all the other wonders of the world, great and small.

In memory of Pat, who taught me how to be a lawyer, and introduced me to the original grudge tiger.

And for Larry.

Siempre Adelante

Praise for The Case of the Grudge Tiger

"…This story can best be described as wholesome. Helms' writing style, with accessible but detailed prose, gives the tale an overall feeling of nostalgic comfort, a warmth and simplicity that's present in animal-centered family movies like Free Willy and Homeward Bound. These traits pop in the dialogue as well…This simplicity is a strength and is partly what makes the story enjoyable. Another high point is the trial, particularly when Dr. Nigel Lucas, the English tiger expert, delivers passionate, clever testimony…."

"A charming tale about a loving family and their beloved tiger."

Kirkus Reviews

***

"A thoroughly engaging legal drama packed full of interesting, often charismatic, characters."

A Wishing Shelf

***

"A tale of intrigue, empathy and drama…uniquely detailed and flawlessly written novel."

Susan Coryell, Author of A Red, Red, Rose,
Beneath the Stones, Nobody Knows,
A Murder of Principle, and Eaglebait.

ACKNOWLEDGMENTS

Many people provided me with such valuable assistance with this novel that their names belong on the cover of The Case of the Grudge Tiger, along with mine. I thanked them when this book was originally released (as Grudge Tiger) in 2021, and I thank them again here. They are Betsy Ashton, Judith Budner, Dr. Lynne Foreman, Col. Dan Fournie, Holly Hale, Lily Helms, Mayor Don Huffer, Grace Kotre, Diane Langhorst, Max Langhorst, developmental editor Anne McAneny, Anne Moore (1947-2023), Bill Sparer and Mary Ann Sparer, Mary Beth Trybulec, Rev. Cheryl Wade, Eileen Watson, and the Lake Writers of the Virginia Writers Club.

This book would not have been possible without the insights, encouragement, and vision of Ally Robertson, Crimson Editor of The Wild Rose Press. She is an absolute pleasure to work with. I continue to be immensely grateful to her and to all of the talented people at my wonderful publisher.

Finally, my deepest appreciation is always for my trusted first reader, my husband, Larry.

Chapter 1

Kenny

Kenny's eyes latch onto Dean because it's impossible to *not* watch him, especially when he parades his perfect body around—shirtless. He comes from the direction of the petting zoo, where Marietta, her gorgeous older sister, is painting one of the supply sheds. Kenny doesn't think Dean sees her since she's standing under the branches of one of the enormous weeping willows that divide the back yard from the rest of the forty acres of the zoo. He scowls as he passes, like an old, pissed-off camel about to spit. He stops mid-stride, leans down the way a pitcher does to wind up, and throws a shiny, flat object up over the high fence and into Ms. Benni's cage.

Kenny's gaze zips to Ms. Benni, who doesn't move except to raise her head a couple of inches—just enough to show she's seen or heard the thing land. Then Dean is at the doorway, pushing the digits on the keypad so quickly it takes Kenny a moment to realize what he's about to do. He walks through the first steel chain-link door, does the same thing with the second, and saunters in, real casual, like he's strolling through the mall. After Dean takes about six steps, Ms. Benni rises and slips into a crouch, her belly coming off the ground as she stares intently at him, her ears back. She lifts one paw slightly, and her tail shoots straight out. Anybody who owns a cat can guess what's about to happen. Kenny screams bloody murder just before Ms. Benni lets out a thunderous roar and flies from the shade of the tree all the way to the spot where Dean scrambles to the door he just came through. Dean is too slow. Ms. Benni's right front claw rips through his left arm and leg.

As her screaming drowns out the donkeys braying in the next pen, Kenny sees Charlie, their lead maintenance man, grab Dean and pull him through the two gates, which slam behind them. Ms. Benni ambles back to the shade, lays herself down, and yawns. Kenny calls 911 and takes a deep breath so she'll be able to talk to the operator. Her phone has been in her hand the whole time because she's been recording Dean to share with her best friend Becca, something she always tries to do on his delivery days. She knows Dean's injuries are serious, because a 300-pound Bengal tiger doesn't serve out boo-boos that aren't. Her brain fights to catch up with what she's seeing because in the eight years they've had Ms. Benni, she's never tried to attack anybody.

Marietta comes running from the supply shed. Their mother sprints from the house to where Charlie has Dean on the ground just outside Ms. Benni's enclosure and looks up at Kenny standing beside the open gate in the picket fence, just beyond the trees. Her mother yells to get some clean sheets. Kenny nods, then dashes through the yard, bolts into the house, screen door slamming behind her, and takes the stairs two at a time up to the second-floor linen closet. She fumbles as she tries to hold onto a large pile of sheets and almost falls head-over-heels running back down the stairs. As she flies through the back yard, her heart pulses fast, blood rushes to her head, and her tongue grows thick. She wonders if she might have a heart attack.

Once Kenny makes it, she sees that her mother has tied her apron around Dean's leg and is using her baby blue blouse to wrap his upper arm. Kenny is embarrassed that other people see her mother in just a bra, a concern she realizes may be more about herself. Her mother grabs the sheets and uses them to cover Dean's blood-soaked wrappings. It isn't working. Within seconds, the sheets turn the color of their raspberry preserves. Dean lies flat on the ground, shaking like he's having some kind of seizure, his face as white as the sheets were. It's as though every bit of his blood is in a race to make it to the wrappings. Kenny hears the ambulance siren wailing in the distance and yells at it to hurry up. She notices her sister standing back, maybe ten yards away. Marietta holds a large paint brush, dripping red paint all over her legs and the grass, like a little girl with a melting popsicle. The next time Kenny glances at her, Marietta is sobbing into her left elbow.

Kenny figures it takes the ambulance about fifteen years to arrive, but it's only been fifteen minutes according to her phone. The driver parks in the gravel driveway, the closest he can get to Dean, and three men in tan uniforms come running through the back yard with their equipment. Once they reach him, one of them wraps Dean's arm and leg in large sheets of gauze, while the second guy crams plastic into Dean's nose to give him oxygen. The third man sticks a needle into him and connects it to a tube and a bag of clear liquid which he then holds above Dean's head. Another year seems to pass before they move him onto a stretcher, carry him to the ambulance and slip him inside. One of the attendants jumps in the back with Dean. The other two slam the back doors, jump in the front, and peel out with sirens screaming. Huge dust clouds trail the ambulance, then disappear as quickly as they bloomed. As the air clears, Kenny realizes she has no idea why Dean threw the thing and then followed it into Ms. Benni's cage.

Chapter 2

Marietta

Fifteen minutes before Kenny's first hysterical scream, Dean walks around the side of the supply shed looking for Marietta. She hears his footsteps on the gravel and knows it's too late to hide, so she grimaces and braces herself for another unwanted overture. The grinding sound of the movement of gravel stops a few feet from her. Without looking away from her painting, she says, "Hi, Dean," as unenthusiastically as she can.

"Hey, Marietta."

She glances at him. He isn't carrying anything, so she knows he must've already finished his feed delivery. Dean wears only a pair of jeans, so Marietta returns her gaze to the large can of red paint rather than give him the satisfaction of thinking she is admiring his physique. "What's up?"

"I just finished my delivery, so I thought I'd stop by and say hi."

"Yeah. You did that." She flushes, embarrassed at her ability to speak so rudely to another human.

"Are you trying to get rid of me, Marietta?"

"No. Not really. We can talk. That would be cool. I just don't want you to ask me out again."

"Well, it just so happens that I have two tickets to a concert you might like."

Marietta knows she won't enjoy any concert if she goes with Dean. She tries for a reasonably friendly voice because she thinks Dean is generally an okay guy, except for his obsession with her. "No thanks. I really don't have any time for dates, what with my work schedule, helping Mom with this place, and taking a summer course."

"You always do that."

"Do what?"

"Find a reason to say no to me."

She stops painting and turns to look at Dean. "How many times?"

"What?"

"How many times have I said, 'No thanks?' "

"One hundred percent."

"Not percentage. How many times do you think it's been, Dean?"

"Hundreds?"

"Exactly. You have to stop." She really doesn't want to hurt his feelings, but he's been panting after her since fifth grade, and it's become intolerable.

"How can I stop when I'm in love with you?"

Marietta doesn't respond because she doesn't know what else there is to say.

"Listen. All I'm asking for is a chance—one date. If you spend some time with me, you might actually like me. I really do love you. Also, I might have some news about me that will surprise you. How can you not want to find out if we'd be a good couple?" He pauses, lifts his perfect right eyebrow a notch, and adds, "You're the only girl who's ever said no to me, ya know?"

The word "narcissist" almost jumps off her tongue. But what she actually says is, "Of course I don't know.

How could I know a thing like that? And doesn't your mentioning it suggest it's the reason you're so infatuated with me? Obviously, you just want what you can't have."

Dean seizes the opportunity to look right at her with his impossibly stunning green eyes which are the deep color of wet seaweed. "You're wrong, Marietta. It's not just that. Seriously, why won't you go out with me? Just tell me the truth for once. Then I won't bother you anymore."

"Really?"

"Um-hm."

"Are you sure you want to hear this, Dean?"

"Yeah. I'm sure."

She takes a deep breath and searches for something to stare at, settling on a rake leaning against the wall. "Okay. Here goes. You're not a bad guy. And you're the best-looking boy I've ever seen. In fact, if I first met you on one of my flights, I'd probably go out with you. But then I'd just find out what I already know. You're not what I'm looking for." He doesn't say anything, so she goes on. "You were always a terrible student, never went out for sports or anything else. You're nothing special— not especially brave, or funny, or ambitious. Do you think I forgot that you finished high school two years behind our class? And the only job you've ever had is your minimum wage gig, helping your dad with the Feed 'n Seed. The truth is, Dean, you're not even average. And I wouldn't settle for that." She knows what she's saying is cruel, so she tries to think of a sincere compliment. "You don't need me. Off the top of my head, I can think of ten girls who'd think they'd died and gone to heaven if you asked them out. Seriously. I can give you their names."

Marietta realizes the encouragement must not have worked when she glances up and sees he is looking down, grimacing and shaking his head. He turns away, lets out a long breath, and disappears. She bites her lower lip hard and it draws blood, warm and metallic. Talking to Dean like that was unconscionably mean, and she knows what made it so cruel was that everything she said was true.

Before, Marietta always tried not to hurt Dean's feelings, but he responded to that modicum of kindness like it was encouragement. As painful as it was to say the words, and as terrible as she feels that they're out there, she knows she really didn't have a choice. Dean invited her to tell him the real deal, with a promise to let her be. It wasn't something she wanted to do. It was Dean who backed her into a corner with the simple choice: tell him the truth and feel like crap for it, or continue to allow him false hope and cringe every time he's around. She leans over the paint can and dips her brush too far down. A few minutes later, she hears Kenny's blood-curdling cry and knows instantly it has to do with Dean. A second later, a full-throated tiger-roar shakes the ground.

Marietta runs towards the scream and stops cold when she sees Dean lying on the ground with Charlie kneeling over him, just outside Ms. Benni's area. She freezes. Her heart races and her breath comes in short spurts which make her feel nauseated. Since she can't see past Charlie, she takes two steps to her left then gags at the sight of the puddles of blood. An instant later, her mother also ministers to Dean. Marietta still holds the paintbrush as she vomits into the grass. She wipes her mouth on her other hand, drops the brush, and begins to wail. It strikes her that she doesn't want her crying to distract anyone from helping Dean, so she places her elbow over her mouth to stifle the sobs.

A minute passes before Marietta can get a grip and process what's going on. She can't believe it, even as she sees it happening. Dean went into Ms. Benni's enclosure. But what the hell was he thinking? One minute he's slithering off after insisting he wants an honest answer to his question, and the next he's outside Ms. Benni's area spouting rivers of blood. It's obvious whatever happened was because of what she said to him, and she wishes she could take back every word. She'd so much rather put up with Dean's creepy, puppy-like devotion than see him hurt. She hovers between disbelief and self-loathing and then starts to dry-heave, all the while praying Dean isn't as badly hurt as it looks.

Chapter 3

Carolyn

Just over a week after Dean got hurt, Carolyn gets up early to try to finish her bookkeeping before the crowds start to arrive at ten a.m. Through the dining room bay window, she catches a glimpse of a sheriff's car pulling up and parking, but since she's in the middle of a list of numbers, she keeps banging them into her computer until the doorbell rings. When she opens the door, she sees it's an old friend from church who'd been much closer to her husband than to her. "Hello, Fred. Won't you come in?"

"Thank you, Carolyn." Fred removes his hat as he walks through the door, leaning forward as though he's accustomed to being too tall for doorways. As he steps into the small foyer he looks around, almost like he's looking for Tom. It strikes her that Fred hasn't stopped by since the day of Tom's funeral, just over two years before. Of course, she sees him and his wife at church every Sunday, but that's the extent of it.

He rubs his right hand over his chin. "Too bad about that thing with Dean."

"It was just awful, Fred. I understand he was in the hospital for three or four days, which doesn't really surprise me. He was hurt pretty badly, from what I could tell." She shakes her head and adds, "I'll never in a million years understand why that boy let himself into Ms. Benni's enclosure. He had to know how dangerous it was."

"Yeah. Hard to understand."

Since he offers no explanation for his visit, and Carolyn has no idea why he's standing in her foyer, she thinks it best to be hospitable. "Will you have some iced tea, Fred? Maybe a slice of apple cake?"

"No. Thank you kindly, but I've got a number of stops to make this morning."

"Well then, thank you for swinging by to check up on us." The front door stands open. Carolyn takes a step toward it, but Fred doesn't move.

He says, "Actually, I stopped by to serve these legal papers on you." He's holding the envelope behind his hip in his left hand.

As he hands it to her, she says, "Legal papers? Really?" She twists the tab on the manila envelope and folds the top back.

"Go ahead and take it out. I'll just stick around for a few minutes to see if you have any questions."

It's a pile of typed pages stapled to a blue backing. She reads the heading on the first sheet: *Dean Alcott vs. Carolyn Warren, individually and d/b/a Warren Family Zoo.* "Dean's suing me?"

"Yeah. He's got Henry Perdue representing him. Now, Hank's on the feisty side of aggressive for sure, but he doesn't have a reputation for filing entirely frivolous lawsuits. My advice is to get yourself a lawyer as soon as possible."

The gut punch sucks the air out of her. Carolyn stumbles into the dining room, over to the sturdy oak table, manages to pull out a chair, and falls into it. Fred follows her into the room and remains standing just inside the doorway. Her heart races as she pages through the papers. The further she reads, the more her hand shakes. "It says here Dean's looking for something in excess of a million dollars." She looks up at her husband's old friend. "Fred, I don't have a million dollars. In fact, I'd be hard-pressed to come up with $5,000 cash. Everything I own is tied up in the zoo."

His deeply lined face arranges itself into a grimace before he shakes his head and sighs. "Listen, Carolyn, I can't give you legal advice. Wouldn't be any good if I did. Just get yourself a lawyer." He nods once for emphasis and heads for the front door.

Carolyn mumbles, "Okay," and rises to walk with him. She's struggling to comprehend the assault of accusatory words she just read. Most of the sub-paragraphs begin with the word "negligently."

Fred is putting his hat back on when he stops so abruptly that she has to catch herself to keep from walking into him. He looks down, rather than at Carolyn, and says, "Oh, one other thing I should tell you. The state's attorney says he's planning to look into this—whether you can keep your animal."

The statement wrenches her out of her fog. "What? Fred, the boy went into a tiger cage!"

"I'm just sayin' what I heard. I'm sure somebody will be in touch with you about that." He quickly shakes her hand and hightails it to his car.

She feels his nervousness but can't muster any sympathy for him. As she stands in the doorway watching him drive off, gravel popping beneath his tires like tiny gunshots, a wave of fear washes over her. She grows so weak she fears she'll collapse, so she stands absolutely motionless for a minute until the light-headedness passes.

Carolyn walks to the back door and calls to Charlie to fetch Marietta and Kenny, who are scheduled to be doing a check on the animal food dispensers and the swizzle-sticks for the bird sanctuary to prepare for the crowds. She tells him she needs to see the girls right away—no excuses. She remains at the door and can't help but watch Charlie hurry off. At sixty, he has the physique of a much younger man, probably from the physical demands of zookeeping, and a dark farmer's tan. She generally tries to resist the temptation since it annoys her that she often feels a visceral Pavlovian response to him.

In a few minutes, her girls come running. Carolyn leans against the kitchen sink as they stand a few feet from her, flushed from hurrying in out of the heat. She states in one quick sentence that she's been served with a lawsuit brought by Dean, and that the sheriff heard the state's attorney is looking into whether Ms. Benni will be allowed to remain at the zoo.

Marietta throws both hands up to her mouth. "Oh, no!"

"Yeah. This really sucks," Kenny says.

"No, Kenny. It doesn't just suck. It's all my fault. I'm so sorry." Though Marietta is looking at Kenny, the apology seems to be directed to Carolyn.

"Don't be silly, Marietta," Carolyn says. "This isn't anybody's fault but Dean's. He's always seemed like such a nice boy. But he proved last week that he's a very, very foolish young man."

"Yeah. You didn't push him into Ms. Benni's cage," Kenny says.

"Actually, I kinda did. The things I said to him by the shed were hideous. I'm appalled they came out of my mouth. I made him angry enough to do it."

"Marietta, I know you're just trying to be understanding, but what you're saying doesn't make any sense. If you told Dean he's the devil incarnate, it's still no reason for him to stroll into Ms. Benni's enclosure."

"Mom's right. Dean knew Ms. Benni was in there. No matter how mad you made him, this is on him, not you."

Marietta grimaces.

"But we do have a problem here, girls. Dean is suing me for a million dollars." Carolyn pauses, wanting to be completely accurate. "Actually, the complaint says he wants in excess of a million dollars." Feeling light-headed again, she adds, "Let's go sit in the dining room. I left all the paperwork on the table in there."

By the time they all sit down, Marietta's apologetic mood has evaporated. "Over a million dollars? Really?"

Carolyn nods her head.

"Well, that's just ridiculous. Mom, how in the world can you be responsible for Dean's moronic decision to trespass inside a Bengal tiger's enclosure?"

"I don't know. But I'm not a lawyer. I think Fred was right that I need to find one right away."

"Shouldn't we do some research first to make sure we find the right kind of lawyer? Don't they have like different specialties?" her younger daughter, who prides herself on being methodical, says.

"I'm sure they do. But how do I find out? I guess I should go online." Then it hits her. "Wait, girls. We do know a lawyer. Remember? My cousin Eileen's an attorney in New York. I'll call her."

"You think she'd come down here and defend you—like in that movie about the cousin from New York who goes to Alabama?" Kenny bounces up out of her seat.

"Heavens no. Her specialty is environmental law. But I do think she'll be able to tell me how to go about finding an appropriate kind of lawyer." Carolyn hurries into the kitchen, finds her address book, and reaches for the wall phone. Her cousin answers on the first ring. After a brief conversation, Carolyn says, "Thanks so much, Eileen." She steps into the doorway to the dining room to tell her daughters what she learned. "She reminded me that what I need to do is call our insurance company, and they'll hire a lawyer for me."

"That's a relief," Marietta says.

"It is. I should've thought of it myself. I don't know where my head is."

"Your head is just fine, Mom," Kenny says. "It's just the stress."

"So, where's the insurance policy?" Marietta asks.

"In the basement." Carolyn turns and crosses the kitchen to the stairway and hurries down. She can't believe she didn't think of the insurance—Tom would have. Of course, they faithfully carried insurance since they began building the zoo over ten years before. They never missed paying the premium on time, always to the same company. She makes her way through rows of storage boxes, past the washer and dryer, to the far wall where the file cabinets stand, holding every detail of the business, over ten years of the zoo's history. Carolyn takes a moment to slow her breathing, then pulls open a heavy bottom drawer which screeches its displeasure at the disturbance. She rummages through the files labelled neatly in Tom's handwriting, which jars her, as always.

Once she's found the right one, she tucks it under her arm and hurries back up the stairs. She's forced to pause for a moment on the landing to catch her breath. Her girls are still sitting at the dining table looking stunned. She takes a seat across from them and sweeps away the piles of bills to make a space. The insurance policy is the only item in the dark green folder. Its top sheet has the policy period: two years—January 1, 2018 to December 31, 2019, and a brief summary of the coverages. She runs her index finger down the list until she finds the general liability limit, $500,000 per person. A whistle escapes her lips.

"What is it?" Marietta asks.

"The insurance information. We have $500,000." Carolyn can feel herself relax.

"So, you think that's enough?" Kenny asks.

"I certainly hope so, sweetie." She looks at her daughters, both of whom appear doubtful. "It's a lot of money, girls."

"Of course it is," Kenny says. "But didn't you say the complaint, or whatever they call it, says Dean's after a million dollars?"

"It does. In excess of a million, actually. But that can't be right. I don't want to sound mean, but his injuries were his own fault. I just can't imagine—"

Kenny hurries to reassure her. "You're right. There's no reason to worry about anything until we talk with your lawyer." She actually pats her mother's hand, which feels odd to Carolyn. "Is there a phone number for the insurance company?"

Marietta grabs the policy and quickly finds the 1-800 number, which she jots down for her mother. Carolyn again uses the phone on the kitchen wall and gives some basic information to a machine, after which the recorded voice tells her someone will call back within twenty-four hours.

The girls return to their chores, and Carolyn tries to concentrate on her bookkeeping by speeding up her work. Still, apprehension battles for her attention. It has only been an hour when the phone rings, and Carolyn jumps up to answer it. A woman identifies herself as Helen Huffer, the insurance adjuster assigned to the matter. She asks about what happened, instructs Carolyn to send the complaint to her as an e-mail attachment, and says someone will be in touch after that. Carolyn hurries back to the corner of her bedroom where she keeps her computer and printer and spends what seems like an hour on the maddeningly slow process of scanning the twelve-page document. The task keeps her from actively analyzing what is happening but does nothing to slow her heart rate.

She knows she has to keep busy or go crazy. Her daughters are out doing their chores, so there's no one around to tell what Ms. Huffer said. Carolyn returns to her ledger book, working even faster at the distraction, but lays down no memory of what she's accomplishing. It's almost five p.m. when the phone startles her back into full scale anxiety. She jumps up at the sound and knocks over her chair getting to the kitchen to grab the phone. The loud bang of the wood hitting the hardwood floor makes her jump again a second later. This time it's the voice of a younger woman. She says her name is Jackie Bauer and that she's been retained by the insurance company to defend Carolyn and the zoo. She asks if she may stop by to speak with her and her daughters the next morning, Tuesday, and they settle on meeting at ten a.m. Although Carolyn thinks of herself as an optimist, she feels only dread, and suspects she won't get a wink of sleep that night. She wonders whether she'll even be able to keep breathing.

Chapter 4

Jackie

Helen calls with the new assignment late on Monday afternoon, as Jackie is dictating a brief in support of a motion for summary judgment. When she sees who's calling, she answers on the first ring, quickly putting down her Dictaphone and grabbing a pen and legal pad. "Hey, Helen. How are you, sweetie?"

"I'm fine, dear."

Jackie laughs. "Sorry. I was just being southern."

"Well, don't stop being that. We need your drawl in the courtroom down there."

"You make it sound like I'm at the ends of the earth."

"That's how we Chicagoans think of you guys in the sticks. Especially in your overly profligate county," she says.

"Hey! That's just when we're on juries. We're not generous with our own money."

Helen laughs. "Fair enough. Listen, I've got something different for you."

"Great. You know how tired I get of doctors who make their patients sicker and those damned punch presses that seem to prefer fingers to metal parts."

"It's a tiger attack."

"No kidding?" Jackie sits up straighter in her chair.

"Seriously. Apparently, there's a little family-owned zoo down in Heartsville. Plaintiff got into the tiger's enclosure somehow and had his left arm and leg ripped up."

"Did you say ripped off or ripped up?"

"Up."

"Oh good. Leg-offs and arm-offs are going for big dollars down here. But I haven't heard of any cases where both were eliminated in one fell swoop."

"I don't know how bad the injuries are, but we could have a problem."

"I think we already have one," Jackie says.

"True. But guess what the zoo's limits are."

"If I must guess, I'd say the traditional small business one or two million, hopefully with an umbrella. But, if there were reasonable limits, you wouldn't have asked me to guess. How bad is it, Helen?"

"Five hundred."

"Damn. So, I assume there's no umbrella."

"That would be a correct assumption."

"Did they use an agent?"

"Unfortunately for Mrs. Warren, they came straight to us. So, she doesn't have an agent to sue for underinsuring her."

"I assume the plaintiff brought the suit under the Animal Control Act."

"Sadly. That, plus a negligence count."

She scrawls notes of everything Helen says. "Great! At least we have a shot at winning one count."

"Yeah. But that won't help Carolyn Warren very much."

Jackie grimaces, already seeing the difficulty for Ms. Warren. "She's the owner. Right?"

"Yeah. She had it in a partnership with her husband for a decade. But it appears he passed away a couple of years ago, so now it's a sole proprietorship."

"Have there been any other claims against the zoo?"

"Not so much as a slip-and-fall on a snow-cone."

Jackie nods, pleased her new client's zoo doesn't have a history of problems. "Which plaintiff's shop?"

"Henry Perdue and Associates."

"He's such a liar."

"What do you mean?"

"He's only got one associate."

"That doesn't offend me much, as long as it's the only lie he tells."

"I know him well from lots of cases, Helen. It won't be."

"Tell me about him."

"Hank's probably in his late thirties—a few years older than me. He started out with a defense firm but sold out and slipped over to the dark side after a couple of years."

"How's he done?"

"Not bad. He's gotten some decent verdicts. He's basically a macho jerk who likes to come across as the most aggressive guy in the courtroom. Then again, I suppose we can all be jerks."

"Not me."

"Of course not. I was referring to we lawyers."

" 'Wee' as in little?"

"Ha, ha."

"Wait. I think I do remember him. Wasn't he opposing counsel in a gas line explosion case you handled for me a few years ago?"

"You're right. That was he."

"Hm."

"So, do you have time to shoot the complaint over this afternoon? I'd so much rather be reading about a tiger attack than finishing this choice of law brief."

"Definitely. I'll get it right out to you. As I said, Jackie, I'm a little worried about the limits."

"I'll jump right on it. If it's a policy limits situation, Hank may take your money and run."

"Honestly, I kind of hope it is. From my files, this looks like a good, clean insured. I'd hate to see the Warren family lose their zoo over this. So, I'll get my letter out today letting Mrs. Warren know the plaintiff claims damages in excess of her limits."

"And I'll see if I can get them to meet with me tomorrow morning. I'll read everything tonight after my hot date." Jackie rolls her eyes as she says the last two words.

"Anything I should know?"

"I have no idea. He's just someone I met online. We're just grabbing dinner after work."

"Well, make sure it's a public place, and all that… And thanks for jumping on this file, Jackie."

"Any time, sweetheart." Jackie leans back in her chair and puts her feet up on her desk—something she likes to do when her office door is closed and she needs to think. It isn't all that risky since her desk chair doesn't face toward the door.

The truth is, Hank will be a fairly worthy opponent. As far as Jackie is concerned, the worthier the better. She mentally reviews the elements of the Animal Control Act. It's generally tough to defend cases that are brought under the act, although not necessarily impossible, like it would be in a state with a vicious animal statute. Jackie sees the challenge as a good thing because she hates cases that don't test her creativity. She won one case under the Illinois statute, which most people still call the "Dog Bite Act." That one wasn't terribly difficult to figure out. A man tripped over a sleeping dog which was lying on the landing of a staircase and the guy fell down the steps, suffering serious injuries. Jackie pointed out to the court that the plaintiff wasn't hurt by a dog, qua dog. It was more like dog-as-tripping-hazard, something for which the act has no application. Unfortunately, if this tiger attacked a person, it would definitely be tiger, qua tiger. She just hopes there will be some little chink in Hank's case she can work with to craft a defense for the zoo.

Chapter 5

Kenny

Jackie Bauer, her mother's lawyer, waltzes through the front door like she's the guest of honor at a party—very upbeat and friendly. She takes her time greeting each of them with a handshake and a smile. She asks them to call her Jackie, which Kenny thinks is very cool. Tall and slender with an open face, she isn't especially beautiful, but her personality kind of lights up the room. Her dark auburn hair drapes down her back in a sleek ponytail, and she wears blue jeans, hiking boots, and a casual tan blazer. Kenny notices that when her mom points Jackie into the dining room, she waits until each of them is seated to choose a chair. As it turns out, Marietta, Kenny, and their mother take seats on one side of the rectangular table, and the lawyer sits in the center on the other side. Jackie puts her small pile of papers down in front of her and pulls an empty yellow writing pad out from the bottom of the stack. She doesn't have a briefcase, or even a purse, which Kenny assumes she left in her car. She pulls a pen out of her jacket pocket. "Shall we get started?"

Her mother says, "Of course," and they're off and running. Kenny sees it as running because Jackie covers so much information in the time she spends with them.

Jackie says, "Ms. Warren—"

"Carolyn, please."

"All right. Carolyn, can you tell me all about your zoo? How long you've had it, what's here, who helps you operate it, and why you chose such an unusual small business? By the way, please ignore my notetaking. I'm sure I'll remember most of what you all share with me. Frankly, it's mainly a habit." She grins, and Kenny notices what a bright toothy smile the lawyer has.

Her mother seems a little nervous talking, so Kenny hands her one of the glasses of iced water she put on the table in case her own mouth dries up—something that happens when she has to give a presentation at school. Her mother takes a lot of sips of hers while answering Jackie's questions. The first thing out of her mouth is, "My husband, Tom, passed away two years ago."

"I'm so sorry," the lawyer says, and it seems genuine.

"Anyway, he and I inherited this house and the forty acres about twelve years ago. I had an aunt I'd been close with who lived down here. She was in her nineties when she died, and her own children and her husband had predeceased her. It hadn't been operated as a farm for a while, so there were no crops to speak of. Of course, we thought about just selling the property. We were both elementary school teachers, so we could've used the money. But we got to talking about it, and the idea of opening a zoo came up."

"Well, that's different," Jackie says. When Carolyn doesn't respond, Jackie adds, "What I mean is, most couples' first thoughts about what to do wouldn't have been, 'Let's open a zoo!' " Jackie smiles, but is met with quiet, as if her comment had been insulting.

"Of course not. But, you see, Tom and I first met at

the Milwaukee Zoo when we were teen volunteers. We both lived in Milwaukee's burbs and decided to go to U—W, Milwaukee so we could continue to work at the zoo as we made our way through college. We were both able to get paid positions, which we kept until we graduated."

Jackie says, "Then the idea of opening a zoo makes perfect sense. In fact, it's pretty darned romantic."

"Well, it was our dream. When the inheritance came up, we'd been married thirteen years already. Marietta was ten and Kenny was five. Other than taking off a year with each baby, I'd been teaching for almost a dozen years by then. Tom also taught elementary school—English and history."

"What did you teach?"

"Mainly science and math."

Jackie nods and smiles. "So, you moved the family to Heartsville and opened your zoo."

"Hardly. We moved pretty quickly, but it took the better part of two years to get everything ready so we could open. I taught down here while Tom worked on getting all the preliminary things done. We had to borrow a lot of money for everything—the barns, animal enclosures and display areas, restrooms, and of course, the animals. We studied what all of the animals would need and how to care for them properly. We also had to get all of our compliance approvals. And it took a while to find good, reliable employees to help with all the work. Today, I have five workers, three full-time and two part-time—plus Marietta and Kenny and myself. I manage the operation and Charlie Russell, our full-time maintenance lead, is in charge of all of the upkeep." Carolyn pauses, then adds, "Jackie, these people depend on this employment. It's not a hobby. This is their only source of income. And mine." She takes a long sip of water, which Kenny suspects is to help her mother keep from crying.

"I understand. So, what did you start with?"

"What do you mean?"

Jackie tilts her head. "I was just wondering what animals you started with."

Kenny is riveted to her mother's every word since she doesn't remember hearing about the beginning of the zoo in such detail before. She has a crazy idea that maybe every family should be interviewed by a lawyer so they can learn their parents' stories. Also, she misses her father.

Carolyn smiles. "The truth is, we had a weird menagerie at first. Tom focused on animals we could afford since price was the most important factor at that point. Let me think." She closes her eyes and leans her head back. "One bison, two kangaroos, two ostriches, a bobcat, ten prairie dogs, one camel, and assorted birds." She pauses, then adds, "Oh, and we had goats, pigs, rabbits, a couple of donkeys, and three ponies in the children's zoo."

"No tigers?"

"Oh, no. Ms. Benni was our first when we bought her two years later from a safari park kind of place—you know, the customers drive their cars around to look at the animals."

Jackie startles. "Wait. You don't mean they drive right up to tigers?"

Carolyn laughs hard. "No, Jackie. Some of their animals, including the camels, were free to approach the cars. But the tigers were enclosed in an area that the cars could only drive by—without entering." The lawyer doesn't seem to be offended at all at being laughed at.

Kenny interrupts. "Mom, why haven't you told us all this before?"

Carolyn looks at her and then at Marietta. "Haven't I?"

"Not really." Kenny tries to remember how much of this is actually new to her. "But still…"

Marietta just stares at her mother.

"That helps me a lot. So, the tiger that attacked Dean is called Ms. Benni?"

"Yes. The girls named her that because she's a Bengal tiger."

"I named my first cat Kitty." Jackie then turns to focus on Kenny's sister. "So, let's get back to Ms. Benni a bit later. Marietta, tell me about yourself."

She is quiet for a moment, then says, "May I ask why?"

Jackie gives her a wide smile, like she expects the question. "The more I know about you all, the better I'll be able to handle the case."

"It seems irrelevant to me. But sure. I mean, if it might help. I'm a flight attendant with a regional airline. I fly out of St. Louis."

"So, a two-hour commute to work?"

"Yeah. I want to live here and save my money so I can move up to St. Louis or Chicago eventually. I have my associate's degree from our community college, but I'm still taking courses that'll transfer. My plan is to finish college and get a full-time gig with one of the national airlines."

"Then flying will be your career?"

"Yes. What most appeals to me about it is being able

to use the benefits to see the world. I know I'll never make a ton of money, but I won't need so much, since my airfares will be covered. I've dreamed of travelling since I was a little girl." This is a fact about her sister that Kenny has never heard before.

"A well-constructed plan, then. Are you in school now, Marietta?"

"I have one on-line course this summer. I'm mainly flying and helping Mom out here when I'm at home. If I were a brainiac like Kenny, I'd have a scholarship. Since I'm not, I'm making it happen inch by inch."

Jackie nods. "Boyfriends?"

"Tons. But none at the moment." She pauses. "I suppose this conversation will eventually make its way to Dean Alcott."

"Oh, was he a boyfriend?"

"Never. But he's been the most persistent person in the world about wanting to be one."

Jackie makes a note on her pad. "I see. And you're right. We will definitely be getting to Dean." She turns to Kenny. "What can you tell me about yourself, Kenna?"

"I go by Kenny."

"Right. You told me that when we met. Sorry."

"That's okay. So, like Mom said, we didn't have any tigers at the beginning. We got Ms. Benni in 2011, when I was nine and Marietta was fourteen. So, we can tell you a lot about her—when you're ready."

"Great!" She nods. "But what about you, Kenny? High school?"

She's a little nervous to start answering Jackie's questions because she's seen how quickly her mother and sister responded, as though just talking to the lawyer made them nervous enough to spill their guts. Getting people to tell her the truth is probably something the lawyer has to be good at for her work. Or maybe it's not because she's a lawyer, but more because of how non-judgmental and encouraging she is. "Yeah. I'll be a senior in the fall."

"And then?"

"I'm hoping to go to Northwestern or the University of Chicago if I stay in Illinois. Otherwise, maybe St. Louis University. I'll have to work my way through, so a scholarship would help a ton."

"Do you think your chances are good?"

Marietta jumps in. "She's brilliant. She totally aced the PSAT and her first ACT. And, in her entire school career, my sister has never made anything less than an A-."

"That was only because I overslept and missed a test."

Jackie chuckles. "I think you'll do just fine. Tell me about your friends?"

She takes a couple of seconds to think how to explain herself. "I don't have much time for a social life since I come home to do chores right after school. I guess you'd say I'm more of a loner."

Jackie nods, then says something Kenny finds amazing, "I was always an extrovert in the classroom and an introvert on the playground." Kenny is shocked because it's exactly what she, herself is, although she never thought to describe it that way. Then Jackie asks, "So, any friends at all?"

"Oh, sure. Becca's my best friend—my only friend, really." She laughs so Jackie won't feel sorry for her. "It's cool. She's really great. We do everything together." She pauses, then tells Jackie something she hasn't yet mentioned to her mother or her sister. "Plus, there's this girl at school who just invited me to a really cool party—like two weeks ago. And it was great!" Both Carolyn and Marietta kind of squint at her because they are hearing about the party for the first time.

"Well, thanks for the information. And really, ladies, I appreciate you opening up about your lives. I can't promise that anything you've shared with me will help with the case, but background information has helped before. So, shall I reciprocate?"

Kenny is dying to know more about their totally cool lawyer. She says, "Definitely."

Jackie's eyes light up as she studies Kenny for a brief moment. "I grew up in a county to the west of here—over in Sander." Kenny looks at her blankly, and Jackie adds, "I know. No one's heard of it. Population 1,200—on a good day. I went to Chicago for college and law school, but really prefer small town life. So, I moved back shortly after I started practicing law."

"To Sander?" Kenny asks.

Jackie laughs. "No. I thought I'd do better in the county seat…since there's a courthouse there. I joined a small defense firm and have been with the same five people for the past nine years…but, who's counting?"

"Wait," says Marietta. "You're saying you gave up Chicago for this parochial little…" She glances at her mother. "…this rural area?"

Jackie smiles. "I did."

Marietta persists. "How do you feel about that decision now?"

Jackie grows more serious. "I think there are pros and cons to small-town life. I'm glad I'm here."

Marietta just nods.

Kenny sits up straighter, and asks in a mock-serious voice, "Boyfriends?"

Jackie laughs. "There were some when I was still a blooming rose. Now I try to fit in a date whenever I feel like people will start to talk about me if I have no social life whatsoever. But I'm kind of picky, so I don't usually see the same guy more than once."

Kenny doesn't understand how she can meet so many different guys. "Then who are they?"

"People I meet online. I just use a dating service to save time."

"Really?" Carolyn says.

"Yes. But it's not like I'd recommend it. I'm very happy on my own, so dating is a pretty low priority right now."

"I agree with that," Marietta says. "If you have a life plan, dating has a good chance of messing it up."

"Me too." Kenny nods for emphasis. "At least, that's the story I'm sticking with from now on."

"Good. Then we're all in agreement." Jackie pulls out the complaint. "Now that we know a little bit about each other, let's talk about Dean Alcott and Ms. Benni. Which one of you saw Dean first on the day of the accident?"

Kenny says, "I guess that was me. I was watching him just before he went into Ms. Benni's enclosure. After that, I kept watching and saw the whole thing."

"Okay. We'll start with you, Kenny."

Marietta raises her hand like a schoolgirl. "Actually, Jackie, I think we'd better start with me—since I'm the reason Dean went into Ms. Benni's area."

"Well, that's an interesting statement. What do you

mean, Marietta?"

"Dean delivers feed for his dad's business every other Monday. Every time he's here, he looks for me."

"Why?"

"Because, since I was twelve years old, he's been obsessed with me."

"You said you never dated him, though. Right?

"Definitely not. I mean, sometimes in school, he did things with groups of kids I was with. Even though I was one of those horrid queen bees in high school, I still couldn't really insist on a Dean-free zone."

"That would be awkward."

"Darn right, it was."

"Tell me about Dean, Marietta."

She sighs like it bugs her to even think about him. "Gorgeous. Medium brown hair, dark green eyes, and, of course, killer dimples. And he has the body to go with it."

"Really?"

Kenny jumps in. "He walks around here without a shirt. I'm not sure if he's working on improving his bronze finish or trying to work on Marietta. He's really beautiful—like the David."

"Oh, my."

Kenny purses her lips, then adds, "What I mean is that he's got a nice six-pack, but not in a gross way like a body-builder."

"Is he charming?"

"I'm not sure I'd go that far," Marietta says.

"Let me ask it this way. Does he have the voice and the mannerisms to go with the body—so that people kind of bend over backward to give him what he wants?"

"Yeah. That's a good description," Kenny says, then

adds, "Except for my sister, of course."

Jackie turns to Marietta. "You said you've had tons of boyfriends. Why haven't you gone out with Dean?"

Marietta sighs again. "Now we're getting to the heart of it. How about I tell you what I said to Dean when he pressed me to answer that exact question?"

"Please."

When Marietta finishes describing their conversation, Jackie says, "I see. When was this?"

"Right before he let himself into Ms. Benni's enclosure."

Jackie nods, then makes a quick note on her legal pad.

Kenny pats her sister's hand. "It's not your fault, Marietta."

"I know."

"Marietta, did you see Dean enter Ms. Benni's area?"

"No. I went back to painting the shed until I heard Kenny scream bloody murder."

"Kenny?"

"I didn't know about what Marietta said to him. I was just watching Dean from under our willows as he walked in my direction."

"Why?"

"You've never seen Dean…shirtless."

"He's that good-looking?"

"Yes," Marietta and Kenny say at the same time.

"Okay. So you were watching him to enjoy the view. There's no law against that."

"Good. I was also recording him on my phone."

Jackie raises her eyebrows. "Really?"

"Yeah. I was."

Jackie breaks into a big smile. "This could be very helpful. So, why were you recording him?"

Kenny hesitates a moment, trying to think of a way to make herself sound less creepy. Then she blurts out, "I just had my phone out because I thought Ms. Benni looked especially sweet, stretched out at her full length on her tummy with her head between her paws. Yeah. That's it. That's why I was taking pictures."

Jackie says, "Oh." But Kenny can tell she knows it's not the whole truth, and nothing but the truth.

"Then when Dean came into view, I kept shooting so I could share it with Becca. See, she doesn't run into Dean very often, and never when he's shirtless, so I figured she'd want to see it."

"He must be some boy," says Jackie.

"You have no idea," Kenny says.

"So, do you have a recording of the whole Ms. Benni attack?"

"Not all of it. Just the part before I screamed. I've got everything before that—where Dean threw something—now I'm thinking it was probably his cell phone—into the enclosure and where he came around and let himself in through the two gates, and then walked on in."

"Why do you think he threw it?"

"He was walking really quickly from the shed, wearing a furious face. All of a sudden, he stopped, leaned way down like a pitcher winding up, and flung the thing. I don't know for sure, but I got the feeling he just needed to throw something, so he threw the only thing he could get his hands on. He pulled it out of his back jeans pocket and just flung it as hard as he could."

"So, the reason he went into Ms. Benni's cage was

to recover it?"

"I think so. See, he pushed the codes on the keypads really fast. Then he just strolled on in, and right towards the thing I'm assuming was his phone. He acted like Ms. Benni didn't even exist."

"Was Dean supposed to know the digital code to get in?"

"No," Carolyn says. "He did need to know the four-digit code for the other enclosures, since he often had to enter those to make his deliveries. But I had the lock to Ms. Benni's cage coded differently. Only Charlie, my daughters, and I knew it."

"Then how did Dean—"

She answers before Jackie finishes her question. "I've discussed it with Charlie. He remembers something that happened one day when he asked Dean to help him remove a downed tree limb. Of course, Charlie had first secured Ms. Benni in her holding pen. Then, when he and Dean approached the main entry, he felt like Dean was breathing down his neck. When Charlie turned his head, Dean smiled at him in a way that convinced Charlie that Dean saw him enter the code. It would've been simple for Dean to remember it because the first two digits are the same as on all of the other locks. And I chose the year of Charlie's birth for the last two so he wouldn't have any trouble remembering it."

"Did Charlie ever say anything to Dean about it?" asks Jackie.

"No. Charlie told me he never brought it up after that."

"Did he consider changing the code after Dean saw it?"

"He told me he never gave it another thought. Of

course, now he wishes he had."

Jackie nods. "Have you retrieved the phone yet?"

"No. I looked for it through the cage. I could just barely make out a bit of white in the tall grass. I told Charlie to leave it where it is in case its location might be evidence."

"Perfect. Are you're sure Dean knew Ms. Benni was in there?"

"Oh, yeah," Kenny and Marietta say at the same time.

Their mother adds, "Ms. Benni's never anywhere else. See, we built her enclosure large enough, and with interior holding areas, so that she'd never have to be moved. Dean's been dropping off feed since he was thirteen years old. He started out helping his dad, then took over the deliveries once he could drive. So, he knew Ms. Benni was in there, all right."

"How old is Dean now?" asks Jackie.

Marietta says, "My age. He was in my class at school until he had to repeat—twice. So, he didn't graduate with me. He's twenty-two."

"Kenny, where was Ms. Benni when Dean walked through the gate?"

Carolyn speaks up first. "Actually, there are two gates, an exterior one and an interior one. They can't be opened at the same time. It's just an extra precaution to make sure Ms. Benni doesn't ever escape. Dean had to have pushed the buttons on two keypads."

"Yeah," Kenny says. "I saw him do it. Twice. It's all on the video."

"Good. So, was there any other way for Ms. Benni to exit?"

"Just into her shelter or her holding pen. But there's

no exit from those," Carolyn says. "The fence around her main enclosure is twenty feet high, and curves inward at the top another four feet, so there's no chance she can jump out. It's above and beyond the AZA requirements for tiger enclosures. I don't mean to suggest that we're an AZA zoo. We just try to follow all their guidelines for Ms. Benni because she is a tiger, after all."

"And AZA stands for?"

"Association of Zoos and Aquariums."

"Ah. So, Dean had to have thrown his phone, or whatever it was, twenty feet high to get it over the fence?"

"Exactly," Carolyn says.

"Kenny, where was Ms. Benni when the thing fell from the sky?"

"There's a big tree in the center of Ms. Benni's area. It was early afternoon, so there was decent shade. She was lying just under the tree, and the thing landed probably seventy-five feet from her."

"Did Dean go directly to the gate after he made the throw?"

"Yes. It was like he just realized what he'd done and went to get it without giving it much thought."

"Interesting," Jackie says.

"I wasn't super worried at first because I've been in there when Ms. Benni's resting, and she never even got up," Kenny adds.

"What?" her mother says sharply.

"We didn't tell you because we didn't want you to get mad."

"Who's the 'we?' " Jackie asks.

"Becca and me. It was no big deal, and it was over four years ago." Her mother's eyes are still shooting daggers at Kenny, so she adds, "I'm alive, aren't I?"

Jackie says, "Does Dean know about it?"

"Becca and I might've mentioned it to him. We were always looking for reasons to talk to him."

"How far into the cage did you get?" Jackie asks.

"Just like one or two steps, since I was nervous."

Jackie turns to Marietta. "Have you been in the enclosure?"

"Does it matter?"

"It could."

"Yes. I have."

"Oh, my Lord," Carolyn says. "How could you girls be so stupid?"

"Mom, it was when I was in high school. Ancient history. Anyway, nothing happened. Ms. Benni just watched me, and never moved."

"How far in did you go?" Jackie says.

"No more than five feet. I'm not crazy, you know."

"You are crazy. Both of you," says their mother. "Ms. Benni can cover twenty feet in a single bound."

"I know that now, Mom," Kenny says.

"What do you mean?" Jackie asks.

"It's what Ms. Benni did when Dean got through the gate. One second, she was lying down, resting like a baby, and the next, she went into a crouch, her belly coming off the ground as she stared at him with her ears back. She lifted one paw slightly, and her tail shot straight out. Anybody with a cat could've guessed what was about to happen. That's why I screamed my lungs out. I could tell she was going to pounce." Kenny pauses to catch her breath. "And then Charlie pulled him out of the cage and Mom came running."

"Let's back up a minute," Jackie says. "First of all,

Marietta, did Dean know you'd been inside the enclosure?"

"I'm sure he did. He may even have seen it. There was a small group of kids watching me. And anybody who wasn't there probably heard about it at school."

"Okay. And Kenny, how far into the enclosure did Dean get before he turned back?"

"Not far. Nowhere near the object. See, I think he must've seen Ms. Benni go into the crouch too. Or maybe it just hit him that he shouldn't be there. I guess it was maybe fifteen feet—at most. I'd say he'd taken five or six steps."

"Did he turn back before or after you screamed?"

Kenny takes a moment to think about it. "I'm not sure. It all happened so fast. I think it was right when I screamed."

"But you have it on the recording?"

"Yeah. But just up to where Ms. Benni crouches and I scream."

"May I see it now?"

"Sure." Kenny pulls her phone out of her pocket. Jackie watches the video without showing any reaction, then slides it over the table to Carolyn and Marietta. They both shake their heads as they view it. Jackie pulls a business card out of her jacket pocket and asks Kenny to forward the video to her.

"I have to ask." Jackie looks at Carolyn. "Have you ever gone in while Ms. Benni was present?"

She lets out a long sigh. "I've been tending to Ms. Benni for eight years. I suppose I feel like I know her pretty well. I wouldn't even consider entering her cage while she's asleep and risk surprising her. But there was one time, probably five years ago, when I judged I might need to go in. Kenny's new kitten had gotten herself up the fence and was teetering on the edge of the drop-off over the tiger's area. I let myself in through the first door, then just stood in the doorway of the second to see what would happen. Thank God, the silly kitten turned around and jumped into a tree on the outside of the enclosure. I did have my body partly inside Ms. Benni's enclosure. I can't lie about that. But believe me, Jackie, I had no idea my girls were so foolish. I just thank God they weren't hurt."

"I can't believe it, Mom! You never told me about that. So, Apple Juice could've been eaten by Ms. Benni?"

"I thought so. But you loved that kitten so much. I just did what I could."

"Oh my gosh. I'm so sorry she got out of my room. You could've gotten killed for a kitten."

Carolyn looks right at her and slowly nods her head "Exactly."

"Listen, ladies. I'm sorry I had to dredge that up. But I do need to know all of this." Jackie pauses for a moment and looks lost in thought. She jots a note on her pad, then looks back up at them. "Say, was Dean ever inside of Ms. Benni's enclosure apart from the time he helped Charlie with the heavy lifting?"

Kenny says, "Beats me."

"Not that I know of," Marietta says.

"I don't know that he was," Carolyn says. "I'll double-check with Charlie."

"Thanks. If there's anything at all I should know, please give me a call." Now Jackie hands business cards to Carolyn and Marietta.

"I'll talk with him about it this evening."

Jackie stands up. "Say, why don't we get some fresh air and you can introduce me to Ms. Benni."

They take the back door since Ms. Benni's cage is just beyond the back yard. Carolyn offers Jackie a tour of the zoo, but she says she'll have to take a rain check, and just has time to meet Ms. Benni. As they approach the front of the tiger enclosure, Jackie asks why there are no visitors.

Carolyn says, "We're closed on Mondays and Tuesdays, and for all of January and February due to the winter weather. As you know, we don't get the bitter cold like northern Illinois, but we do get a heck of a lot of snow down here. So, we do our major cleaning, maintenance and any expansions without the families under foot. Except for that, we're open from ten a.m. to six p.m. Wednesdays through Saturdays, and noon to six p.m. on Sundays."

Jackie actually gasps when she first spots Ms. Benni, stretching her lean, muscular body and looking like she's seven feet long, not including her tail. The tiger is magnificent in the morning light, her stunning deep golden and black coat rippling when she moves. Jackie whispers, "She's gorgeous."

Knowing approximately where to look, they are all able to make out the contours of Dean's phone, lying in tall grass between the maple tree and the gate to the enclosure. Jackie jots down some notes and takes several pictures from different angles of the double gates and the area where Dean got attacked. Then she says, "Marietta, can you show me the shed where you were painting? And Kenny, how about replicating the exact route you saw Dean take to Ms. Benni's enclosure?"

They spend almost an hour reenacting ten minutes

worth of events. "I think that's enough for today," Jackie says. "Carolyn, do you have the plans with the measurements for the layout of Ms. Benni's enclosure?"

"I'll have to look for them."

"Great. Let me know when you find them so I can have them copied and returned to you right away. And could you arrange to have Dean's phone retrieved? I'd also like to have an exact measurement of how far it is from the door and also from where Ms. Benni was resting. Maybe you could have someone spray paint the spot in case anyone else wants to make measurements. Then I'll have the phone returned to Dean."

"I'll ask Charlie to attend to it this evening."

"Great. Thanks so much, ladies. I'll work up an assessment for you—how the law is likely to apply to the facts, and what your prospects are. And I'll call Dean's lawyer to see if he'll share what medical information he has at this point. Once I put everything together, I'll call to set up another meeting so I can give you my initial evaluation and recommendations."

"When?" asks Carolyn.

"A couple of weeks or so. I'll give you a call."

Kenny wonders how her family can possibly wait for two weeks to find out if her mother could really end up owing Dean over a million dollars. She says, "Could it be sooner, Jackie?"

"I'll try."

Chapter 6

Hank

He didn't expect a call on the case quite so soon, since he only had the papers served a few days before. Then again, maybe the zoo is underinsured, and the insurance company is eager to dump its limits. He worries it could be worse than that—no policy. It will be much messier if Ms. Warren has to sell the zoo to make good on the verdict. It's probably all heavily mortgaged anyway.

The message on his machine is from Jackie Bauer, who called after he left the office at seven p.m. the night before. Hank likes the idea of having her as his opponent—not that she'll have much to work with, since the Animal Control Act imposes virtually absolute liability. She'll know immediately that he only filed the negligence count because it would be malpractice not to. That, and the fact that it will give the jury the solace of giving Dean nothing under that count while awarding him everything for the claim based on the statute.

Hank thinks of Jackie as an attractive woman who knows the law and can be almost as aggressive as himself. But somehow, she manages to do her thing in a way that doesn't come across as combative. It's an illusion—she's a barracuda. He likes her, but he tries to believe he doesn't care a whit what she thinks of him. Of course, he's kidding himself. Despite having a happy marriage and four daughters under the age of twelve, Hank still wants to be attractive to interesting women, and of all the women practicing law in the county, she's the most interesting.

He first realized he cares what she thinks of him one afternoon when he was arguing a motion against some boring old fart defense lawyer. The judge was letting Hank get away with ranting and raving about how the guy had wronged his client in some way. The courtroom was almost empty, but a couple of lawyers whose motions were scheduled to be heard after Hank's were wandering in. Hank was in mid-rant when he chanced to see Jackie enter the courtroom. He immediately ended his tirade and told the court he'd concluded his argument. He doesn't even remember if he won or lost. What stayed with him is that Jackie's very appearance stopped him in his tracks, as he didn't want to look foolish to her. No one ever had that effect on him before. Jackie is definitely the collegial type, but he knows not to get caught off guard by her friendliness. He'll underestimate her at his peril.

She answers on the second ring. "Hank, thanks so much for returning my call. As I mentioned in my message, I'm defending the Alcott case."

"Wonderful! It's been a while, Jackie. How've you been?"

"Just great. How are your darling daughters, Hank?"

"Growing up too fast. Say, when are you going to take the plunge? "

"Nothing percolating at the moment. But how could I possibly drag myself away from lawsuits like this tiger thing to do something as mundane as dating?"

"Fair enough." He feels it's been enough chit-chat and gets to the point. "Who's got the coverage here?"

"As you know perfectly well, I could make you wait for our answers to interrogatories for that. But I'm in a good mood today, so I'll tell you. It's one of Benevolent's. The adjuster is Helen Huffer."

"From the pipeline explosion case. What? Maybe three or four years ago?"

"Yeah. That's she. A real hard-ass about settlements."

He smirks. "I remember. Of course, she had something to work with on that one."

"As opposed to…"

"Listen, Jackie, you may as well tender the limits now."

"Why in the world would I do that?"

"Because your client doesn't have a prayer." Hank, enjoying having the law on his side, leans back in his chair and crosses his legs.

"Oh, really? So, you don't think Dean's little stroll into the tiger cage was just a little bit negligent? Say, a tad more than fifty percent?"

"Maybe. But as you well know, that's my throw-away theory. How do you plan to get around the statute?"

"Good question." She pauses. "I don't know yet. But, heck, I've only had the file for forty-eight hours. I'll think of something."

"Good luck with that."

"Thanks. Say, Hank, what I really wanted to talk to you about is getting a look at Dean's injuries."

"Seriously? Photos won't do at this stage?"

"No. I'd like to see."

"Maybe. If you disclose the insurance limits."

"Maybe. I'll need Helen's consent, and Ms. Warren's. I'll see what I can do."

"Good. And I'll check with Dean to see if he'd like to meet you."

"Fine. Take care, Hank."

"You too."

Hank hangs up the phone and swivels his leather desk chair to stare out the window. It's pure bullshit. Forty-eight hours is more than enough time for Jackie Bauer to know her ass is grass. She's got nothing, and she isn't going to have anything. This will all be about how high he can build Dean's damages.

Chapter 7

Jackie

She assumes that once Hank finds out the limits are only $500,000, he'll make a policy-limits demand. Maybe. Unless, for some reason, Dean wants to go after Mrs. Warren's zoo for the money in excess of the limits. There could be a lot of it.

Jackie is tied up all day on Thursday in meetings on another case. On Friday morning, she calls Helen. "Hi. Good time to talk about the Alcott case?"

"Absolutely. What have you got for me, Jackie?"

"I met with Carolyn Warren and her daughters."

"What do you think of them?"

"Really lovely women. Marietta, the twenty-two-year-old, is a beautiful blonde in that California girl kind of way. The jury won't have trouble understanding why Dean's been after her for almost a decade. She was a bit standoffish though, like she isn't entirely sure she can trust me. But don't worry, I'll win her over with my wit and refinement."

Helen laughs. "Of course you will."

"The younger daughter is a rising high school senior. Very bright, and not as gorgeous, but Kenny is charming. She has this curious way of staring intently at whomever is speaking, as though she's trying to memorize every bit of what they say. I like her, and so will a jury."

"And Carolyn?"

"Quietly contained. Sensible. Likable. I'm about to press 'send' on my full report on what the women told me about Dean and the accident. Do you want me to go over what it says?"

"No, thanks. I've got to get into a meeting in a few minutes. I'll read it tomorrow morning."

"Understood."

"What do you need from me, Jackie?"

"I spoke with Hank earlier today. He'll arrange for me to meet his stunning client as soon as I tell him what your limits are."

"I don't see a downside, do you?"

"Nope."

"Good. Get Mrs. Warren's agreement, then let me know what we're dealing with on disfigurement. Pictures too."

"Will do."

Jackie calls Carolyn, who seems to have no interest in trying to evaluate the pros and cons of revealing the limits information earlier than necessary. She accepts Jackie's explanation that she needs to meet Dean as soon as possible to begin to gauge how he'll play in front of a jury.

Jackie calls Hank to let him know she has authorization to share the limits information if he has Dean's agreement to let her stop by and take a look at his injuries.

"Dean says he's not doing much anyway but sitting in his bed writhing in pain," says Hank.

"So, that's a yes?"

"Yeah."

"When?"

"We can go this afternoon if you're available, Jackie. I leave tomorrow for some depositions in California that should run all next week."

"This afternoon would be great. What time?"

"Let's meet at his dad's house at four o'clock. Now, don't go knocking on the door before I get there."

"Please, Hank, you know I wouldn't do something like that. Especially since it would be a violation of the ethics rules."

"Yeah, it would. So, it's your turn, Jackie. What're the limits?"

"$500,000. No umbrella."

"Shit." He pauses. "Sorry."

"No. I completely agree. They're shitty low limits. Hopefully, Dean's damages will be substantially less than that."

"Dream on."

"See you at four, Hank."

****

Jackie arrives at the Alcott home early because she wants to drive around a bit to get a sense of the neighborhood. It turns out to be a semi-industrial area, with the house sitting just across the street from Alcott Feed and Seed. A small warehouse connects with the retail storefront. The house, a two-story brick building with a wrap-around porch, recalls the Warrens' home, both probably dating back to the 1950s. The freshly mowed lawn is the highlight of the small, no-frills front yard. She takes a quick photo with her phone.

Hank pulls up next to Jackie's car in his black Mercedes. She knows he only drives his older model Ford during jury trials—in case one of the jurors might see him coming or going. He's also early. Jackie swings her legs out of her car and walks over to where Hank is closing his door and pressing his fob to lock up his prize. "Hi, Hank. I've been waiting in my car like a good girl."

"Hey, Jackie." He steps back, and motions for her to go ahead of him down the sidewalk. Jackie wonders whether he stepped aside out of courtesy or for a view of her backside, but dismisses the thought as cynical—even for her. When they reach the front door, Hank knocks softly, and Dean's father greets them. "Hey, Hank." They shake hands. "And this must be Mrs. Warren's lawyer. Pleased to meet you, ma'am."

"It's nice to meet you too, Mr. Alcott. I'm Jackie Bauer." She assumes Dean must take after his mother.

Mr. Alcott says, "I've made the sunroom into a bedroom for Dean so he won't have to drag himself up the stairs. If you'll follow me..." He leads them down a narrow hallway to the first door on the left.

Jackie pays attention to everything she sees since she never knows when she might lay eyes on something that will have meaning later. The house is clean and tidy, and the layout again brings the Warren home to mind. Mr. Alcott knocks on the door, and she hears Dean say, "Come in, please." They all enter the small room, and Mr. Alcott introduces Jackie to his son. Then he excuses himself and leaves them to it.

Dean is sitting up in bed with sheets pulled up to his waist. He is shirtless but has a wrapping around his left upper arm. His face and chest wear a patina of perspiration. He smiles. "It really is nice to meet you, Ms. Bauer. My lawyer told me you're really good." Jackie feels as though she's been hit upside the head. The Warren girls weren't exaggerating. Dean is exquisitely handsome with a dazzling smile, piercing deep green eyes, and a muscular build. He's also polite and proficient at dishing out flattery. Even at this very first introduction, it's obvious that, somehow, he has even more going for him than the sum of these qualities.

"Well, it was nice of Hank to say that. So, how's your convalescence going, Mr. Alcott?"

"Oh, please call me Dean. Otherwise, I'll think you're talking to my dad."

Even the cliché is charming coming out of Dean's mouth. "Of course. How are you feeling, Dean?"

Hank interrupts. "Don't answer that. We'll supply all those details in discovery."

"Sorry, Hank. I really only meant it as a common courtesy. I wasn't trying to trick Dean into saying, 'Fine, thank you. How are you?'"

Dean laughs at them and rolls his eyes. "Lawyers." This makes both Hank and Jackie laugh, as well.

Hank says, "As I mentioned on the phone, Ms. Bauer would like to take a look at your wounds. It'll help her and the insurance company evaluate your case."

"I'm sorry to have to ask you to remove the wrappings," Jackie says.

"Not a problem, ma'am. It's about time for my dad to change the dressings anyway."

"Shall I fetch him?" says Hank.

"Not necessary. I can just pull these tabs to get the wrapping off." He grimaces as he continues, and Jackie thinks he's genuinely in pain. "I'll just need my dad's help to put the fresh dressings on. I'll do the leg first, okay?" Dean pushes away the sheet and is wearing cut-off sweatpants above the area that's bandaged.

"Certainly," Jackie says.

As the dressing is pulled away from his leg, Jackie tries not to look horrified. The gash is a two-inch deep canal down the middle of his thigh, almost twelve inches long. Yellow liquid oozes around the edges as the dressing pulls at the reddened skin while separating from the wound. Once it's pulled away, Jackie sees that it is saturated with darker yellow liquid and speckled with blood. She wishes she hadn't had an egg salad sandwich for lunch, and seriously wonders if she can keep it down. It's not that she hasn't seen bad wounds before. One plaintiff was so badly burned, he had to wear a mask at home, which terrified his children. Another, an older electrician, lost everything up to his elbow from an electrical shock. What flesh remained had a gnarled, monstrous look. She was a young lawyer at the time and actually teared up...not an especially great strategy for keeping the settlement amount down. But Dean's injury seems even worse because it disfigures such a beautiful young body. She knows it's important not to show any reaction, so she shifts her face to neutral. "Hank, may I take a quick photo for the insurance company?"

"Dean?" says Hank.

"Oh, yeah. Do you need more light, ma'am?" He asks the question in spite of the fact that the afternoon sun is pouring in the three oversized windows.

"No. This is fine. Thank you, Dean." She snaps a close-up of the wound.

"So, now I'll pull these wrappings off my arm. Okay?"

"Yes. Thanks." The upper arm is sliced exactly like the leg, but not as deeply. The yellowish liquid oozes there, as well, but the dressing isn't as soaked with the stuff. She wants to ask why the wounds haven't been sewn up, but knows she agreed to just a viewing. She asks Hanks's and Dean's permission again, then takes a quick photo. This time, she makes sure to step back far enough so that the photo captures his face, as well as the wound.

Dean says, "Do you need anything else, ma'am?"

"No. Thanks so much." Turning to Hank, she says, "I'll just let myself out. I appreciate your arranging this for me."

"Sure. I'll get Mr. Alcott to come in and dress the wounds. Then I need to talk with my client for a while."

As Jackie walks toward her car, she tries to think how best to describe Dean to Helen. The boy has a quality beyond handsomeness, more like magnetism. She gets into her car and carefully backs out of the driveway, aware of the proximity of the Mercedes. She has a lot of questions she wants to pose to a doctor friend, and she needs to call Helen.

Chapter 8

Hank

It's on his forty-five-minute drive to the Alcott home that Hank thinks through his situation. He's already given Jackie the list of medical bills and projected future costs that the treating plastic surgeon helped him put together. Of course, pain, suffering, and disfigurement will also be a large part of the verdict. Unfortunately, with only a partial disability and minimum-wage employment, the lost wage claim doesn't quite get him to where he wants to be—which bugs the hell out of him. An idea starts to worm its way into his mind. There just might be a believable way for Dean to bolster his damages for the interruption of his work life. Of course, all of this is designed to get Helen to cough up the $500,000 as soon as possible. There is little point going after Carolyn, since the bank probably owns the zoo. Not to mention that Jackie will fight like a wildcat to protect the Warrens. Actually, like a tigress. He laughs at his lame joke. His plan is to persuade Dean to take the policy limits and call it a day. Hank just needs enough damages to convince the insurance company to tender its limit before he has to put a lot of hours into the case.

It becomes glaringly obvious—a large wage loss claim will cinch it. He knows he's not dishonest enough to outright ask Dean to lie. But he's perfectly comfortable helping Dean recognize the potential he had before the mauling. The kid looks like a movie star, and he knows how to juice up the charm. Hank was actually a little intimidated when he first met the boy, since he's always felt a little uneasy around other men who are far superior to him in any realm. What is it with men, anyway? It strikes Hank as pathetic that nurture has conspired with nature to relentlessly push boys to compete with each other. "Man up!" "Make a man out of you." "Be the best." The deafening drumbeat of penis-measuring sickens him. Hank's older brother used to compete with him in everything—from who got ready for school first to which one was the better high school wrestler. His brother is in California now. A neurosurgeon—of course. Some people tell Hank they don't envy him—raising four girls. But he knows the truth because he's lived through it. He thanks God every day he doesn't have to raise boys.

Hank has a feeling Dean is a client who will understand how to work with him. So he feels fine about casually mentioning to Dean that he probably could have made a lot of money modeling. Of course, he would've had to move to a town larger than Heartsville—maybe St. Louis or Chicago. Then again, New York might've offered the best opportunities. Hank knows how to say it without stepping over the ethical boundary—plant the seed, but not outright ask Dean to lie. He'll just hover over the line, like a drone, and simply be careful not to hit the ground on the wrong side of the divide.

It's just after Jackie leaves the Alcott home following her viewing of Dean's wounds. Hank suspects she wanted the early meeting because she was told about

Dean's extraordinary good looks—before he was mauled. Hank waits until Mr. Alcott finishes dressing his son's wounds and leaves the room. "You know, Dean...well, I'm sure people have told you that you look like a magazine model. I suppose you've thought about making that your career."

"Not really."

"But people have told you how handsome you are? That is, you're exceptionally attractive."

Dean looks down at his hands for a long time before he speaks. "Mr. Perdue, I really do appreciate everything you're doing for me. But I just don't swing that way."

Hank is confused. "What way?" He stumbles all over, trying to extricate himself from the misunderstanding. "Oh, no, Dean. That's not what I mean. I'm not...like that...either." When he adds, "I have a wife and four daughters," he realizes he's only making it worse. "Listen, Dean, I think you are misunderstanding me because I'm not being clear enough." The drone is now coming in for a landing on the far side of the line. "Let me make it simple. Your case would be worth more money if you testify that you've been planning for a potentially high-paying career like fashion model—as opposed to the minimum wage work you do for your dad. If I had to guess, I'd say you've probably been saving up your money to pursue that dream." Damn. Hank is so discombobulated that he's saying more than he intended. Once the divide is breached, there's no way to un-breach it.

Sure enough, the green eyes light up. "Now that you mention it, that was exactly my plan. I was living at home to save up money to move to Chicago and get started on my fashion model career. I just didn't tell anybody because all the guys around town already want to smash my face in for the way I look. More like, for the way their girlfriends look at me."

"That's exactly what I figured, Dean. But it would actually be better for your case if you could remember telling one or two people about your secret plan. It was probably someone you trusted."

"Thinking about it a little more, I did tell two people about it, my best buddy Jimmy and my dad."

"Well, that does make sense. It would be hard to keep an exciting plan like that to yourself. But anyone would understand why you didn't want to blab all over town about it."

"That's very true." Dean was smiling now, seeming to enjoy their little game of a conversation.

Mr. Alcott knocks on the door before entering. "Excuse me, Mr. Perdue, but I just need a word with my son."

"Of course." Hank steps back into a corner of the small room.

"Dean, I was just about to run out to check on a delivery problem. Is there anything you need before I go?"

"No. I'm good. Thanks, Dad."

Hank decides he may as well test out the older Alcott's willingness to support what his son will say. He certainly can't give Jackie the old man's name as a witness on the wage loss claim without knowing that Mr. Alcott is on board. Hank takes a step forward and smiles. He'll approach it like he did with Dean, but this time, without overstating the kid's gorgeousness.

He doesn't get very far with his insinuations about Dean's modeling career when Mr. Alcott, still standing next to the door, shakes his head and spits—right on the hardwood floor. He says, "Mr. Perdue, when I was thinking about which of you lawyers knocking on his hospital room door Dean should hire, I looked into your reputation. It's not that good. But I was told you don't go in for outright lying and cheating. Now I know I made the wrong decision."

"Mr. Alcott, I think you got the wrong impression."

"No, I didn't," says Dean's father. "After you leave, Dean and I will talk about whether to keep you on. But I can tell you right now, I will not lie for you, or Dean, or anybody else. Now if you talk Dean into perjuring himself for money, there's probably nothing I can do about it. The boy is of age. All I can testify to is that my son never mentioned becoming a male model. I know for a fact he's never considered it. But I can't prove that, can I? I'd be trying to prove a negative. That's hard to do, isn't it, Mr. Perdue?"

"Yes, sir."

"And I can't prove he didn't mention his dream of a modeling career to Jimmy. That's where you're going next, isn't it?"

"I don't know, sir."

Mr. Alcott turns abruptly and leaves. He mutters under his breath as he walks out the door, "It's starting to smell like something rotten in this room."

As soon as they hear his father's car start up, Dean says, "I still want to do it. Jimmy will be in."

"What about your father?"

"Oh, he'll get over it."

"Aren't you worried he'll lose respect for you?"

"He doesn't have any now. Never did."

"Why's that, Dean?"

"I can't be sure, but I think it has something to do with how much I look like my mom."

"Where's she?"

"Ran off with another man when I was three."

They end their meeting with Dean's last sentence hanging in the air as Hank walks to his car. So, the kid is being punished for the sins of his mama. And he won't have his dad's help in building up his damages. Fortunately, Dean has the wherewithal to pull this off with just Jimmy's help—and Hank's guidance.

Chapter 9

Jackie

While Jackie was in college, she became friends
with Pavana Bharam, an Indian woman who moved to
Philly for medical school, and then her residency at the
University of Pennsylvania. Jackie feels sure Pavana will
be happy to do her a favor by giving her some insights
into Dean's injuries since Pavana is studying to become
a plastic surgeon. But Jackie has no idea if she'll know
anything about tiger maulings.

It's almost six o'clock that Friday evening when
Jackie emails Pavana, first catching her up on her life,
and then explaining the favor she needs. Jackie details
what's happened and how the injuries look and attaches
the two photos. Pavana responds within the hour, first
reciprocating with news of her career and family life.
Pavana writes, *"Based on the pictures, I'm guessing that
Dean spent a few days at the hospital and is now
recuperating at home. His surgeon is, no doubt, waiting
for the wound to do some healing from the inside out. We
call it granulating in. Mainly, they're guarding against
infection. As you probably know, cat claws carry a lot of
bacteria, and cat scratches are highly prone to infection.
(I have no experience with tiger gouges, so I'm focusing
on smaller felines. Sorry.) It's likely Dean will undergo
several surgeries and skin grafts. His thigh and upper*

arm will remain somewhat scarred, and he may have some permanent impairment of the use of those limbs, depending on the degree of muscle damage. I'd love to see Dean's medical records, once you get them through your legal processes. Without them, I'm afraid all I can offer are these generalizations and guesses..."

After thanking Pavana and promising to keep in touch, Jackie lets out a long sigh, blowing the air upward. She needs to call Helen with all the bad news. She picks up the phone right away, knowing if she puts it off, she'll get caught up in something else since her cases are erupting like popcorn in a microwave. She plans to leave a detailed message since she really doesn't expect that Helen will still be at her desk.

"Helen Huffer."

"You're at work at 6:45 on a summer Friday?"

"I have to sit in on a child dart-out case going to trial Monday morning in Peoria," she says.

"Enough said. Listen, this Alcott case is going to be a bear."

"I thought it was a tiger."

"Ha. Good one. So, here's what I've learned. We're probably screwed on liability. Of course, we'll win the negligence count since Dean's is obviously more than fifty percent the cause of the accident. I mean, it was basically his own fault. Plus, our client was in compliance with all the rules and regs."

"So far, so good."

"Yeah. But Hank probably only included that count to let the jury throw us a bone when they award the big dollars to Dean under the act."

"So there's no way to beat this under the statute?"

"It'll be difficult. The three elements Dean needs to

prove are simple. He just has to show that he was attacked while conducting himself peaceably, in a place he had a lawful right to be, and without 'provoking' Ms. Benni. If he proves the elements, there's no set-off for his own culpability. I've watched Kenny's recording of the attack. I don't see how we can argue that Dean wasn't behaving 'peaceably.' He calmly opened the two gates, walked through, and continued on toward his phone. He wasn't running or acting raucous in any way. I believe he'll satisfy that first element pretty easily. As to trespass, we can certainly argue that he had no lawful right to be inside of Ms. Benni's enclosure. His duties didn't require it, and the presence of a wild animal was a 300-pound hint that Mrs. Warren wouldn't approve."

"Yet, you don't sound convinced, Jackie. What are the negatives?"

"Some of the facts hurt us on this. Each of the Warren women ventured in—barely. Nevertheless, they were on the tiger-side of the door, and Dean knew about two of them. Also, Carolyn told me Dean himself was inside the enclosure once before the accident, at the request of one of the zookeepers, Charlie Russell. Apparently, a couple of years ago, a storm knocked a large branch off the mature maple tree in the middle of the pen. So Dean helped Charlie cut the piece up and haul it out of there. Of course, we'll point out that Ms. Benni was safely locked away in her holding pen at the time. Although Dean basically stole the code by looking over Charlie's shoulder, we have no good explanation for why Charlie never called him on it. Plus, Charlie could've changed the code after that, but never did. All of this does undermine our position that Dean was not in a place he had a lawful right to be."

"So based on what you know right now, what are our chances to beat this on trespass?"

"I'm not happy about all of the visits to the tiger-side of the enclosure. I'd feel better about it if this were a bench trial, but frankly, I don't think a jury will buy our argument. If you want a percentage, the truth is we're probably around twenty-five percent chance to win on trespass, as things stand today."

"Okay. What about the last element, provocation?"

"As I mentioned, there's a recording showing Dean basically strolling toward his phone. It's not like he kicked dirt in the tiger's face, or anything like that. After the three uneventful incursions into Ms. Benni's domain by the Warren women, I don't see a jury believing that Dean's mere presence was provocation enough to have caused the attack. Of course, I can make the argument; it's just not a persuasive one."

"Basically, you're saying we've got no real defense," says Helen.

"Basically."

"Okay. How bad are the damages?"

"Bad. His thigh looks like someone took a two-inch-long nail, stuck it in, then ripped the flesh open for about twelve inches. The upper arm looks almost as bad. Both canals are filled with oozing yellow liquid. My plastic surgeon friend says to expect several surgeries and skin grafts, permanent scars, and possibly some loss of function in both limbs."

"I see."

"Yeah. And what makes his wounds even worse is that they're on an unusually gorgeous young man."

"I saw the pictures. He looks like a fashion model. What's his personality like?"

"Polite, soft-spoken, charming."

"Of course, he is."

"Actually, Helen, and I know this will sound hyperbolic…"

"But…"

"But there's something about Dean that's more than just handsome."

"As in, what? Irresistible?"

"More like charismatic."

"Great. Just what I was hoping for. Well, you know what to do. I'm interested in medical bills, of course. But at this point, I'm more curious about the kind of lost wages Hank will be able to put up on the board."

"I'm on it. I'll let you know as soon as Hank demands your limits."

"I'd say they're his for the asking, once you confirm all the damages estimates."

"At least the nightmare will be over for the Warrens if we can settle this thing," Jackie says.

"Yeah. I'd love to put this to bed for them."

Jackie says, "Catch you later, sweetie."

Helen laughs. "Bye."

Chapter 10

Kenny

Kenny trusts Jackie, but she's still worried that the complaint says Dean wants over a million dollars, and her mother has only $500,000 in insurance. The family isn't talking about it, but the "it" is like a silent stranger who moved in with them. The first week was so oppressive that Kenny got absolutely nothing done besides her chores. She needs to keep up with her research on colleges and scholarships, but nothing can hold her attention.

This second week after Carolyn received the lawsuit is worse. Marietta is away flying five days in a row, so the stranger spreads out and takes over the living room as well as the kitchen and dining room. Kenny spends what energy she has seeking reassurance from Becca by phone. She doesn't want to go out and leave her mother alone with the stranger.

It's Friday evening and she's desperate for a hit of encouragement. She rings Becca. "Hi. Good time to talk?"

"Of course. I'm here for you."

"Thanks. So, have you heard anything about how Dean's doing?"

"I just overheard at the grocery store that he's home, and that he won't let any of his friends visit—except for

Jimmy, of course."

"Why not?"

"Seriously, Kenny?"

"You're saying he doesn't want them to see his injuries?"

"Would you?"

Kenny thinks about it. "Not if I suspect they just want to see if I look like a freak. So, have you heard what Jimmy's saying about it?"

"Apparently, Dean's wounds are gross. He doesn't complain much about pain, but he grimaces a lot, so Jimmy thinks he's pretty bad off."

"What does Dean do all day?"

"I hear he's playing video games and drinking beer with Jimmy," says Becca.

"Hm. I guess he won't be able to help his dad for a while." Kenny pauses, thinking about how this fact could cost her mom.

"Yeah. Guess not. You know, you sound really down. Are you okay?"

"Sure. I'm just worried about the lawsuit. What if Dean wins for way more than Mom's insurance money? I get the feeling she doesn't have a lot of extra dollars."

"How do you know that?"

"You know how you know. She's really careful with money. And she tells me and Marietta that there's no extra to pay us for working at the zoo—which is fine. But, duh. Plus, she always looks miserable on days she pays the bills."

"You're probably right then. But like I've told you a million times, there's no way a person can walk into a tiger cage, get mauled by the tiger, and then win a bunch of money from the tiger's owner. I mean, if you were on the jury, would you give the dumbbell who did that any money?"

"No—not when you put it that way."

"There's no other way to put it. That's what he did. You recorded it."

"Yeah, I did. But—"

"What?"

"I just have a feeling it may not be so simple. I mean, our lawyer, Jackie, is super nice, and I think she'll do a great job. But the thing is, she didn't actually say anything encouraging."

"Oh."

"And I can tell Mom's totally freaked out. She doesn't talk about it much. But I catch her just staring out the window, for like ten minutes at a time. Becca, she never did that before. I think she's worried we'll actually lose the zoo."

"Crap."

"Yeah. I don't think this stress is good for her health. She's already got that heart arrhythmia. I wish she'd just start drinking or something to help her relax."

"Crap."

"Do you have anything more helpful to suggest?"

"I do. Kenny, you have to call Jackie and tell her she needs to buoy up your mom."

"Buoy her up?"

"Exactly. Buoy. It's on one of the ACT vocabulary sheets."

"Hm. That's actually a good idea. I could use some buoying up myself so I can get back to my research on scholarships."

"Why are you acting surprised? You may be first in our class, but I do come up with a passably decent idea from time to time."

"'Passably?'"

"Ha-ha."

"Thanks, Becca. I'll call her right away."

"Good. Wait. Before you go, I should probably tell you I overheard something else about it. Apparently, Jimmy's been spreading some manure that Marietta heaped some really mean insults on Dean before he got so mad that he threw his phone."

"Really?"

"That's the rumor."

"Well, I know what things she said, Becca, and it was only because he insisted that she tell him the absolute truth about why she won't date him. So, Jimmy's version is so far out of context that a hundred-foot line on your dad's best rod couldn't reel it back in."

"Good. That's what I figured. See ya, Kenny."

"See ya. Thanks again."

****

Kenny feels a little guilty talking with Becca since she hasn't told her how she's made some new friends. Also, when Jackie interviewed Kenny in front of her mother and Marietta, Kenny was careful not to say too much about the recent seismic shift in her social status. She thinks it was because she is still having trouble believing it. As best Kenny can reconstruct things, she's starting to be accepted by one of the popular groups of girls because she sobbed at a memorial service. She realizes she might be imagining it, but she's pretty convinced it's true, and she definitely feels bad about getting a social promotion out of someone's death.

How it happened was that, way back in fifth grade, Kenny became friendly with Marietta's friend, Sadie.

When Sadie came over to the house to hang out with her sister, she always made time to talk with Kenny, too. At the time, Sadie was way nicer to Kenny than her sister was and was always telling her what her little sister Roxy was up to. Roxy must've been in third grade, since she was two years younger than Kenny. Apparently, Roxy was so full of energy and curiosity that she pretty much never stopped moving, for which reason all of her babysitters quit, and Sadie had to take care of her whenever their mom and dad went out.

Roxy was the kind of girl who did things like build mud castles on the hardwood living room floor and mix cake batter and cookie dough so wildly that the whole kitchen ended up coated with flour, all to the blaring of rock music popular with teens. Sadie showed Kenny pictures, and the two of them didn't remotely resemble each other. Sadie has black hair, pale skin, and is super-pretty, while Roxy's hair looked orange and frizzy, she was covered with freckles, and she had a big gap between her front teeth. Sadie tried to make it sound like she and her parents were totally exasperated, but Kenny could tell she absolutely adored her little sister and was really proud of what a free spirit Roxy was.

Last fall when Kenny started junior year, Roxy showed up at the school as a freshman. Kenny often saw her in the hallways since she was hard to miss with her orange hair, but they didn't have any classes together. Whenever she caught a glimpse of Roxy, it reminded Kenny of how much it had meant to her that Sadie had treated her a little bit like a friend.

But one day this past spring, Roxy made the tragic mistake of hopping on the back of a motorcycle, without putting on a helmet. Although Kenny didn't really know the girl, she knew how much Sadie loved her. The school held a memorial service and all of the students were required to attend. There was one part where each of them had to walk up to the front of the auditorium and drop a carnation on the table in front of Roxy's picture. So, up they paraded, hundreds of kids, row by row. When Kenny got to the front, she happened to glance at the first row of guests, and there sat Sadie with her parents, all dabbing their eyes with tissues. Kenny burst out bawling as though it had been her own sister who'd died, which was exactly the weird thought she'd had in that instant. Luckily, she had a tissue in her pocket. Kenny was definitely the only student who fell apart walking across the front of the auditorium—in front of the entire student body.

Becca told her not to worry about it because everyone is so wrapped up in their own lives, they would forget about it by the next day. She was wrong—but not in the way Kenny expected. The next day at school, girls who never talked to her went out of their way to say hi. This went on, day after day, and Kenny couldn't figure it out. At first, she wondered if it was because her braces had finally come off, which did make her look tons less bad. But comments made to her, and ones she overheard, made it crystal clear what was happening. Those girls admired Kenny's sensitivity. For a boy to have shown his feelings would've gotten him dumped on—possibly injured. But apparently, for a sixteen-year-old girl to look so emotional and empathetic was highly valued in the subculture of cool girls at Heartsville High. She wondered if the school's name was a little clue.

There were only a few more weeks of school and the weirdly friendly atmosphere persisted right through to the last day of the semester. Then, a couple of weeks after school let out, one of the girls in a popular group invited Kenny to a party at her house. It was just a group of girls, and they hung out in the girl's back yard. There was a fire pit, burgers and dogs, and lots of Cokes and even beer—which Kenny didn't try. She had fun, and she realized that the girls weren't particularly mean or insensitive. They were just decent students, who talked about their crushes, parents, summer jobs, and colleges they wanted to try for. Kenny decided she was wrong to have been prejudiced against them for being cute, and for their parents having money.

The only negative was that none of them picked up on the hint when Kenny brought up how cool Becca is. She tried not to let herself think about what the reason could be, but it was like that old joke about asking someone not to think of a pink unicorn. She'd overheard comments at school that were impossible to unhear, a lot of which were about Becca's eyes. So, Kenny did wonder a smidge whether the reason could possibly be a tiny bit…racist.

She didn't mention any of this to Becca because she felt guilty about going to the party without her, and even more guilty for not telling her about it. And now, Becca is showing her again how she doesn't deserve to be left out of Kenny's news. While she is failing her, Becca is still doing what a true friend does—helping. So, Kenny does as Becca suggested, and texts Jackie about how miserable her mother is.

Chapter 11

Carolyn

Carolyn is relieved when Jackie calls and asks if she can drop by on Monday evening to give a preliminary evaluation of the case. Jackie says she has meetings all afternoon, but will stop by after work at around six thirty p.m. However bad it's going to be, Carolyn prefers knowing.

Kenny helps her clear off the dining table and prepare some iced teas. Marietta returned from St. Louis earlier in the day but says she has a headache and can't join them for the meeting. Carolyn opens the front door to Jackie at precisely six thirty. This time, her lawyer wears a gray skirt suit and heels. Her hair is straight and pushed behind her ears, and her small pearl earrings glow in the hallway light. It's the first time Caroline sees Jackie in a skirt and she thinks she looks like a TV lady-lawyer. She visualizes her cross-examining Dean about his stupidity, which relaxes her a little.

"Will Marietta be joining us?" asks Jackie, as she takes her usual seat at the dining table.

Carolyn says, "I'm sorry. She's upstairs with a headache. Is that all right?"

"Of course. Will one of you fill her in for me? I want to be sure you all know where things stand as this moves forward."

"I will," Kenny says.

"Great. Thanks, Kenny." Again, Jackie has neither a purse nor a briefcase with her, just a yellow writing pad and a pen. She explains the situation with the negligence count and with the Animal Control Act count.

"So, what you're saying is that Dean won't get any award for his negligence count because he was more than fifty percent at fault," Carolyn says.

"Exactly."

"But we'll lose under the other count, the Animal Act thing."

"Most likely. I wish we had something to work with there, but as I said, we know exactly what happened, and Dean's pretty much checked all the boxes to win. We do have a bit of an argument of trespass, but it's weakened by the history of others entering the enclosure—and the fact Charlie knew Dean had the code. Of course, Dean still has to prove all of his damages and I'll do everything I can to keep him honest there."

It's hard for Carolyn to concentrate after that, but she needs to know what the inevitable loss will mean for the zoo.

Her daughter says, "Why not throw in the towel and just argue about the damages stuff?"

Jackie smiles. She is always especially encouraging to Kenny. "Good question. Actually, we do that sometimes. But in this case, I'd like the jury to know exactly what happened, assuming the judge doesn't grant Hank summary judgment on the statutory count. Jurors aren't stupid. They'll see that you did absolutely nothing wrong, and it's possible they'll factor that in when they decide how much to award Dean."

"But I'll bet they're not supposed to do that," Kenny

says.

"That's right. But they're human beings and they won't have forgotten it."

Carolyn doesn't find much solace in this. "How much do you think a jury will give Dean?"

Jackie takes a sip of her tea. "Delicious. The way it works is that Dean's lawyer has to prove all of the losses he's suffered or will suffer because of this, and at the end of the trial, he'll list them for the jury. Let me show you what I mean. Jackie takes her time to make a list on her legal pad, then pushes it across the table to Carolyn, who reads it silently, then slides it over to Kenny.

Medical bills-current————-$70,000

Future medical bills————-$100,000 to $175,000

Lost wages, at minimum wage, to date————-$2,800

Future lost wages————-(Assuming partial disability until age 65, at roughly his current wage, reduced to present cash value) —————(over $1,000,000)

Pain and suffering————-$500,000

Disfigurement————-$200,000

Total————-roughly $2,000,000

Carolyn asks, "How did you come up with these terrible numbers?"

"They're guesses," Jackie says. "I'll make sure we only consider what Dean and his experts will be able to prove."

"How good do you think your guesses are?" Carolyn says. "I mean, based on your experience."

"I think they're very conservative."

"Oh, my God," Carolyn gazes out the front window,

but sees nothing but her deceased husband's face.

"There may be good news, too," Jackie says. Carolyn looks at her intently. Hopefully.

"Thank goodness! What?" Kenny says.

"You have $500,000 in insurance, Carolyn. That, plus the fact that there's no limit on what your insurance company will pay for your defense."

"That is good news," Kenny says.

"Oh, no," Jackie says. "That's just how liability insurance works. The good news is the insurance company may decide to tender its full limits—offer Dean the whole $500,000 to settle his case. And he may take it."

Carolyn purses her lips as she lets this sink in. "How does Hank get paid?"

"Hank's fee will be one third of whatever Dean gets. I know, it sounds like a lot of money for not very much work. But remember that Hank doesn't get a dime for whatever work he puts into this if Dean loses the case."

"But he won't," Kenny says.

"Probably not this particular case, no," Jackie says.

It still doesn't make sense to Carolyn. "Why would Dean and Hank accept $500,000 if they could get a jury to give them so much more?"

"Two reasons. First of all, a good settlement is always better than a great verdict for the plaintiff. See, if we settle, it's all over. There won't be any appeals or delays. But, if they get a huge verdict, they know we'll appeal. We could win, at least as to some of the issues, on appeal. And even if we don't, Hank will need to spend a lot more time on this case—possibly years. Second, your insurance company can write the check for $500,000 as soon as Hank agrees. But if Dean gets more than that from a jury, and wins all the appeals, he would still need to collect the amount above the insurance coverage from you. I don't need to know right now, but you may not be able to come up with the money, even after you sell everything. He can't get blood out of a turnip."

"Well, I'm not quite a turnip. But, as you can imagine, Jackie, I really don't want to have to sell my business. It's all I have left of Tom." She hates to cry in front of others, but it is all too much for her, and tears run freely down her cheeks. Kenny puts her arm around her mother.

Jackie waits until Carolyn stops crying, wipes her face with a paper napkin which Kenny hands to her, and blows her nose. Jackie says, "Are you okay?"

"Yes. I'm so sorry. Please go on."

"There's nothing to be sorry about. But what I was going to say is that your worry about the zoo is exactly why a settlement for the policy limits would be a good result for you, Carolyn."

It makes sense to her, so she nods.

Kenny says, "Then you need to make that happen, Jackie."

"I'll do my best." Jackie turns to Carolyn, "I want to make sure you received the letter from Helen Huffer about your exposure in excess of the policy limits."

"I did. I'm glad you reminded me because I want to be sure I'm understanding it correctly. I read it to say that Benevolent will hire an additional lawyer to defend me because the verdict may be more than my coverage, and my personal assets are at risk. Am I reading it correctly?"

"You are. Basically, I have allegiance to both Benevolent and you. But this new attorney would consider *only* your interests. "

"So you're saying I can have this additional lawyer in case I'm worried you'll put Helen ahead of me?"

"Essentially. But the new lawyer would be in addition to me. So he or she would offer input on our defense and settlement strategies purely from your standpoint. It's completely your choice, Carolyn."

"I see. But I'm comfortable with just you. Frankly, I can see another lawyer mucking things up. All my life, I've gone with my gut, and I don't plan to change now."

"That's fine. I'll send you a letter to confirm. And, Carolyn, feel free to change your mind at any point."

"Okay. I'll let you know if I have a change of gut." She smiles at Jackie, relieved to have one decision behind her.

"I think that covers everything for now. I'll keep in close contact." As she rises from the table, Jackie adds, "Oh, and I hope Marietta's headache isn't anything serious."

"She hasn't got a headache," Kenny says.

Carolyn looks at her daughter. "What did you say, Kenny?"

"I said she doesn't have a headache."

"Do you know why she didn't want to join us for this meeting?" asks Carolyn.

"Yes."

"Kenny, please answer my question."

"You know Marietta, Mom. She's just being a grudge tiger."

Kenny hesitates, and Carolyn says, "Go on."

Kenny looks first at Carolyn and then at Jackie. "She just thinks Jackie told people all the things she said to Dean just before the accident."

"What?" Jackie sits back down at the table.

"Well," Kenny says, "it got around that she said really mean things to Dean, and Marietta assumes you spilled the beans, Jackie."

"I certainly didn't."

"I know," Kenny says. "I tried to tell her it was Jimmy—Dean's best friend—but she won't believe me."

Jackie turns to Carolyn. "Would you do me a favor and let Marietta know that the only person I shared the information with is the insurance adjuster, Helen. She needs to know the whole story."

"I will, Jackie. I'm sorry my daughter wasn't here to hear this herself. We appreciate your help. Don't worry about Marietta. I'll speak with her."

"Thank you. We'll talk soon." Jackie picks up her writing pad and lets herself out the front door.

Carolyn plans to let Marietta know how her childish behavior embarrassed her, but that's the least of her concerns after what Jackie said. She feels like she's been run over by a herd of elephants. Jackie made it clear there's no hope for her but a quick settlement, which means she'll have to agree to give Dean the entire $500,000. Carolyn doesn't really mind spending the insurance company's money if it will make the nightmare go away. But she's terrified at the prospect that Dean won't accept the offer.

Chapter 12

Jackie

Later that evening, Jackie sits at the counter in her apartment eating a salad, sipping a beer, and checking emails. She sees that Hank sent her a tentative list of Dean's damages. Nothing on the list surprises her until she gets to the wage loss claim, which is exorbitant. The parenthetical below the number says, "elimination of modeling career."

"Shit," she says under her breath. Why is Hank trying to build up the damages when he probably already has enough legitimate items to warrant a limits settlement? Maybe he just wants to pressure Helen to offer the $500,000 sooner. This new claim is something she'll have to look into right away. She wonders whether Dean ever worked as a model and whether he has contacts and realistic prospects. Jackie also wonders why no one mentioned the modeling thing to her.

Suddenly she's completely out of steam. She walks the few feet to her living room, eases herself into the cool suppleness of the leather couch to watch something on PBS, and quickly dozes off. Her phone shows one a.m. when she awakes with an urgent thought. *What did Kenny say? That Marietta is a grudge tiger? Of course, I understand the meaning—that Marietta holds grudges generally and was too angry with me to come downstairs and join us in the dining room. But why "tiger?" Why "grudge tiger?"*

She leans over her laptop which now sits on her coffee table, having traveled with her to the couch like a child who won't let go of her mother's hand. She shoots an email to Kenny, whom she suspects might still be up at one o'clock in the morning.

Jackie: Hi, Kenny! Why did you call Marietta a grudge tiger? I get the "grudge" part. Why tiger?

The response comes right away.

Kenny: *Hi, Jackie. It's just a thing we say in our family—for a person who holds a grudge. Because Ms. Benni holds grudges big time, since we first got her when she was two years old, we just use that phrase.*

Jackie: *Thanks. What do you mean when you say Ms. Benni holds grudges? Examples?*

Kenny: I've got lots of examples. Here's three (but there are more):

1. Last year, Charlie had to shoot Ms. Benni with a tranquilizer gun so we could get her teeth cleaned, and Ms. Benni saw Charlie shoot at her. For like a week or two after, every time Charlie went near Ms. Benni's enclosure, she went crazy, growling and pawing at the ground.

2. I was around twelve years old when I used to try to give Ms. Benni a grooming with my dad's extra-long backscratcher. I'd just stick it through the fence when she was lying close enough to reach. So, one time I was doing her ear and I accidentally poked her right in the eye. She didn't even growl at me at the time. As a precaution, my parents wouldn't even let me go near her for two weeks. Sure enough, when I finally was allowed to go up to the fence to see her, Ms. Benni growled at me and went crazy—just like with Charlie last year.

3. Mom is the only one who gives her meat to her because it's so gross. You'd think Ms. Benni would love her the most, wouldn't you? Well, about six months ago, Mom accidentally gave her some meat that had turned. She said Ms. Benni kind of stuck her tongue out which looked like a frown, but Mom didn't think anything of it and gave her the meat anyway. Ms. Benni ate it, got sick pretty quickly, and vomited all over the place (tiger vomit: not pretty). The next day Ms. Benni took her meat, but she also growled at Mom and pawed around in the grass acting crazy. She did that every time Mom fed her for at least a week.

Jackie: Thanks. You know what I'm going to ask you next, don't you?

Kenny: You're right!

Jackie: What happened? And when?

Kenny: OMG! I forgot all about it. So, it was about ten days before the accident. No. It had to have been two weeks because Dean only comes by every two weeks—always on Mondays. He went off to talk to Marietta by the monkey cage, and he looked furious on his way back. Ms. Benni was sunning herself right next to the fence and had her head resting against it. As Dean stomped by, he walked like ten feet out of his way, hopped over the barrier glass wall, and went right up to her cage. Then he hauled off and kicked at Ms. Benni hard, right at her head, through the fence—and Dean was wearing those work boots with metal toes.

Jackie: Then what happened?

Kenny: Nothing. Ms. Benni just watched him. Dean kept walking until he was out of my sight.

Jackie: Good. So, did you record it?

Kenny: I know you must think I'm a crazy stalker. But yeah. I did. He was shirtless, so Becca would've killed me if I didn't get it.

Jackie: Do you still have the video?

Kenny: Sure. So does Becca.

Jackie: Okay. I have a court appearance at 9:00 tomorrow morning. Do you think it'll be okay with your mom if I stop by around 10:30 tomorrow? I mean today?

Kenny: Yes. Definitely yes. Could this be it?

Jackie: What?

Kenny: That "provocation defense" you told us about.

Jackie: A long shot. But, yes, Kenny. Could be. I'll see you later 😊

Chapter 13

Marietta

Neither Carolyn nor Marietta has any idea why Jackie needs to visit with them again so soon after stopping by the night before. Kenny simply said she has an idea but doesn't want to say it wrong and confuse things. Marietta accepts her mom's assurance that Jackie wasn't the person who told folks about her conversation with Dean. With that behind her, Marietta is eager to meet with Jackie again and get back up to speed. Her mother was right that she also needs to apologize.

When Jackie pulls up, all three of them meet her at the door. She looks very professional in a navy pin-striped pantsuit and, Marietta thinks, very pretty. Maybe depending on Jackie for the zoo's survival makes her see her mom's lawyer as more attractive than on the first day they met. They put out the usual tea and some cookies and take what have become their usual positions at the table. Jackie has just a blank yellow legal pad with her, which she sets in front of her on the table. No one touches the cookies.

Jackie accepts Marietta's quick apology, then says, "Let's dive in, shall we? Last night, I learned of two major developments in the case."

Carolyn says, "Last night? You mean, after you met with us?"

"Yes, after I got home. Let me explain. First, I received Hank's list of Dean's damages. The surprise is that Dean is claiming a large loss of future income from his career as a model."

Marietta is studying her iced tea as she takes this in. She slowly raises her head. "What?"

"You didn't know about Dean's modeling career?"

"I know Dean never had one—and had no plans to start."

"Carolyn? Kenny?"

They both just shake their heads.

"Let me put it this way, Marietta. Can you think of any reason that Dean could not pursue a modeling career?"

"You mean, other than the scars?"

"Yeah. Before the accident, would that have made sense to you as a possible career for Dean? He is very handsome."

"You've met him?"

"Yes. This past Friday."

"Obviously, he's very good-looking. And he can put on the charm, which I'm sure he did for you."

"He did."

"But the thing is, he doesn't have an ambitious bone in his body. Like I told you, he was a terrible student and non-athlete, and he seems perfectly content making deliveries for his dad and hanging out with Jimmy. Honestly, nobody who knows Dean would believe he'd move to a big city and start pounding the sidewalks and go to cattle calls to get a *modeling career*." She uses air quotes for the last two words.

"Okay. I understand. You know, the jurors won't be people who know him. But you've given me some ideas as to where I might be able to chip away at this."

Marietta nods her head once. "Good."

"What's the second development, Jackie?" asks Carolyn.

Marietta interjects, "Let me guess. Dean also claims he was going to become a rocket scientist."

Jackie laughs. "No. The second may be a defense I can develop."

"I thought you said we don't have a defense to the statute count," says Carolyn.

"I did. But that was before Kenny told me that Ms. Benni is a grudge tiger."

Marietta and her mother speak at the same time. "She is."

"Kenny also told me that she saw Dean kick Ms. Benni two weeks before the attack. He was walking along looking angry, hopped over the glass barrier wall, and went right up to where Ms. Benni was lying. Then he did his best to wallop her in the head with his steel-toe boot."

"What?" says Carolyn.

Marietta turns toward her sister. "Why didn't you tell me?"

"I didn't want to get Dean in trouble."

"You're darn right he would've been in trouble." Marietta thinks for a moment, then adds, "Plus, the fact that you didn't tell us will probably make it harder for a jury to believe it even happened."

"I have a video," Kenny says.

At the same moment, Marietta and her mother say, "What?"

"I don't get it," Marietta says. "How do you have a recording?"

"Yes. How do you, Kenny?" her mother asks.

Kenny's face turns bright red.

"Tell them," Jackie whispers.

"Okay. Wow. This is going to be embarrassing to say."

Jackie urges her on. "Go ahead. Take your time."

"It wasn't just the video from the day of the accident. Remember how I said I was taking a picture of Ms. Benni because she looked so sweet when I happened to record Dean? Well, that wasn't really the reason I had my camera on." Kenny takes a sip of her tea and swallows hard. "The truth is, I always recorded Dean when I saw him on his delivery days in the summers. Since I was in school, I didn't see him much the rest of the year. It's just that he's amazing to look at, and Becca didn't have all the chances to see him that I did. So, I recorded him for her."

"Since when?" Marietta asks.

"Since I turned thirteen and got my first phone."

"Wait. Do you have all those recordings on your phone?" Marietta says.

"Of course not." Kenny pauses. "That would use up too much data. They're all stored in the computer."

Carolyn says to Jackie, "Is what Kenny did any kind of violation of Dean's privacy? Could we get her in trouble by using the recording?"

"No and no. Walking around in the outdoors, on your property, Dean had no expectation of privacy. And, we have no choice but to produce the two relevant videos to Dean's lawyer in the course of discovery."

Kenny says, "With the two recordings, and all the proof we have that Ms. Benni is a grudge tiger— shouldn't we win?"

"Maybe. I mean, yes, theoretically."

Marietta has no idea why she suddenly feels sorry for Dean. She says, "But then Dean wouldn't even get his medical bills paid."

"Oh, no. Those are being paid by his own insurer. If Dean wins enough money from your mother's insurer, Helen would just reimburse Dean's insurance company for the medical costs. Or his insurer may waive their lien so Dean could keep whatever money he gets from your mom's insurance company."

"Good. This was all Dean's own fault, and I hate him for kicking at Ms. Benni. But I honestly don't want to see him stuck with all those doctor bills. He's got enough to deal with."

"Of course," says Jackie.

Kenny asks, "Why did you say *theoretically* we should win?"

Marietta sees Jackie smile at her sister, whom she really seems to like. "Because it's a long way from here to there. First, I have to convince the judge to let me put on evidence that there is such a thing as a grudge tiger—that the experts recognize the category. Then we have to prove that Ms. Benni is one. The examples you gave me last night are great, Kenny, but the jury may discount your testimony since you're defending your zoo. I'd love to have a witness who's not a family member, friend, or employee who could testify that Ms. Benni really is a grudge tiger. Finally, even if we are persuasive that she is one, we still have to show it's more likely than not that the attack was actually a result of Dean kicking Ms. Benni two weeks earlier. As you probably know, in civil cases, the plaintiff has to prove his case by a preponderance of the evidence. If he can tip the scale at all in his favor, he wins. So, my job is to convince the jury that our grudge tiger theory is more likely the correct view of the facts. Assuming we are able to get our defense all the way to a jury, there's no way to predict what they'll do with all of this. So, theoretically, we should win. But we have a lot of work to do."

Carolyn seems energized by this shot at winning the case. She says, "Understood. What can we do to help?"

"Make a list of every example of a Ms. Benni grudge you can think of, when it happened, and who witnessed it. Try to think of someone who is not connected with the zoo who knew Ms. Benni to be a grudge tiger before Dean's accident. Kenny, please send me the first video—the one of Dean kicking Ms. Benni. And don't talk to anyone about this defense. I have an idea how to hide it in plain view from Hank, and then use it at the most opportune moment."

Kenny smiles. "So you plan to pounce?"

Jackie laughs. "Exactly."

Marietta's heart swells with a bit of optimism for the first time since this whole thing began. She senses the same sentiment from her mother but doesn't want to risk breaking the spell by mentioning it.

Chapter 14

Jackie

As soon as she gets back to her office, Jackie calls Helen, who answers on the first ring. "Hello?"

"Hi, Helen. Has the child-dart-out case started?"

"No. After I spent all weekend reviewing my file, the plaintiff's attorney asked for a continuance and got six months."

"Well, at least you won't have to spend the week sitting in a courtroom in Peoria."

"True. How's my favorite tiger case coming along?"

"Surprisingly."

"Really? What've you got for me to kick off the week?"

"Bad news and good news."

"Hit me with the worst. Then once I finish choking on my donut, you can resuscitate me with the other."

"Dean's claiming a wage loss of two and a half million dollars, based on his anticipated fashion model career which Ms. Benni took a bite out of, so to speak."

"Okay. I'm officially choking."

"Yeah. Hank broke it out at $100,000 a year for twenty-five years."

"Good of him to explain his math."

"Of course. Our teachers down here in the sticks taught us to show our work."

"So, did the kid actually have a modeling career?"

"Not that your insured or her girls knew of, and I really think Marietta would've known. The problem is that Dean really does look like a fashion model. And it won't help us on that point that Carolyn's younger daughter recorded him every chance she got."

"Why'd she do that?"

"Just to enjoy showing him to her best friend, who didn't have the same opportunities."

"Ouch."

"I know. But the older daughter, with whom Dean was obsessed, says he never could've done the modeling career due to lack of both brains and ambition."

"Well, I hope she'll testify to that more delicately."

"I think she will. I believe she could be very deliberate if she wants to be. The younger girl is thought of as the brains in the family, but I don't think much would get by Marietta either. Anyway, my guess is that Hank is behind Dean's sudden-onset career choice, and I wouldn't put it past him to try to persuade a couple of Dean's friends to rhapsodize about how it had been Dean's lifelong dream."

"Got it. Well, start chipping away."

"I've got some ideas."

"Okay. I'm ready to be resuscitated with some good news."

"We may have a way to win the Animal Control Act count."

"What?"

"There's been a development." Jackie doesn't need to remind Helen that lack of provocation is one of the elements Dean must establish under the act. Helen knows tort law like an attorney, and as to certain points of law she's dealt with repeatedly, she knows it better than most. "The last time I stopped by the Warren's house, Kenny explained her sister's absence from our meeting by saying she's a 'grudge tiger.' Apparently, Marietta was angry with me for blabbing about what she said to Dean just before the attack. Which, of course, I didn't do. Anyway, late that night—last night, actually—it hit me that it's an odd phrase. I emailed Kenny right away, and she explained it's a family term, based on Ms. Benni's trait. I met with the women this morning."

"I see. So, Dean did something to Ms. Benni before the attack."

"Exactly, Helen. Dean hauled off and tried to wallop Ms. Benni in the head the last time he visited the zoo before the attack. The tiger had her head resting against the fence where Dean aimed his foot. Unfortunately, it was two weeks before, but Ms. Benni's grudges have lasted that long in the past."

"I like it. Of course, I wish it had been two days rather than two weeks. But how do we prove it?"

"You know how I told you a few minutes ago that Kenny took video of beautiful Dean whenever she could?"

"She recorded it?"

"Yep. She's got video both of the kick and the attack two weeks later."

"That's amazing. How will you use it?"

"I need to find an expert on grudge tigers, get an interview, and then either get the expert into the courthouse to testify or take a video-taped evidence deposition I can show at trial. By the way, that bit will cost you some money."

"Of course it will," says Helen.

"And I want to lock down witnesses to testify about Ms. Benni's grudge behavior, and hopefully find someone independent of the Warren's operation to confirm that."

"Any prospects, Jackie?"

"Not yet."

"Okay. Go find your expert. Work on this defense, but keep chipping away at the damages. I assume you've subpoenaed all of the medical and school records."

"Two weeks ago."

"When should this one go to trial?"

"As you know, down here in the boonies, the judges' caseloads are smaller. Plus, Judge Marcus runs a rocket-docket."

"Marilyn Marcus?"

"Yeah."

"As I recall, she's not usually a friend to the defense."

"True. I expect she'll absolutely hate our grudge tiger defense. I just want to persuade her to let it go to the jury."

"Agreed."

"Also, Hank will probably try to expedite getting this to trial since he looks at it as easy money."

"What basis does he have to expedite?"

"None. But I suspect he'll think of some lie."

"Thanks, Jackie. This case keeps getting more interesting."

"I know. Take care, hon."

****

Jackie can't do much on the damages side since the records from the hospital, treating doctors, and high school aren't due for another two weeks, so she starts her research on grudge tigers. After three hours on the internet, she hasn't found any leads from U.S. zoos or circuses. There are several stories of revenge tigers in the wild from eastern Russia, Myanmar, and India. A few books came out in the past couple of decades which reference specific cases of tigers in the wild hunting down men who either injured them or took the remains of a kill from them. Apparently, the revenge tiger would walk right past the huts of numerous other villagers, and then destroy the hut of the guy who disrespected him. Jackie opens her Amazon account and orders the books for overnight delivery. She can't go any further on it but has a pile of work on other cases. It's going to be another late night at the office.

****

The books arrive and the revenge tiger stories make the Ms. Benni incident seem like a kitten scratch. The two books, now filled with yellow post-its, sit to her left as she summarizes her findings. One of the animals, a tiger in the farthest eastern reaches of Russia, was wounded by a poacher. The tiger tracked the man down and destroyed everything that belonged to him—including the contents of his little cabin. Then he destroyed the man. It was 1997, and this reverse-hunting situation seemed to be something newly discovered at the time. Of course, tigers in the wild have always set upon humans when they come across each other in inauspicious ways. But the attack on the poacher took place three days after the man was believed to have stolen the animal's kill. What happened to the man was said to be the result of a focused, intentional attack. Though somewhat stunned that such a thing could happen, the professionals involved in the investigation agreed it was clear that revenge was the motive.

The second book focused primarily on a similar attack, by a tiger in Myanmar. The tiger briefly left its freshly killed antelope unguarded. When the tiger returned, a local hunter was commandeering the antelope. The man dragged the thing to his jeep, slung it in the back seat, and drove back to his cabin in a small village nearby. Over the next week, witnesses saw a tiger prowling around the perimeter of the village, but each time, the tiger quickly faded into the woods. It was ten days after the hunter absconded with the antelope that the tiger slinked into the village after dark, passed by a dozen other cabins and parked itself outside the man's home. When the man went outside to use the outhouse, the tiger pounced. He ripped the man to shreds but ate only a small amount of the guy's remains. The theory was that the tiger hadn't been hungry—just pissed. The tiger was never seen again in the village.

Jackie is thrilled with the stories, which seem consistent with Dean's experience with Ms. Benni— without the fatality part. But there is a huge problem. Two anecdotes—even two well-documented anecdotes—do not a pattern make. What she really needs is a well-credentialed witness who has thoroughly studied the issue. He or she could testify about the "revenge tigers" featured in the two books, but also about tigers in general, about memory and vindictiveness, and whether there really is something that qualified experts agree is a "grudge tiger." And she needs to find the expert soon.

Also, she realizes her instinct about what Hank would do was correct when she receives his motion to expedite the trial. He probably thinks of the case as a slam-dunk and wants to get his fee as soon as possible. His basis for the motion is Dean's affidavit that he needs to move out of town because the trauma of the attack will stay with him as long as he remains, and he wants to alleviate the problem by moving in with an aunt and uncle in Cairo, Illinois. Jackie knows the scenario Hank sets forth is probably bullshit, and that, once he has his money, Dean is likely to continue to live in Heartsville.

But Judge Marcus is sympathetic to the plaintiff, as she always is to plaintiffs. She sets the trial to begin in two months—on September 30th. It's an extraordinarily short amount of time in which to complete discovery and file all pre-trial motions. Jackie's top priority becomes locating an expert witness. She searches the national defense bar association's expert database, but it has nothing on grudge tigers. She also sends notes out to defense attorneys all over the country who are listed as counsel of record on cases brought under statutes similar to the Illinois act, or who defended any exotic animal cases. She receives several interesting suggestions in response to her query, but none are appropriate for her case.

It's already almost lunch time, and Jackie needs to catch Helen to provide her with a quick status report. When Helen returns her call in the early afternoon, Jackie explains the situation.

"I think your search is too narrow, Jackie."

"Maybe. But what we're looking for is a pretty narrowly focused expert."

"Of course. That's not what I mean. I think you should do a world-wide search."

"Really?"

"Sure. You just told me how two of the unassailable

examples of revenge tigers are from Eastern Russia and Myanmar. Why would you expect to find your expert in St. Louis?"

"Are you saying you'll approve hiring an expert from far, far away? I mean, the expense may be prohibitive."

"There's no such thing. If you're asking whether I'd spend $100,000 to save $500,000, the answer is, duh."

"But even if I find the right expert, and the jury believes him, we could still lose for other reasons."

"I know how it works, Jackie. I've been doing this job for over twenty years."

"Sorry."

"Don't be so negative. You have a creative idea for how to win this case. You're a better trial lawyer than Hank, with your hands tied behind your back."

"Maybe. But I'd have a hell of a time marking my exhibits."

"Run this down. Let's see if we can't save my limits and Carolyn's zoo."

"Got it."

"And keep me posted."

"Will do."

Chapter 15

Kenny

As Kenny enters the kitchen from the back deck after grooming the ponies, her mother announces she has some bad news, and Kenny's heart sinks. She's so tired of hearing those words used as a preamble. "Just tell me, Mom."

"Hank got the case expedited, so now the trial will start on September 30th."

"Wait. That's only eight weeks from now. Is it enough time for Jackie to get everything ready?"

"She said she'll do what she has to and make it work."

Kenny doesn't like the wording, which sounds as though she'll have to cut corners or something. "Yeah. That is bad news."

She's starting to head upstairs for a shower when her mother adds, "There's more. She also says the state's attorney filed a civil complaint against me and the zoo. She just learned about it late this afternoon. She asked me if she could accept service for me, which I appreciate, since I'd just as soon not have a repeat of Fred's visit."

"What's the complaint for?"

"He claims we're harboring a wild animal in such a manner that she's a threat to public safety."

"That's stupid. Ms. Benni never escaped, did she?"

"Well, apparently, he wants the court to order us to remove her to somewhere out of Illinois, and if that can't be done, to destroy her."

"What?" Kenny says, too loudly.

"I know. It's ridiculous."

"No kidding."

"Jackie says this state's attorney, Mr. Babcock, is just grabbing for a headline since he's up for reelection next year. She assumes he wants to be seen as protecting the public."

"Figures. And lots of people won't read past the headline to see that what he's doing doesn't make any sense."

"I think you're right."

"So, does Jackie think he can win?"

"She doesn't seem to. She says the case has also been assigned to Judge Marcus. And even though the judge usually favors plaintiffs—like Dean—she absolutely hates frivolous filings. Apparently, the woman is quite a formidable taskmaster in her own courtroom."

"Good. We need a hard-ass judge." Kenny's language apparently surprises her mother, but she doesn't say anything. "So what can Jackie do about it?"

"Helen Huffer authorized her to defend this one for us too. Jackie plans to file a motion to dismiss the state's complaint. She wants to attack it...well, her word was 'viciously,' and she'll seek costs and fees, which means if she wins the motion, the state might have to reimburse the insurance company for whatever they have to pay Jackie to get the thing dismissed."

"Wow."

"She expects all of the supporting papers will be

scheduled to be filed over the next couple of months. Then, the judge may or may not allow oral argument. According to Jackie, it's only when Judge Marcus is very angry about a filing that she goes straight to a written ruling—no oral argument."

"But Jackie definitely thinks she'll win. Right?"

"I got that impression. But, even if she does win, she says it's likely the judge will allow the state to file an amended complaint after that."

"Crap. So for how long can this Mr. Babdick keep amending?"

Again, Carolyn doesn't comment on her daughter's language. "I don't know, Kenny."

"So, maybe forever?"

"I have no idea. But because the briefing schedule will run for a couple of months, we shouldn't expect much to happen on the state's lawsuit for a while."

"So, it just hangs over our heads. Well, that really stinks." Kenny takes a deep breath. "Did she say anything else?"

"Yes. She said Helen also authorized her to spend whatever is needed to hire a grudge tiger expert, if one can be found."

"What does she mean, 'if one can be found?' "

"I don't know, sweetie. I guess they aren't that easy to come by."

"You're probably right. Do you mind if I email Jackie to ask her about that part?"

"Not at all. You two emailing each other was how Jackie discovered we may have a grudge tiger defense."

"It was, wasn't it? Okay, I'll shoot her a note after my shower. Thanks for keeping me up to speed."

"Of course, sweetie. This thing is very important to

all of us."

"To put it mildly."

After Kenny showers and dresses in comfy shorts and a t-shirt, she sits on her bed to send the email from her phone.

"Hi, Jackie. Mom says it may be hard to find a grudge tiger expert."

"It is, Kenny. Any ideas?"

"Maybe. Do you want me to do a search?"

"That would be great. I've got a brief due tomorrow in another case, so I'll be immersed in that most of the evening."

"I'd love to do it. I'll let you know as soon as I have something."

"Thanks tons, Kenny."

"Sure thing."

Kenny's thrilled to have something to do to help defend the zoo, and she's pretty good at internet research. She really wants to help her mother, but she realizes part of her motivation is to impress Jackie. She spends the rest of the evening and until early in the morning at her desk, pounding away at her laptop looking for leads, running them down, and moving on to others. As she kind of expected, there are many tiger experts, both in the United States and abroad at universities, nature conservancies, veterinary clinics, zoos and circuses. But she can't find anything specifically addressing "grudge" or "revenge" tigers beyond references to the couple of instances in the wild that Jackie read about.

Kenny runs out of leads and ideas, so she closes her

laptop and stares into space, trying to leave room in her head for whatever she's missing. Her mother taught her that you have to let things go sometimes to leave room for the answer to pop up. She glances at her bookshelf. There, in a corner of the bottom shelf, are her children's books—the ones so special she's saving them for her own children.

She reboots her laptop and searches for children's books on big cats and has no idea why she didn't think of it before. Kids' books on tigers outnumber adult books by about five to one. They range from baby books with thick cardboard covers and cut-outs to put your fingers through to make the tiger's tail, to baby's bathtub books, to scholastic books for older kids, with pages of interesting facts about animals. Unfortunately, Kenny can't see the text beyond the first couple of pages, and only a small percentage of the books even have tables of contents. For all she can tell, the books might all have a paragraph or two on grudge tigers. But she can't buy hundreds of kids' books just to look through them.

She figures the whole grudge tiger idea would probably scare little kids, and she assumes no author in her right mind would try to sell books guaranteed to give children nightmares. So, she focuses on books written for fourth graders and up. She studies the covers, clicks once to see the first couple of pages, and then on any tables of contents she comes across. She's been through about two dozen books and is about ready to call it a night at four a.m. when she stumbles upon a book called *Odd Behaviors of Wild Animals* by Dr. Nigel Lucas, which seems promising. Kenny rubs her eyes and leans in, hoping more attention will transform the table of contents into what she's looking for. There are chapters on elephants, polar bears, giraffes, monkeys and finally, at Chapter 8, tigers. Of course, she has no idea what "odd" tiger behaviors Dr. Lucas is referring to. Sadly, the darn book isn't available as an e-book.

She emails Jackie a short summary of her research and gives her the information on Dr. Lucas's *Odd Behaviors*. It seems weird, but Jackie writes right back, which makes Kenny wonder if the woman ever sleeps. Jackie says that she just ordered it for expedited delivery and will have the book in two days. Kenny knows she should continue her search, but she's too tired to do more. She doesn't want to bother Jackie again, so she decides to ask her the next day whether she thinks Kenny should keep looking while they wait for Dr. Lucas's book to arrive.

****

The next morning Carolyn tells Kenny that she forgot to mention one thing Jackie told her. Kenny is supposed to start thinking about how she'll answer all the questions about why she took the two video recordings. Kenny thinks about this for a while and arrives at the obvious conclusion that her life is officially over. She'll be humiliated and dumped on her entire senior year once it comes out at her deposition that she recorded Dean every chance she got, like a creepy stalker. She knows that anyone who hears about it—that is, the entire school—will think she's a pathetic sneak, because that's exactly what she would think of someone who did that. She assumes her days—okay, day—of hanging out with the popular girls are over.

Kenny can't moan about it to her mother because she's already totally stressed out. It's so ironic that the good Kenny did by capturing Dean on video as he tried to wallop Ms. Benni in the head is the cause of her complete mortification. How stupid she feels to have been so proud, patting herself on the back for making the recordings that might save the zoo. There is no way to put the genie back in the bottle. She's majorly screwed.

Although all of this means the end of her world as she knows it, it's nothing compared with how miserable it makes her to think of telling Becca that her own name is likely to come out for having watched the videos. Kenny's deposition is scheduled to be the last of the four to be taken on August 19th, the day she'll have to betray her best friend. She toys with the idea of not telling Becca until after the deposition is finished. It's always possible that something will intervene before that date—third world war, zombie apocalypse, the Rapture. But, if she does have to give her deposition, she knows Dean and his snarky friend Jimmy will spread the news like a computer virus, and Kenny just can't let Becca find out about it like that. She considers dropping by her house, which is only five miles away. She's sure her mother will let her borrow the car. But she can't do it—she can't bear to see the look on Becca's face.

It's around nine o'clock on Friday night when Kenny finally works up the courage to call Becca. Her cell phone rings about four times before she answers, and Kenny starts to hope for a reprieve.

"Hey, Kenny! How's it going?"

"Okay, I guess."

"Good. I've been worrying about what'll happen to you guys if Dean wins the trial. It's not that far off."

"Yeah. I know." She pauses. "So, what're you doing tonight?"

"Babysitting my little sister. Mom and Dad won't be

back till after midnight. It's some kind of fundraiser for the clinic where Mom works."

"That's nice."

"It's fine. How's the case looking? Did you find a grudge tiger expert yet?"

"We have one lead, a guy named Dr. Lucas, but really no idea if he'll pan out." She pauses again, then dives in. "Say, Becca, there's something I need to tell you."

"It sounds like it's gonna be bad news. But what could be worse than maybe losing the zoo?"

"I guess it depends on your perspective."

"What does that mean?"

"Crap. This is hard to say."

"Now you're scaring me, Kenny."

"Okay. Here goes. When I give my deposition on August 19th...."

"Yeah. A week from Monday."

"Right. Well, it's very likely Dean's lawyer will ask me why I have a recording of the day Dean kicked Ms. Benni, and also of the day Dean went into Ms. Benni's enclosure."

"Ah. I get it. Yeah. That'll be embarrassing. I mean, what can you say? The truth doesn't sound too good."

"I know."

"Could you say you were trying to keep a record of how well Dean does his job?"

"No. My mom and Marietta already know the truth."

"But they're not going to rat you out if you want to go with another story, are they?"

"Wait. Are you saying I should lie under oath and ask them to lie, too?"

"Maybe. I mean, what difference does it make *why*

you made the recording. Isn't the point just that you have it, and it proves your lawyer's theory is right?'

"I can't lie under oath, Becca."

"You're probably right. I think it might be a crime."

"Yeah."

"But who's even going to know what you say at the deposition? Isn't it done in private?"

"Everyone will know."

"How?"

"Dean's lawyer will be asking me the questions. And why I happened to be recording his client is a pretty obvious question. So, after the deposition, he'll tell Dean, who will tell Jimmy. Once Jimmy knows, the whole town will know."

"Crap. You're right."

"Yeah. Also, there will probably be reporters at the trial. I mean, it's not every day a tiger case goes to trial. So, it could also be in the newspaper."

"Crap."

"Crap is right."

"I'm so sorry. You'll be humiliated."

"I know. But Becca, the reason I'm telling you this is that your name is likely to come out too."

After an agonizing moment of silence, Becca finally speaks. "Why would it?"

"Because, the reason I recorded him was to share it with you."

"But you don't have to tell him that part, do you? Can't you just say you wanted it for yourself?"

"Maybe I could start with that. But if the lawyer asks me whether I showed the recordings to anybody—which I'd say he's pretty likely to ask—I'll have to give up your name."

"But you can't."

Kenny doesn't respond.

After a few seconds, Becca continues, "I couldn't take it. Being the only Asian kid in school's bad enough. Being a science geek kind of seals my fate as an outcast—with you, of course."

"Of course."

"But being known as a creepy voyeur is another whole level of deplorable."

"That has occurred to me."

"Kenny, I can see you're trapped. But you just have to think of a way to keep me out of this. I mean, your mom already knows what you did—and she hasn't killed you."

"So far."

"Right. But my parents are different. We have this honor-code-thing in the family. So, if I dishonor my parents, they may never speak to me again."

"Becca, I'm every bit as devastated as you are. But I do know your parents, and it's hardly an honor-killing situation." Becca doesn't respond, so Kenny says, "All I can do is hope Dean's lawyer doesn't ask me who I showed the video to. I mean, I'll leave you out entirely when I explain why I recorded him—since I really did make the videos for myself too. But if he asks the follow-up question, I'll have to tell the truth."

"Damn."

"Yeah. This has become majorly messed up."

"I'm going to think about this some more, Kenny. I have to go now. I have a lot of crying to do."

"I know. Bye, Becca."

"Bye."

Of course, Kenny should be worrying about her

mother, and the zoo, and Ms. Benni. But her worry-meter is stuck in the "me" position. Now she needs to fret over hurting her best friend (in more than one way), losing her new friends, and having the whole school think she's a creepy stalker. She'll just have to trust that Jackie will take care of everything else.

Chapter 16

Carolyn

Carolyn's house is in an uproar since Kenny realized that in order for the two video recordings to be introduced into evidence, she'll be asked under oath why she recorded Dean. It will come out that she did it approximately once every two weeks, whenever school wasn't in session, for three years. Of course, Carolyn understands why that will be humiliating for her daughter—and for Becca. Unfortunately, there's no way it can be avoided. Almost no way. Actually, Jackie explained that the one thing that could prevent Kenny from having to give her testimony would be a settlement before the deposition date. Apparently, Jackie and Hank agreed that all three of the Warrens will testify on August 19th. If Helen has enough information to persuade her to offer her entire policy limit to Dean before that date, and if Dean accepts it, the whole thing will be over, and no one will ever know what Kenny did. Carolyn also understands why that might be difficult to achieve.

Until Jackie tells him there is a recording of the kicking episode, and that Ms. Benni is a grudge tiger who was provoked, Hank will continue to think he has an iron-clad case. And Jackie prefers to keep it hidden in plain view, hoping to catch Dean in a lie about it at his deposition. Therefore, unless Dean just wants to be a nice guy and not go after her zoo, it's doubtful to Carolyn that he'll agree to take just $500,000 for a case that is apparently worth much more, and one his lawyer believes he's sure to win. After all, a third of the settlement will go directly to Hank. The $330,000 that will be left isn't anywhere near what Jackie thinks Dean will end up with if he wins before a jury.

The next morning, Jackie calls to report that Helen has authorized the payment of the entire limits if Carolyn agrees, which she does in a heartbeat. Jackie says she'll call Hank right away. Carolyn knows she shouldn't get her hopes up, but she can't help herself. She feels a lightness creep in and actually keeps her fingers crossed, pending Jackie's next phone call. Unfortunately, in under an hour, Jackie calls back to tell her the bad news. While Hank appreciates the offer, he can't persuade Dean to take it. His client says he wants his day in court. Following that, Helen asks Jackie to withdraw the settlement offer and prepare for trial.

The whirlwind of activity leaves Carolyn first flummoxed and then desperate. Suddenly, losing her zoo seems to be setting in concrete. She's fairly certain her daughters don't fully appreciate how devastating the financial consequences will be if she loses the case to Dean. Just selling the heavily mortgaged zoo, whether as an on-going operation, or as individual animals and forty acres of land, wouldn't yield enough money to satisfy the amount Jackie said the verdict could be. Carolyn would also have to sell the house. She mentally shoves aside the probability that none of them would ever fully recover emotionally. It's the financial impact that would be downright ruinous.

Carolyn suspects she might be able to get some kind

of teaching position, even after the ten-year hiatus. Still, she'd have no choice but to rent an apartment in town, a new home that wouldn't remotely resemble their prior existence. And she would own nothing.

Kenny may well receive a scholarship to college. But her daughter has no idea how much room and board, books, and miscellaneous expenses can add up to. Had Dean's lawsuit not happened, Carolyn could've easily co-signed for a student loan. With no collateral, what bank would agree? She doesn't have the heart to discuss this scenario with Marietta and Kenny and sees no reason to do so. If everything goes badly, they'll have months and years to learn the consequences firsthand.

In the meanwhile, there is no way around Kenny's immediate humiliation of being viewed badly for basically stalking Dean. It would be one thing if her daughter were leaving for college shortly after the trial, but Kenny has another year at Heartsville High, and no way to avoid her classmates learning what she did. Carolyn suspects that her daughter's videotaping will also feed into Dean's narrative that he is so handsome he surely would've succeeded with his modeling career.

Carolyn watches Kenny blanch when she learns the case is definitely going to trial. Someday, her daughter might look back at this and laugh, but that day is a long, long way off. Instead, she's slamming doors, crying and spending a lot of time in the bathroom. As the stress mounts, Carolyn is too embarrassed to ask her doctor for something for her anxiety. Instead, each evening she forces herself to drink some of the chardonnay Marietta keeps stocked in the refrigerator. She's never liked the taste of alcohol, so she uses a straw to force-feed herself. Unfortunately, even though it makes her a bit dizzy, it does precious little to calm her nerves. She certainly can't suggest that Kenny turn to alcohol, and she really has no idea how to ease her daughter's foreboding and barely-below-the-surface rage. Carolyn wonders if Jackie realizes what a difficult position Kenny is in.

Shortly after closing time, Carolyn decides to get a jump on her weekly survey of the general condition of the animal enclosures. She's at the far west end of the zoo to check the wallaby and giraffe cages when she notices someone walking around near the employee cottages, which are just beyond the zoo fencing. It's Charlie. He's all cleaned up, and wears khaki slacks and a light blue, short-sleeve shirt which highlights his tan. As he heads toward his car, Carolyn notices he's carrying a bouquet of flowers in his left hand. Her heart skips a beat and her mouth goes dry. She bites down on her lower lip, and squeezes her eyes tightly closed for a brief moment. Then she tries to distract herself by focusing on every detail of the Bennett's Wallabies' enclosure.

Chapter 17

Jackie

It's Thursday, August 8th, the day Jackie and Carolyn plan to go over the information and documents Jackie will have to produce to Hank as part of the discovery process. Jackie leaves for the appointment early so she'll have time to tour the zoo. It's her first time to visit when it is open to the public, and it starkly contrasts with the quiet of her prior visits, when she only occasionally heard the call of an animal. She decides to park in the public parking lot out of curiosity about what a visit looks like to a family out for a summer vacation afternoon. Cars are lined up in rows of about twenty, with probably a half dozen rows already filled, and more vehicles flowing in. As she steps out of her car, music, chatter and children's laughter wash over her. The sun shines brightly, so she immediately reaches into her pocket for her sunglasses.

Jackie walks up to the ticket booth, following closely behind a large family group. The younger children are so excited they are literally jumping up and down. She pays her ten dollars to a zoo employee to whom she's not yet been introduced, and wonders how the business can succeed with such modest ticket prices. The ticket woman hands Jackie a one-page full- color map of the zoo. There are restrooms just inside the ticket booth area, and she ventures in, purely out of curiosity about upkeep and sanitation. She finds it simple but pleasant and clean, with the walls painted a sunny yellow and bordered with zoo animal stencils along the top near the ceiling. The gift shop is just across the blacktop walkway, and she dashes in for a bottle of water since it's already hot. This answers her question about the low admission price. Like movie theatres, the zoo obviously makes its money on refreshments and gifts. So, with her three dollar bottle of water in hand, she steps back into the sunlight, again lowering her sunglasses, and looks down to study the map.

The zoo is basically a large oval, with four smaller ovals protruding from points along its perimeter like a series of suburban cul-de-sacs, with exhibits lining each of them. Jackie is glad she arrived over an hour early, because just to speed-walk through and spend a minute eye-balling each enclosure will take her that long. Noting that Ms. Benni is at the far end of the oval from where she enters, Jackie decides to save her for last and walks in the opposite direction.

As she heads for the first cul-de-sac, she passes a charming, antique-looking carousel with brightly painted wooden zoo animals chasing each other around and around to the tune of "All Around the Mulberry Bush." Little girls in pigtails and boys with shirttails hanging out adorn the ride as though they were chosen by central casting. Young parents beam and take pictures of their brave little cowgirls and cowboys, riding lions and zebras, and camels and rhinos—bareback. A sign lists the very limited hours it runs each day and, surprisingly, says the ride is free.

The first oval features hippos, Asian black bears,

chimpanzees and a couple of other kinds of monkeys, Andean condors, and ring-tailed lemurs. Jackie appreciates that there is a large, printed sign in front of each exhibit, with details on the country to which the animal is native, its gestation period, how many offspring it produces at a time, adult weight, and diet. An interesting fact is also included, like that llamas typically spit only at each other, or that chimpanzees are very social animals and live in communities of forty to sixty chimps in the wild.

As she hurries past the families luxuriating in the slow pace of a vacation day, she notices how beautifully the center area has been done. Inside of it is another smaller fenced-in space in which pelicans, Chilean flamingos, and rheas frolic in and around a sparkling blue pond. An aeration fountain in the center keeps the water moving and shimmering in the sunlight. Daylilies, delicate cosmos, and bold zinnias are scattered in pretty groupings, and white wooden benches sit at roughly twelve-foot intervals for folks who want to take a break and enjoy the loveliness of the scenery or of each other.

It's a fairly long walk to the second large cul-de-sac on the path, which features an impressive exhibit with two African elephants, and then a bird enclosure that guests are allowed to enter. As she continues west, she comes upon a number of the larger animals. Zebras, camels, reticulated giraffes, and Bennett's Wallabies, which look a lot like kangaroos, surround a central grassy space. There is also a second building with restrooms, hidden between the camels and the wallabies. Each animal enclosure includes a small building, toward the far back of the exhibit, which Jackie assumes is partly for shelter for the animals, and partly for food-storage, cleaning supplies, etc.

She finally arrives at the third large cul-de-sac, which includes the tiger exhibit. To reach Ms. Benni, Jackie makes her way past the African crested porcupines, Eurasian lynxes, and a cougar. Ms. Benni's is one of the larger enclosures, and like with the other exhibits, a forty-five-inch-tall tempered glass barrier wall keeps guests at least ten feet from the cage. Jackie pulls out her phone and takes photos from every angle she can manage, realizing she must look like a creepy tiger-stalker. Then she focuses on the large sign which describes tigers in general and includes a map showing where wild tigers can be found. The text says:

The Bengal Tiger is native to India, Nepal, Bangladesh and Burma, and it has a lifespan of 15 years in the wild and 25+ years in captivity. The Bengal Tiger is the second largest subspecies of tiger; only the Siberian is larger. Average males weigh between 400 and 500 pounds, and females are smaller and weigh between 250 and 350 pounds. Tigers are solitary hunters and only seek out contact with other tigers in the mating season. A Bengal tigress has an average of two to four cubs in a litter, after a gestation period of three and a half months. Its diet consists of deer, boar, Asian buffalo, and antelope. These large cats can consume between 40 and 60 pounds of meat at one time. This gorging activity allows the cats several days between successful hunts. Like all tigers, each Bengal Tiger has its own particular stripe pattern, and the stripes are skin-deep. The patterns are unique, like human fingerprints. They have excellent eyesight and, in particular, night vision. As a result, they hunt after dark. Habitat loss and large-scale poaching are posing the greatest threat to this species. Bengal

Tigers do especially well in captivity.

Jackie appreciates all of the information, even though it doesn't do a thing for her grudge tiger defense. Although she met Ms. Benni on her first visit to the Warrens, today she's interested in every detail of the tiger's home. It's an attractive space with grass covering most of her area, and wood chips around the perimeter. A wooden platform for the tiger to sleep on is near the mature, solitary maple tree in the center. Ms. Benni also has a second wooden structure which looks like a giant child's play area, with ramps with broad ridges on two sides and a slide down the third. Giant tires top the ramp on the fourth side. There is a shallow pool situated at the back of the exhibit, which appears to be about three feet deep and maybe fifteen feet long and four feet wide. Along the side of the enclosure is a wooden building, which must be Ms. Benni's shelter, judging by the open door. Just beyond that, there's a separate rectangular steel mesh cage, perhaps twelve by twenty-four feet. Jackie stands near what looks to be the main entrance to the exhibit. First, there's a door made of the same steel mesh as the enclosure as a whole, with a frame of metal rods. She can see the heavy-duty keypad which a zookeeper would use to unlock the door. Another eight or nine feet in is a ninety-degree turn and then a second door, also equipped with a keypad. Jackie assumes there is also a man-door to the tiger's shelter, so that the attendant can make sure Ms. Benni is locked up before going into the large enclosure to clean. Or maybe that's what the rectangular cage adjacent to the shelter is for.

While Jackie is studying Ms. Benni's home, Ms. Benni is studying her. She lays flat out on her sleeping platform, with her paws stretched out in front of her.

Every time Jackie glances at her, the tiger seems to have her big, almond-shaped, greenish-yellow cat-eyes glued to her. Maybe she's trying to tell Jackie to win the damn case so she won't have to move—or be murdered.

Jackie glances at her watch and sees she has only ten minutes before her meeting with Carolyn. As she heads for the exit, she passes by the last cul-de-sac, a children's zoo with llamas, fallow deer, goats, cows, donkeys, and pony rides. She notices a sign that says the children may purchase pellets from a vending machine to feed the animals through the fences, but the kiddies aren't allowed to enter the exhibits. So, a feeding zoo, rather than a petting zoo. Probably for the best.

Jackie exits where she entered, walks around the exterior perimeter of the zoo, and finds a path leading to the Warrens" back yard. She lets herself in through the gate in the picket fence, walks past the willows toward the house, then takes the stairs up onto the back porch. The door opens as soon as she knocks. "Good morning, Carolyn. I just gave myself a tour. I hope I didn't frighten you using the back door."

"Not at all. I saw you coming."

"Your zoo is just lovely—a great place for families to relax together. It breathes joy. I can see why you love it so much."

"Thank you. We work hard to keep it that way."

As Jackie steps into the kitchen, she says, "Where shall we…?"

"Let's use the dining table. That way you can spread out your papers."

Jackie has already inserted all of the information into the answers to interrogatories, so Carolyn just needs to review it to be sure it's correct. The request for documents requires Carolyn to run to the basement for a plat of survey and papers on the purchase of Ms. Benni from the safari park. Jackie mentions she already has the two recordings Kenny forwarded to her, and she reminds Carolyn that she should have her daughter start giving some thought to how she wants to explain how she happens to have them.

It doesn't hit Jackie until she's driving home just how embarrassing it will be for both Kenny and Becca that they shared the footage of a hot boy who works at Kenny's mom's zoo. But as an essential part of the defense, there's no way to avoid it coming up, now that Dean has dug in his heels about refusing to settle for the policy limits. Jackie's not so old she's forgotten what high school is like—especially since she imagines that Kenny's status at school is a lot like her own was. It definitely has the potential to be pretty miserable for the two girls.

****

Two days after Kenny gives her the information about the kids' book, Jackie expects to see it in her mailbox. Instead, she receives an email that the book is now out-of-stock. However, the on-line seller provides her with contact information for four bookstores, each of which claims to have one copy. Since she's running out of time and can't afford to lose any more, she orders all four books, and requests expedited delivery from each. Unfortunately, it will be a few days. The book is fifteen dollars, but with all the delivery charges, she spends almost one-hundred twenty-five dollars to get four kids' books that might not even have what she needs. Of course, Helen will reimburse her if she remembers to list it on her expense account.

Another several days pass. It's already Saturday, August 10th, only one week from the deadline to name the expert witness, and two weeks before all expert witness reports need to be exchanged. Jackie is excruciatingly uncomfortable with her lack of progress in pinning down a grudge tiger expert. Her whole defense hinges on having one—and a good one. Yet, here she sits in her PJs, having her morning coffee, with only the remote prospect that a children's book she hopes will arrive that day will reveal her path to success.

Her doorbell rings, and she bolts to the intercom, where a man's voice says he has a package for her. She says she'll be right down, leaves her apartment door wide open, and takes the four flights of stairs in a sprint. She flings open the glass front door to her building and takes the package. She's pretty sure she says "thank you" so dramatically that the guy probably figures the package is a mental health medication for a deranged woman.

Jackie takes the elevator up but resists the temptation to rip the package open until she's back in her apartment. Her heart races, but she slows herself down by taking a couple of deep breaths before carefully opening the package at her small kitchen table. There it is: *Odd Behaviors of Wild Animals* by Dr. Nigel Lucas. It's a large, slim book, probably nine inches by twelve inches, with a colorful cover featuring a lion, a tiger, and an ape. She flips past the chapters on elephants, giraffes, monkeys and polar bears, and heads straight for Chapter 8—the one Kenny's e-mail said is about tigers. Several stunning full-color pictures of tigers, including a white tiger with her cubs, pull her eyes to the page on the left. Text covers the next two pages.

She quickly skims the information, looking for the

words grudge tiger. She sees it. At the end of the first page of text is a sub-heading: "*Revenge tigers*." The three paragraphs which follow briefly explain what she previously read concerning the documented cases in Northeast Russia, Myanmar, and India, but there's no mention of any revenge tigers in captivity. The section concludes with an author's note: "*Based upon the author's research and decades of study of tiger behavior, it is his opinion that the tendency toward holding grudges, or being a revenge-seeker, is basically a personality trait. This propensity is simply who the particular tiger is.*"

Jackie hasn't really thought of Ms. Benni this way before, but it makes sense. The Warrens' tiger was raised in captivity by kind zookeepers, so it isn't like she's been abused. The idea that it's a personality trait is consistent with the fact she's displayed the behavior as far back as when Carolyn took her in as a two-year-old cub. Most important, Dr. Lucas's interpretation will work for Jackie's defense.

She flips to the back of the book to study the "*About the Author*" page. Dr. Lucas, English born and raised, received his undergraduate degree at Oxford. He pursued his interest in tigers by completing his advanced degrees, including a doctorate in Wild Animal Studies, at the Indian Institute of Technology's satellite location in Karnataka, India (home of over 400 wild tigers). At the time he wrote the book, Dr. Lucas was living in London with his wife and son. He was employed by a nature conservancy group and was a member of numerous boards of directors.

The book was published ten years before, in 2009. She opens her laptop, which has settled itself between her coffee and the untouched oatmeal breakfast bar which sits on a saucer on her table. Googling Dr. Lucas, she learns he is still with the conservancy and still living in London. The information includes his date of birth. Apparently, he's forty-two years old, surprisingly young to have published the number of research papers listed in his bio. There is no contact information for him, so she checks out the London conservancy where he works. Luck smiles on her, and she is able to navigate the site to an email address for Dr. Lucas.

Jackie pushes away her coffee cup and plate and puts her elbows on the table, her head in her hands. She closes her eyes and thinks through how to approach the man with a sense of urgency, but not outright panic. If he loves tigers as much as his life's work suggests, he'll be interested in helping her save Carolyn's zoo. From everything Jackie reads, she's pretty sure he'll jump on board—if he can. The big questions are his availability and whether any job restrictions might preclude or limit his ability to serve as an expert witness. And, of course, whether she even has a current e-mail address.

She starts typing away and, after numerous re-writes and about forty-five minutes, pushes "send" at nine thirty a.m. her time. After that, she basically sits staring at her screen. It's 3:30 in the afternoon in London, but since it's a Saturday, she doesn't know if he'll even check his emails. Of course, she should get up and clean the apartment, or at least shower and dress. But Jackie is paralyzed waiting for Dr. Lucas to save her—or not. She taps her fingers on the table, stares at her chipped nail polish, and fidgets in her chair. Amazingly, his response comes within the hour. First, Dr. Lucas expresses his sympathy for the Warrens' involvement in the lawsuit.

Then, he writes of his deep love for the species *tigris*, dating back to his early days, living just next to his family's zoo, outside of Malvern, England. Finally, she sees the magic words: *"I'd be honored to review your materials, and if you think my conclusion would be of interest to the jury, to testify by video."*

A smile creeps across Jackie's face, and she lets out a long sigh as she continues reading. Dr. Lucas explains he'll have to juggle some other obligations, and definitely *cannot* take time away from his work to travel to southern Illinois for a live appearance at a trial that will start on September 30th. However, he will make the necessary adjustments to his schedule so that he can sit for a video evidence deposition in London on the date Jackie suggested, Monday, September 2nd.

She writes back immediately, expressing her deep gratitude, laying out the specific work needed and the timetable, and requesting the doctor's fee schedule, since Helen will need to approve the amount. Jackie hopes it will be in an area that will appear reasonable to a jury, because she's well aware that Hank will try to use the expert's fee to argue that Dr. Lucas is simply a hired-gun, and that his fee should be held against his credibility.

Again, Dr. Lucas responds to her promptly, agreeing to the schedule of activities. Then he writes more magic words: "I will not charge a fee to study an interesting situation for a family zoo or to share my knowledge with a jury."

"Wow!" Jackie says out loud. Because it really is too good to be true, she laughs as she decides she'd better make sure she's not dreaming. She heads directly to the bathroom for her morning shower. If Dr. Lucas's words are still on her computer when she returns, she'll be convinced she's extraordinarily lucky, and get an email out to share the good news with Helen. Then she'll reach out to Carolyn to try to alleviate some of the dread that Kenny told her is hanging over their home.

The words are still on the screen. Jackie turns on the radio and does a little dance to whatever is playing. And she knows it's moments like these that so well substitute for genuine joie de vivre.

Chapter 18

Marietta

She's been getting a vibe from her sister that she and Becca may've had some kind of falling out. Marietta can't put her finger on it, but they will definitely need each other to get through the trial and whatever it leaves in its wake. She runs into Kenny on the back porch as she is coming in and Marietta is on her way out to do chores.

"So, Kenny, what's up with Becca? You guys didn't do anything last weekend and I haven't seen her around in a couple of weeks."

"Nothing's up. Why are you monitoring me?"

"I'm really not. I just noticed, so I thought I'd ask if there's some reason."

"Why do you care?"

"Because she makes you happy."

"Yeah. She does." Kenny just stares at Marietta, then hesitantly says, "The thing is, I might have a chance to get in with a group of girls for senior year. Like I mentioned when Jackie was interviewing us, one of them invited me to a party a few weeks ago. I had a lot of fun, and they're all really nice. So, I'm just kind of curious what it would be like to have more than one friend."

"Nothing wrong with that. But you might want to be careful not to hurt Becca's feelings." Marietta realizes she may be sounding a bit paternalistic. Sure enough, Kenny gets defensive.

"Of course, I'll be careful. I may not be the queen of all social life, but I do know how to be decent to my friend."

Marietta smiles at her. "Have you told Becca about the party?"

"No. But really, you've got a lot going on. You don't need to be in charge of my happiness—or Becca's."

"I know. I just like how you two light up when you're together."

"That just sounds weird. Anyway, I gotta grab a shower."

"See ya later."

She really doesn't want to see Kenny put her relationship with Becca at risk. She suspects her sister would like nothing more than to run to Becca to tell her what a busybody her big sister is, but then Kenny would have to admit she went to the party and didn't tell her best friend about it. One more little drama heaped upon serious vulnerability for the family.

When Marietta learns about the trial date, she assumes the judge must be an idiot, scheduling the trial before Dean's injuries are healed. He'll have to use crutches or a wheelchair to get into the courtroom. And from what she's heard, he is still in a lot of pain. She can't understand why Dean would want to subject himself to the trial while he's still recuperating. Then again, she's not a lawyer. Maybe Hank thinks it will get Dean more sympathy.

Marietta doesn't think things can get worse than they already are. Then Jackie reminds her about her deposition, right after Dean's, on August 19th. She doesn't mind the question and answer part but is horrified at the thought of running into Dean. No matter that it's her mother he sued, she knows in her heart he blames her for what she said to him. Maybe it's from being in school with him, but she has a strong feeling that Dean doesn't accept responsibility for his own failures very well. It was always someone else who let him down, and she's certain he believes she was the cause of the tiger attack. Of course, that is a moronic way to look at it, but she's absolutely sure that's how he sees it. After all, he is a moron.

But as much as she dreads facing Dean, that's nothing compared with the predicament her sister will be in once she gives her deposition. Marietta can't imagine a worse fate in high school than having the entire student body find out she's been sneaking around for years taking videos of a hot guy who works for her mom. It will be especially embarrassing for a goody-two-shoes honor student, nerd-type person, whom the rest of the school probably either ignores or hates for her good grades. And just to add to the calamity, she tries to imagine being Kenny and having to tell her best friend that she's going to go down in flames, too.

Marietta frets over Kenny's and Becca's situation all weekend. She is flying Monday through Thursday, and the drive back and forth to St. Louis gives her time to think it through. She can't prevent what's about to happen, but she imagines it has to be possible to soften the blow. An idea takes shape, as they tend to do over miles and hours. When she calls Jackie to discuss it, the lawyer is enthusiastic and says she wishes she'd thought of it herself. Carolyn agrees as well and promises to make a call to Mr. and Mrs. Kim. They explain that

Becca has been grounded since she told them how her name might come out at Dean's trial. They haven't yet decided on the punishment for dishonoring the family by being involved in the tawdry video-watching, but they're sure she shouldn't have any privileges for the time being. When Carolyn explains Marietta's idea, and what she and her daughter think it will accomplish, the Kims surprise her by agreeing to the plan. They also promise to release Becca from home confinement to meet with Marietta on Friday evening.

At nine p.m. on Friday, Marietta knocks on Kenny's door.

"Who is it?"

"Your sister. May I come in?"

"Sure." As she slips through the doorway, Kenny adds, "But I don't want to talk about it."

"I know."

"So, what do you want?"

"I want you to call Becca and invite her over."

"She's grounded."

"She'll be allowed to come."

"What're you talking about?"

"Just call her. When she gets here, I want to see both of you in the kitchen."

"What is this? An intervention?"

"Kind of. But it'll just be with me. Mom's out to a church group thing, and she won't be back until 11:00."

"What if we don't want to?"

"You don't have a choice. Mom and Becca's folks are on board." Marietta winks at Kenny and then leaves the room, closing the door behind her.

A half hour later, Kenny and Becca are seated at the kitchen table. Marietta prepares a big bowl of popcorn and places it in the middle of the round Formica table. She gets each of them a large glass of icy cola before sitting down and leaning back in her chair. "Kenny, Becca, I just want to tell you how sorry I am that this is happening to you."

Becca says, "Thanks."

Kenny rolls her eyes.

"I won't minimize how bad it is. The thing is, I was one of the mean girls in high school. I don't know how much of this ancient history you know, Kenny, but I was the queen of the main popular group, and whoever I let hang out with me was in it too. You probably remember I was a cheerleader and homecoming queen."

"Right. Congratulations," says Kenny, who isn't looking at her sister.

"You should offer condolences. It wasn't a good thing, Kenny. I was a bitch and nobody called me on it."

Kenny turns toward her sister. "Why were you mean?"

"You know how they say, 'power corrupts?' "

"Yeah," Kenny says.

"It's true. Probably especially for adolescents. Anyway, it wasn't until community college, where we're all pretty supportive of each other, that I realized how horrid I was." Marietta smiles. "Anyway, I've been thinking about your situation for the past few days."

"Thanks," says Becca.

"I've been trying to imagine how I would've reacted if I'd learned of something like this while I was in high school, and it was obvious. I would've been a jerk about it—especially because I'd have been secretly jealous of your good grades. You would have been prime targets for my pubescent wit and sarcasm—two girls for me to take little pokes at."

"This is really helping so much. Thanks, sis," Kenny says.

Marietta looks at her steadily and shakes her head. "Then I thought about what would've taken the fun out of the meanness."

"What?" says Becca.

"If the targets refused to be humiliated."

"But we are humiliated," says Becca.

"That's irrelevant. What you have to do is not *act* humiliated. There are a couple of ways, if you have the confidence."

"Doubtful," Kenny says.

"You may surprise yourself. Just respond to any of their cracks by laughing and saying something like, 'Sorry. We're not sharing the videos. They're all ours.'"

"I might be able to pull that off," Kenny says.

"Not me," says Becca. "That would be like admitting we think Dean's hot."

"Everyone thinks Dean's hot. But there is another approach. Just laugh and go on your way. Laugh and ignore it."

"I get the 'just ignore it' part, but why laugh?" asks Kenny.

"Because having someone laugh at you always discombobulates people. They don't know why you're laughing. Do they have ketchup on their clothes or toilet paper stuck to something? You can't lose with a laugh."

"Thanks for your suggestions, Marietta," says Becca.

"And, guys, keep in mind that there's also a good chance nobody will bother you about this. People in general are pretty wrapped up in their own lives. High school seniors may very well be so absorbed in their dramas, they'll forget all about yours."

"That would be good. We really appreciate your trying to help us," says Becca.

"Well, that was only step number one."

Kenny sighs. "So, what's step number two?"

"Step number two is that we get you two out of this podunk town so you can appreciate how amazingly big the world is. Once you travel, you get a totally different perspective on the things that may happen at your little home-town high school this coming year."

"How do we do that, Marietta? You know as well as I do that Mom doesn't have any extra money for my perspective-broadening travel."

"Of course. But you won't need money."

"I think stowing away might be a crime," says Becca.

"Yeah, Marietta. How do we travel without money? Have you been hallucinating from all the pressure?"

"Not at all, baby sister." Marietta studies the girls and is moved by how young they look—sweet and naive and vulnerable. "Here's the plan. As Mom told us, Jackie contacted the grudge tiger expert we need—in London. The guy you found for her, Kenny. She'll fly there to take a video-taped deposition to use at trial. All expert depositions have to be finished by September 6th, according to the judge's order. So, she set up the London deposition for Monday, September 2nd. She chose the Saturday departure, with a return flight on Wednesday night, because we're closed on Mondays and Tuesdays. So, she and Mom and I thought that would be the least disruptive."

"For what?" asks Kenny.

"For you to go with her to London."

"What about Becca?"

"She's invited too." Marietta turns to Becca. "Your parents have already agreed."

"I still don't understand who's paying for it," Kenny says.

"I'm taking care of that. Now that I have two years in, I get buddy passes for friends to fly free."

"Is it really free, Marietta?" asks Becca.

"Almost. I'll just pay the taxes and airport fees for you. It'll be nominal." Marietta exaggerates the benefit a bit so the girls won't know she'll spend some money on their trip. "And Jackie says she'll reserve a hotel room with two twins and a roll-away, so you guys can just share her room."

"What about meals?" asks Kenny.

"We can live for two or three days without eating," says Becca.

"Jackie says not to worry about that. She's not planning to let you starve."

"So, the deposition is set for Monday. You'll leave on Saturday evening on an overnight flight. The three of you will have Sunday after your flight lands, Monday after the deposition, all day Tuesday, and Wednesday until early afternoon to explore London. Your trip home is Wednesday evening, arriving early Thursday morning."

The girls look at each other. Then Becca shrieks, "We're going to London!"

"Yes, you are," Marietta says. "Kenny, that passport you got for our trip to Toronto a few years ago is still valid. And Becca, your mom says yours is up to date, too."

Kenny says, "I can't believe this. I mean, I get it. You and Mom and Becca's folks all think we'll be able to take whatever crap gets dished out this school year because we'll understand that the world is way bigger than Heartsville High. So we won't kill ourselves or something. But you went to a lot of trouble to do this for us. Why?"

"I could say just because you're my only sister, and I love you. And you are, and I do. But the truth is, it's also a great way for me to assuage some of my guilt over how I behaved at your age. And I think it's a fairly brilliant plan—if I do say so myself."

"You're too cool," Kenny says, as she gets up to hug her sister.

"You're amazing," says Becca. "I hope I'll be a tenth as kind to my little sister when she grows up."

"You will," the sisters say at the same time.

Chapter 19

Jackie

Sunday, August 18th, Jackie prepares the Warrens for their depositions, which will be taken the following day. She thinks they'll all make good witnesses, especially Carolyn, who is as earnest and motherly as witnesses come. She runs through with Kenny several times the likely series of questions on why she made videos of Dean. Jackie tries to desensitize her but expects Kenny will still flush bright red. Marietta comes across as very poised and articulate. Jackie suspects she'd have been an ace student too, if her good looks hadn't resulted in major distractions during her high school years. The jury will understand why Dean pursued her so tenaciously.

Jackie agreed ahead of time that all of the depositions could be taken in Hank's office so Dean wouldn't have to travel to hers for his. She is most curious to hear Dean's explanations for kicking Ms. Benni on June 24th and entering her cage on July 8th. Hank objects when she asks about the kicking incident, but Jackie reminds him that relevance is not a proper objection to a discovery deposition, which he well knows. When Dean vehemently denies that the kicking ever happened, she marks the video as an exhibit, then plays it on a large computer screen for Dean to view.

Hank goes wild. He accuses Jackie of hiding the information and ambushing his client. He bangs on the table with both fists and actually screams at her. When she is finally able to get a word in edgewise, Jackie explains on the record that the kicking incident and the grudge tiger defense were both set forth in the defendant's amended answer and affirmative defenses, which she filed on July 26th. "I hope you're finished with your outburst, Mr. Perdue. It seems that you neglected to read the defendant's amended pleadings. Further, the reason you didn't see the video until today is that the defendant's answers to interrogatories and production of documents aren't due until this Thursday—August 22nd. The record will reflect that I offered to hold off taking all of the depositions until after that date, but you declined my offer and insisted we go forward today. I have a copy of my email and your response, Counsel, and I ask the court reporter to mark them as the next two exhibits."

It isn't a good situation for Hank. Jackie knows his only associate is out on leave, but she never really believed Hank would be so busy that he'd fail to read her amended pleadings—it was more of a vague hope. She doesn't understand why he pushed so hard to expedite the depositions—which resulted in Dean's not knowing about the video before he lied under oath.

Of course, Hank tries to rehabilitate his client by asking whether the video refreshes his recollection. Dean knows enough not to lie again in the face of the evidence. He gathers his wits to explain that it was such a minor thing that he just forgot about it. Basically, he testifies that it was another day on which Marietta was dismissive of him, which embarrassed and angered him. So, he kicked the fence, but his foot barely touched it, much less

Ms. Benni.

Jackie wonders how Dean can massage the truth to such an extent when the aggressiveness of his act is right there on the screen for all to see. She appreciates knowing that any lies he's caught in will undermine his credibility on other points—such as his level of pain and his dream of a modeling career.

Dean tells the story of what Marietta said on the day of the accident pretty much as she reported it, but tearfully—a touch Jackie assumes Hank suggested. Dean claims that throwing his phone into Ms. Benni's enclosure was an "act of passion" and something any man would've done. Immediately afterward, he realized his phone was in the tiger enclosure. Since Ms. Benni was resting under the tree, and since he knew about members of the Warren family having done it, he thought he'd be fine slipping into the enclosure to grab his phone. He didn't see Ms. Benni go into a crouch because his eyes were on his phone. It was Kenny's scream that sent him clambering back for the gate. He almost made it when the tiger, who must've been flying, was on him, mauling him. An older zoo worker he knew, Charlie, pulled him through the gate and it closed on Ms. Benni, so she couldn't follow them out of the cage. Dean explains that he knew the code from seeing it the day he helped Charlie with some heavy lifting inside the tiger enclosure. He thinks Charlie knew he had it, and never told Dean it was a problem. Plus, Dean insists it was important for him to know it in case Charlie ever had an emergency situation in the cage.

Dean lays on the baloney about the modeling career, explaining that it was his secret dream since fifth grade when he realized he'd never be a great student. He claims that the only person who knew about it was his buddy Jimmy, who said, "Go for it, man." Either Hank prepared his client well, or Dean knows instinctively how to fend off Jackie's suggestion that such a career is unlikely because he never modeled and knows little about the profession. He doesn't know the name of any modeling agency, has no idea how the business works, and hasn't taken any concrete steps such as having a head shot taken. Basically, he claims he didn't get that far when his chances were ruined. Dean has an easy smile and an answer for everything she asks.

By the end of the deposition, Jackie thinks Dean's performance was pretty slick, and that the boy isn't nearly as stupid as Marietta seems to believe. And he turned the charm on again, answering questions with "yes, ma'am" and "no, ma'am" and, "I'm sorry, ma'am, but I don't understand the question." In the intervening weeks, her memory of just how compelling the boy is had faded a little. These are all big negatives that Helen needs to know about. As Jackie expected, she concludes Dean's deposition by noon, so he's long gone before the Warrens arrive for their afternoon sessions.

The depositions of the Warren women go well. Carolyn does a nice job answering Hank's questions, and there are no surprises. Marietta is so composed and responsive, it's as though she gives depositions every day. She adeptly explains her relationship with Dean, and how he insisted she tell him the honest truth about why she won't date him. She testifies that telling him the truth was the most painful thing she's ever had to do. She thinks he's a nice boy—she just doesn't want to date him, and he won't take no for an answer. When it's time for Jackie to ask her follow-up questions, she gets

Marietta to talk about Dean's lack of ambition and how unlikely he would be to muster the initiative to pursue modeling. She also testifies that in all the hundreds of conversations she's had with Dean, he never once mentioned it.

When it's Kenny's turn, she testifies truthfully about recording Dean because he is a really good-looking boy, who often walked around the zoo with his shirt off. She leaves it at that, but Hank gets all the rest through more questions: for how long and how often she recorded him, and with whom she shared the videos.

Throughout the women's depositions, something niggles at Jackie. Then it hits her. He stated that he didn't know Ms. Benni had taken off after him until he heard Kenny's scream. She explores this angle while asking Kenny her follow-up questions. "Mr. Alcott—Dean—testified earlier today that he didn't know Ms. Benni had taken off after him until he heard your scream. Kenny, did you see Dean react to a possible attack before you screamed?"

"No. Not really."

"So, if you hadn't been there watching Dean—recording Dean—he never would've made it to the gate in time to be rescued?"

"I don't see how he could've."

Of course, Hank objects. But Jackie makes her point. Kenny may've been unwanted paparazzi, but she was also Dean's guardian angel.

****

Jackie calls Helen to report on the depositions as soon as she gets back to her office. Helen agrees that Dean's testimony that he didn't know Ms. Benni was after him until he heard Kenny's scream could alleviate the Kenny-as-stalker issue—somewhat. After all, it may well be true that Kenny's vigilant Dean-watching, and her timely scream, gave Dean the seconds he needed to make it close enough to the door so that Charlie could grab him. But Helen is concerned with how impressively Dean lied about the modeling dream, and about his charming Deanness in general.

"Listen, Jackie, I want you to spare no expense on the grudge tiger defense. It may be the only thing standing between Carolyn and financial ruin."

"I agree. I've gotten a couple of the partners to cover most of my other cases until I finish the trial. I plan to read everything I can get my hands on about tiger vengeance before I do my interview with Dr. Lucas on the phone. He's agreed to talk with me on Wednesday and get his report written by August 26th, a week before his deposition. Then, if everything stays on track, he'll give his deposition in London on September 2nd—four weeks before trial."

"Good. By the way, how did you locate Dr. Lucas?"

"Are you sure you want to know how this sausage was made?"

"That bad?"

She hesitates. "Okay. Kenny found him. He wrote a children's book on tigers that includes a section on revenge tigers."

"But there's more, right? I mean, he does have the credentials to do this?"

"Oh, yeah. I'll send you his CV. He did his undergrad work at Oxford and has a doctorate in wild animal studies from a university in India. He's published numerous articles about tigers—just nothing about grudge tigers, except for his dissertation and the short section in the kids' book."

"Have you got a copy of his dissertation?"

"He emailed it to me today. It's over a hundred pages long, but there's just one seven-page section on revenge tigers, so I'll just focus on that when I read it tonight."

"Hm. Send me his CV and the dissertation section tomorrow morning."

"You'll have it."

"What materials have you sent to him?"

"The pleadings, Dean's answers to interrogatories and the two videos. I also asked the court reporter to expedite typing up the transcripts of all four depositions, which I'll send to him electronically, tomorrow."

"Was Lucas the best expert you could find?"

"He was the only expert I could find on grudge tigers. And the fact that he agreed to get his report done by August 26th—one week from today—and to sit for an evidence deposition a week after that really cinched it."

"Why is he making himself available?"

"He loves tigers. So he's adjusting his schedule to make this work."

"Good. Any idea what kind of impression he'll make as a witness?"

"None. But I'll know a lot more on that after I talk with him on Wednesday."

"Will you be filing any dispositive pre-trial motions?"

"Yeah. That's another thing I need to squeeze in. We'll move for summary judgment on both counts, once I have Dr. Lucas's report. The facts of what happened on both days that Kenny recorded Dean aren't really in dispute. The best Dean could come up with at his deposition was to try to minimize the aggressiveness of kicking Ms. Benni. So, I'll argue that we should win as a matter of law. As to Count I, Dean was more than 50% at fault for the accident, as to Count II, Dean definitely provoked Ms. Benni."

"But we'll lose, won't we?"

"Of course. As to the negligence count, the respective percentages of fault attributable to Dean and Carolyn are a question of fact for the jury. And as to the statute, at the very least, the question remains whether the kick was the provocation which caused Ms. Benni to attack two weeks later. Hank will file cross-motions, which will also be denied. There's no way Judge Marcus will grant either side summary judgment since neither of us is really entitled to it, and she hates to have her rulings overturned on appeal. But filing is worthwhile because it will educate her in more detail about our grudge tiger defense before the trial starts. It's definitely not the kind of theory I want to spring on Judge Marcus at trial."

"I got it. So, other than hoping Dr. Lucas comes across really well, what else would you like to have that you're missing?"

"I'd like to have a witness to testify that Ms. Benni's always been a grudge tiger."

"You have the Warrens. How about their employees?"

"Maybe. But they're all tainted by self-interest in the zoo's survival. I'd love to find a non-Warren witness who doesn't work at the zoo."

"Then go find one. And don't wait until the last minute. This case has me pacing like a nervous tiger."

"Wait. If I lose, are you going to be a grudge tiger

about it?"

"You really don't want to find out, Jackie. You're my go-to lawyer down there—but I have bosses, too."

"Yikes. I gotta get to work. Bye, Helen."

"Good luck."

Chapter 20

Carolyn

When Jackie calls Carolyn to press her to think of someone not connected with the zoo who knows Ms. Benni is a grudge tiger, she draws a blank. How can there even be such a person? Vets, inspectors, former employees—they are all connected with the zoo, or Carolyn regularly pays them for services. Since Jackie doesn't sound all that up-beat about the case, not being able to produce this witness makes Carolyn even more nervous. She immediately goes looking for Marietta and Kenny, who are on the grounds somewhere doing chores.

She finally finds them at the farthest corner of the zoo, filling the watering troughs for the lemurs and the Andean condors. As they see her approach, the girls put down the hoses and walk toward their mother.

"What's the matter, Mom? Please say it's not more bad news," Kenny says.

"No. It's just that I'm having trouble thinking of someone who can testify that Ms. Benni has always been a grudge tiger."

"What about Charlie?" asks Marietta.

Carolyn fears she blushes whenever his name comes up but hopes the fact she is flushed from the heat will conceal it. "Charlie won't work. Jackie wants me to come up with a witness who isn't associated with the zoo, so the jurors won't think the person is prejudiced in our favor. She needs whatever name I can come up with by four thirty on Thursday afternoon because she has to get all of our witnesses' names to Hank by five o'clock that day."

"Wouldn't one of Ms. Benni's vets work?" asks Kenny.

"I don't think so, since I do pay them to work for us."

"But you pay everyone who works for the zoo," Marietta says. "It's not like we have volunteers lined up to shovel bear poop in ninety-degree weather."

"I know, girls. I guess all we can do is keep thinking about it. Let me know right away if anything comes to mind."

Carolyn needs to take a walk to clear her head so whatever she's missing can materialize. She shudders at the thought of strolling the grounds with the possible loss of the zoo now so imminent. She pulls on her hiking boots and drives the forty minutes to Shawnee National Forest. With her lifetime pass, she's able to drive right in and select a reasonably short trail. She plans to try to forget about Ms. Benni, and Dean, and the zoo, and focus on the nature around her. Her experience is that only by letting a problem go is an answer to it likely to pop.

No other hikers disturb her reverie since it's a midweek day with typical southern Illinois summer weather—sweltering heat, clear blue sky, and humidity like a southeast Asian jungle. But the forest is gorgeous, with gently rolling hills, huge boulders, and thousands of deciduous trees in their summer glory. Wildflowers, ferns, and moss accent the shady areas, and the fragrance of pine needles wafts up as she makes her way through the evergreen patches. Her effort to keep the lawsuit from creeping into her thoughts is only periodically successful. She's soaking wet from the heat and humidity and, even though she sprayed herself, the mosquitoes are keeping the hike from being nearly as refreshing as she hoped.

She hikes in for an hour by her watch, then takes another trail which is posted as also leading back to the parking lot. The fairly steep climb is basically an interminable series of switchbacks, which causes Carolyn to slow her pace considerably. As she stops to catch her breath at the summit of the trail, she's rewarded with a stunning view down a canyon. She spies sandstone cliffs and intriguing distant rock formations which display themselves in an array of muted colors in the late afternoon light. As she sits on a small boulder to take a long drink from her water bottle and blot at her face with a tissue, she recalls when she and Tom took their first hike in the forest, and how they'd stopped at the nature center. She had been rapt, absorbing the facts about how a glacier created all the beauty. She learned that the glacial stage some 200,000 years before provided the ice sheet, the southern portion of which rested in the very area where she now sits. "So much came before," Carolyn says out loud. She pauses and her eyes grow large. "Before. Of course!"

Carolyn is grateful she still has over thirty minutes of hiking to get back to her car, plus the forty-minute drive home. She wants to gather her thoughts about how best to approach getting the testimony Jackie needs. By the time she steps into her kitchen, she feels refreshed by the air-conditioned ride home, and ready to act. She calls Jackie.

"I know who the grudge tiger witnesses are!'"

"Excellent. Who?"

"The people we bought Ms. Benni from when she turned two years old. I have a feeling they may well have seen some of her grudge behavior…if they were paying attention."

"Can you give them a call and find out exactly what they'll say?"

"I think so. But the reason we were able to get Ms. Benni was that Animal Kingdom was closing its doors. The owners were in their seventies, and their kids weren't interested in keeping it going."

"So you don't know if you can find the owners?"

"Oh, no. Their house is just adjacent to where the park grounds were. It's just that I last talked with them eight years ago. It was 2011 when we bought Ms. Benni. So, I don't know if they'll remember anything about her. They probably had hundreds of animals over the years. Also, I don't know if they're still mentally fit. Frankly, I don't even know if they're still alive."

Jackie laughs. "Yeah. Dead witnesses won't help us much."

She genuinely likes Jackie but she finds it hard to understand how her lawyer can joke around so much—in view of what her family is facing. Carolyn doesn't respond.

Jackie seems to catch the criticism in the silence. "Listen, Carolyn, it's important for you to go after this. Today is Tuesday. You have what's left of today, tomorrow and half a day on Thursday to find out if one of them remembers Ms. Benni and can credibly testify that she was a grudge tiger. Can you do that?"

"I'll do my best. I'll get back to you by Thursday

noon."

"Good luck."

"Thanks, Jackie."

Carolyn calls Kenny in and asks her to clean up and put on some decent clothes, while she does the same. She tells her daughter that they're in a hurry and she'll fill her in on where they're going, and why, in the car. An hour later, they pull into a long driveway which leads to a lovely old brick house wearing faded white paint, with graceful vines randomly climbing the walls. Stately white pillars and an elegant, manicured lawn call to mind the plantation mansions of the old south. Giant old oaks stand sentry on both sides of the driveway and are scattered around the yard in a way that keeps the entire area shady with only a few areas of dappled sunlight breaking through.

"Wow, Mom, this place is amazing! The safari park must've made a lot of money."

"Rumor has it that Mrs. Wilcox inherited a fortune. Her family was from Richmond, Virginia, but her husband's people were from this area. Apparently, they spent some of the money buying this house and the grounds for their park. A lot of families around here visited every year. And tourists came from all around— since there was no zoo in the area before we built ours."

Carolyn doesn't see any cars around, but assumes there may be some in the detached two-car brick garage. They walk up the front steps, and Kenny rings the doorbell. After a minute or so, a thirty-something heavy set blonde woman wearing a summer dress and flip-flops opens the wooden door, but leaves the screen door closed.

"Hello."

"Hi. I'm Carolyn Warren, and this is my daughter, Kenny. We're looking for Mr. and Mrs. Wilcox. Are they still living here?"

The woman looks from Carolyn to Kenny, and then back to Carolyn. "What's your business with them?" She says it in a non-committal way, neither welcoming nor hostile.

"I need to ask them what they remember about an animal they sold to me just over eight years ago. It was when they were in the process of closing the park."

"Who did you buy?"

Carolyn finds it interesting that the woman said "who" rather than "what." "We named her Ms. Benni. She's a Bengal tiger. Well, she was around two years old at the time."

"That was Tubbles. I got to name her."

"You did?"

"Yes. I'm their daughter, Rose." She opens the screen door and invites them in. "Please follow me to a spot where we can sit and talk."

Carolyn finds herself in an elegant sitting room, furnished with worn oriental rugs, old dark wood furniture, and a peach-colored crushed velvet couch with two matching chairs. A pile of cardboard boxes, some open and some taped shut, sits in front of a built-in mahogany bookcase which covers the far wall, with a pile of newspapers next to it.

Once they are seated, the woman offers them cold drinks, which Kenny and Carolyn both decline. "All right, then. I'm dying to know. What's going on with Tubbles—I mean Ms. Benni?" Carolyn explains Dean's injury, his claim, and the evidence that he provoked Ms. Benni two weeks before the attack. Rose watches her steadily as she speaks, but says nothing but "um-hm."

Carolyn finishes with, "So, that's why I need to speak with your parents."

"I wish I could help you myself. I have a feeling you're right about Ms. Benni. I don't have any personal knowledge though—I was out of the country when my folks first got her. I only got to see her occasionally when I came home for visits. I'm sorry to have to tell you, but my father passed away two months ago."

"I'm so sorry," Carolyn says.

"Yeah," Kenny says. "That's really hard. My dad died, too." Kenny looks down, and her mother feels she can't face a discussion about dead loved ones.

"Then I'm sorry too," says Rose.

Carolyn asks, "Is your mother living?"

Rose brightens. "Yes. Very much so. She just moved into an assisted living facility near Carbondale. Her preference would be to stay here, but it's too much for her. With me in California and my brother in New York, there's no one around to check in on her or help her out. The main problem with the house is that there are stairs everywhere. It just became unworkable."

"How does she like the assisted living place?" asks Kenny.

"She absolutely hated the idea, but she's starting to warm up to it. They have a darling social director who's very adept at getting people together. Mom's already made a couple of friends."

"Good." Carolyn isn't sure how to phrase her next question.

Rose beats her to it. "Listen. I know you must be wondering about her mental status since you're hoping she can be a witness for your trial. Well, she's still as sharp as a tack. Of course, she'll forget a word or a name once in a while, but I do that too. Unfortunately, she had a hip replacement done about two weeks ago, so I doubt she'd be up to travelling for the trial."

Kenny says, "I'll bet our lawyer could do it by video. I mean, that's how she's going to do our expert's deposition in London next week."

"A London expert witness? There must be a lot at stake."

"There is," Carolyn says.

"Okay. Let's go see Mom and find out what she has to say."

****

They ride in Rose's car since she knows the way. Rose and Carolyn exchange anecdotes about the safari park and the zoo, so that by the time they reach the assisted living facility, the two women have laughed themselves into a place where Carolyn is very comfortable with Rose. Passing through the entrance gate, they arrive in a luxurious, elegant world. The extensive lawns are immaculately groomed with a number of small formal gardens dotting the acres of lush green. The building itself is colonial style but looks to have been built in the last two decades. Like the Wilcox home, it features dramatic white pillars, but the brick is devoid of vines.

As they are led to Rose's mother's apartment, Carolyn expects something like the woman's gorgeous house. Rose knocks and then walks in without waiting for an answer. "Hi, Mom."

Her mother is standing at her kitchenette sink. She turns and smiles at the sight of her daughter. "Oh, sweetie, what a nice surprise."

After they hug, Rose says, "Mother, I've brought you these two nice ladies who want to talk with you about the park."

Carolyn likes Eugenia Wilcox at first sight. Short, and small in stature, she is spry and energetic looking. Her neatly coiffed white hair fits her head like a helmet, and she wears white slacks, sandals and a pale pink cotton tunic top. Her warm smile pulls Carolyn in, and Eugenia's eyes seem to twinkle when she looks at Carolyn—a bit like Mrs. Santa Claus. Carolyn just prays she's been good enough to get what she's asking for.

After introductions all around, they sit down around Eugenia's small mahogany dining table. Carolyn glances around the spacious, tastefully decorated apartment, and feels happy for her that it's every bit as elegant as the home she had to give up. Rose reaches over for the phone and orders four lemonades and a dozen finger sandwiches. She asks Carolyn to tell her mother the whole story. In doing so, Carolyn deliberately leaves out the part about Dean kicking at Ms. Benni because she wants to hear Eugenia's recollection without any suggestion of what she is supposed to recall.

Eugenia nods a lot but doesn't interrupt with any reactions. When Carolyn finishes, all eyes are on Rose's mother.

"Of course, I remember we had a female tiger for just under two years—up until the time we had to close. We got her and her brother as newborn cubs, bottle-fed them and everything. The male left us at around eighteen months. We were able to keep the female until she was almost two." She pauses. "We had so many animals. I really wish I could recall her more clearly." She looks among the others. "It was eight years ago!"

Carolyn's face drops.

Rose says, "It could all come back to you, Mom."

"Yes. It could. I wish I had a picture to help me remember."

Kenny says, "Mom, may I show Mrs. Wilcox the video?"

Carolyn turns to Rose. "Would that be okay with you?"

"Sure. I'd love to see how she looks now."

Eugenia says, "I'm so sorry, but I don't have a projector or anything."

"Oh, Mrs. Wilcox," Kenny says, "I can show you on my phone."

"Really?"

"Sure. Here. This is one of Ms. Benni in the foreground just before Dean kicked at her head." Mrs. Wilcox stares at the screen while Rose waits her turn to watch.

"Kicked at her?" Mrs. Wilcox cocks her head, then looks down at Kenny's iPhone. "Why, that's Tubbles!"

Kenny says, "You can get a better look at her when she raises her head right after Dean kicks."

Mrs. Wilcox looks again, then says, "That young man chose the wrong tiger to kick."

"Why is that?" asks Carolyn, her heart racing.

"Well, our Tubbles had a vindictive character. You see, if we slighted her in any little way, the next time we came across her, she'd be angry...even if it was weeks later."

"When did she start acting like that?" Carolyn says.

"Oh, from the very beginning. At first, when she was a cuddly cub, we thought it was adorable. But as she grew, well, it became somewhat of a problem."

"Who knew about this?" asks Carolyn.

"I'm not sure. I assume the help may've known. And, of course, my husband and I knew and talked about it often."

Carolyn gives it a shot. "Rose told me of your recent surgery. But I wonder if it might be possible for you to come down to the County Courthouse just outside of Heartsville for the trial. It starts on September 30th."

"I'm so sorry, dear. But I'm not going to be able to travel."

Carolyn tries again. "Would you be willing to give a video deposition, from here in your room? You would just talk about Tubbles and then our lawyer will play the video for the jury at the trial."

"Of course. I'd be happy to do it."

"Thank you so much," Carolyn says. "It means everything to me and my daughters."

A staff member arrives with the refreshments and Rose helps her lay everything out on the table.

"Can you tell us about some examples of the things Tubbles did?" asks Kenny.

"My, yes. As I said, at first, they were just cute antics and really funny…"

Chapter 21

Kenny

After a layover in New York, and then an overnight flight, they arrive at Heathrow at ten a.m. on Sunday, September 1st. Two full-length movies and three episodes of an old sit-com battle for Kenny's attention with her worry about losing her reputation and her mother's zoo. She doesn't sleep at all. Although she wasn't seated near either of the others, judging by the way they look when she meets them in the line for customs, they didn't either.

In spite of that, Jackie is her usual upbeat and enthusiastic self. She points out landmarks as the ancient black cab takes them into the city and through a labyrinth of small streets until they reach their hotel on a tree-lined avenue in a residential neighborhood. They're escorted to their third-floor walk-up "family suite" with four twin beds and a microscopic bathroom. Kenny is thrilled.

Jackie needs to meet with Dr. Lucas at three o'clock that afternoon at a coffee house near the National Gallery. She says she has to prepare him for his deposition, which means explaining what the format will be like, what he should do if she objects to anything Hank says, and how to handle answering the questions, all of which is basically what she did with Kenny before she gave her testimony. The deposition itself is scheduled for one p.m. the next day, which will be seven a.m. for Hank, who is participating by video-hookup from his office. Basically, he's going to question Dr. Lucas by a live hookup—or something like that.

Kenny wants to meet their expert witness right away, but Jackie tells her it would be better for the girls to join her and Dr. Lucas for an early dinner after their meeting. Jackie insists she wants them to play tourist until then and on Monday. On Tuesday she'll go with them to squeeze in whatever sights they've missed. She'll work on the trial Wednesday before the flight home. But by then, she thinks the girls will be completely comfortable exploring on their own.

Kenny and Becca settle on the National Gallery for Sunday afternoon because it's near where Jackie has to be for her meeting. They all take the Tube together to the stop nearest the location of the art museum, and then part ways with Jackie. Roaming the halls of the museum in a dream-like state with Becca beside her, Kenny is amazed at what seems like acres of rooms displaying gorgeous artworks, but she has to work hard to keep her eyes open. Becca seems to be dealing with her own jet lag by laughing uncontrollably at things that aren't all that funny, and Kenny is awake enough to worry that the guards might think Becca is drunk and kick them out. Then it occurs to her that Becca probably isn't the first tourist to be in this condition. The guards don't even raise an eyebrow, like they were trained by the same guy who manages the famously stoic Palace Guards. Kenny and Becca force themselves to come back to life to get to their rendezvous with Jackie and Dr. Lucas on time.

Jackie gave them directions to a small restaurant several blocks from the art museum, and they only have to ask two people to find it. As they walk in, Kenny spots Jackie and the expert seated at a table in a back corner, gabbing away. As the girls approach, Jackie sees them, smiles, and motions to come ahead. Dr. Lucas stands as they arrive and shakes hands with each of them as he says hello. After they take their seats, he sits back down. He's tall and slender and has a friendly face. Kenny likes him at first sight and thinks he'll make a perfect expert witness…assuming he'll say what they need.

"Ladies, this is Dr. Lucas."

"Nigel, please," he says.

"All right. Nigel, this is Kenny Warren—"

She interrupts and says, "Kenny, please," then laughs.

"It's Kenny's family who owns the zoo. And this is her friend, Becca Kim."

A waiter appears and takes their drink orders. Dr. Lucas has an uncanny way of making Kenny feel comfortable right away, so she doesn't delay getting to the heart of it. "So, you're familiar with grudge tigers?"

"Yes, Kenny. I've always referred to them as revenge tigers, but it's the same idea. And I'm very familiar. You see, my family also had a zoo, where I worked, from when I could first hold a shovel until I went off to university. Then I'd go back to help out whenever I could. I got to know the habits of all eight of the tigers we had over the years. Most, as you might imagine, were not revenge tigers, but we had one, Tony, who definitely was. I got interested in it."

Jackie says, "Kenny, Nigel really shouldn't discuss this with you before he gives his testimony—since you're also a witness in the case."

"Sorry."

"Nothing to be sorry about. Just a kind of a rule." She smiles, so Kenny knows she isn't angry about it.

"I'm sure you'll do a great job," Kenny says to Dr. Lucas.

"It will be my honor to give evidence about tigers in general, and your Ms. Benni in particular. I hope at some point you'll be able to watch the video of tomorrow's session." He glances at Jackie and raises his eyebrows.

"Definitely. Kenny will be in the courtroom when I play your deposition for the jury."

"Wonderful!" says Dr. Lucas. He's a very enthusiastic man, which Kenny thinks is an important quality for their expert witness.

Becca says, "No juror is going to fall asleep during this trial."

"That's my hope," says Jackie.

The waiter returns with two glasses of wine and two lemonades and recites the specials.

Turning to Becca, Jackie says. "So, what did you two see so far?"

"The National Gallery. But it was weird because Kenny couldn't keep her eyes open and I kept laughing for no reason."

Dr. Lucas smiles. "I hear that's the best way to deal with jet lag. Just force yourself to stay awake until your regular bedtime. You both should feel fine tomorrow."

"Actually," Kenny says, "meeting you has already made me feel fine."

"Thank you. I hope I can be of help. Jackie told me you have only until Wednesday afternoon in London. Perhaps you would allow my son to get you to what you want to see."

"Your son?" says Becca.

"Yes. He heads off to begin university in a month. But Mr. Perdue kindly told Jackie that it would be acceptable for Jamie to sit in on my deposition. You see, my son thinks he wants to be a barrister, so this process would be very interesting to him."

Kenny and Becca look at each other. Kenny says, "That would be great! We don't know London at all, so it'll be hard to be efficient at cramming in the sights we want to see."

"Excellent. I'll tell Jamie that he'll get to play tour guide after the deposition."

Becca frowns. "Are you sure he'll want to?"

"Kenny, Becca, he would never forgive me if I didn't arrange for him to spend time with such lovely American young ladies."

Kenny is surprised by the compliment, but Dr. Lucas looks completely sincere. She glances at Becca, who smiles and nods. Kenny says, "Then we accept."

They are all in great moods as they place their orders. Jackie makes sure to keep the conversation focused on everything but the lawsuit.

Chapter 22

Hank

Hank hadn't loved the idea of examining the defendant's expert witness from afar, but there was no way he'd spend the time and money to travel to London, especially when his only associate is still out. He must've been soft in the head as well as the heart when he offered Bill two months paid leave to help his wife with their twins. Hank is so far behind on everything at this point, he simply can't afford the hours a trip to London would cost. He figures he'll be able to cross examine such a phony expert as a grudge tiger specialist just as well via video-conference set-up as in person. Even if the judge doesn't bar Dr. Lucas's testimony—which she should— any jury with half a brain will find it silly that a tiger would've remembered a little kick for two weeks and then responded to it with a vicious attack.

After the deposition concludes, and the court reporter announces the hour and minute it ended, Hank shuts down his computer and reaches into his bottom desk drawer for the bottle of scotch he keeps for miserable days like the one this turned out to be. He wipes perspiration from his forehead with his shirt sleeve. He despises British accents. They're so damned charming. The expert was good—a real cool customer. Earnest as a choir boy and soft-spoken. Not only that, but

Lucas also told the most fascinating tiger attack stories Hank's ever heard. He feels like shit because it's abundantly clear to him that the jury might very well believe Jackie's expert.

Of course, Hank knows trial preparation has its ups and downs, just like trials do. He'll feel good again when he puts on Dean's case. Hank's medical witnesses are solid, and the gay guy from the modeling agency is enamored of Dean and his potential—before he was scarred for life. Dean, himself, is exquisite—both in his appearance and in how he can slather on the charm. Hank just needs to paint Mrs. Warren as careless and insinuate to the jury that the grudge tiger thing is just a desperate attempt to avoid responsibility for her animal's vicious behavior.

He also knows he'll feel like shit when Jackie puts on her case. Mrs. Warren and Mrs. Wilcox look like everyone's mother and grandmother, respectively. Beautiful Marietta can be almost as enchanting as Dean. And that model student, Kenny, looked like a sweet, humiliated twelve-year-old when Hank questioned her in her deposition about why she recorded Dean. The truth is, she's charming and lovely too, and she looks like the kind of girl who has never told a lie in her life. Plus, she has the videos. And now, Jackie has a fascinating, credible expert witness to tie up her theory with a bow.

This case should never have been so much trouble. Because of the Animal Control Act, Dean could've been 100% negligent, and still win. Jackie has two defenses to the act. She won't get anywhere with her trespass defense, and he's sure she knows it. Hank also suspects she'll pitch it anyway. He can hit that one out of the park with all the evidence of basically the entire roster of zookeepers having entered the tiger enclosure—while Ms. Benni was in there. Hell, even Dean had been in there before—okay, without the tiger. But it had been at the zoo's request.

It's only the argument that Dean provoked Ms. Benni into attacking him that stands between Hank and a very large verdict. He settles on a strategy, the only one he can come up with: belittle the idea and get the jury to laugh the defense out of court. He'll have to mock Jackie's theory mercilessly. Luckily, ridicule is something he excels at. He takes another gulp of the scotch.

Chapter 23

Kenny

On Monday, Jackie texts Kenny at around three thirty p.m. to let her know that Dr. Lucas's deposition is over. Kenny is dying to find out how it went, and she and Becca are also psyched about meeting their tour guide, Jamie Lucas. They hurry back from Covent Gardens to the address for the office of a solicitor who loaned space to Jackie for the video-deposition. Jackie and Dr. Lucas have already left the building and are standing in the shade of a large elm tree, just adjacent to the sidewalk. The young man with them is tall and thin with curly hair the color of honey. It only takes introductions to see that Dr. Lucas's son looks a lot like his dad, and also has the easy, stammering kind of charm like the Brits in the movies. Kenny can't believe their good luck.

"How'd it go?" she asks.

"It couldn't have gone better," says Jackie. "Dr. Lucas was fascinating, and credible, and gave us everything we need on the grudge tiger issue."

"Oh, I'm so relieved!" Kenny lets out a sigh. "You see on TV how sneaky lawyers can trick witnesses into saying the wrong thing."

"Hank tried. But Nigel easily dispatched everything Hank threw at him. I can't wait to play this for the jury." Jackie suggests that Kenny and Becca and Jamie go ahead and grab a late lunch and then tour without her since she has a lot of trial preparation to do. She takes Kenny aside and gives her a credit card for meals and admission fees for the girls. She whispers, "If you mention this to anyone, I'll deny it and claim you stole it from me."

Kenny smiles at her. "Well, I was thinking of posting it but now I won't. Thanks tons, Jackie."

Dr. Lucas and Jackie wish them good touring and walk off together toward the Tube station. Jamie looks between Kenny and Becca. "Would you like to grab a pub lunch? I know a good place not far from here for fish and chips."

"Perfect. That's your traditional lunch, right?' Becca asks.

"For tourists," says Jamie, who then laughs. "Actually, it is quite good. And, as your tour guide, I recommend it."

As they round a corner, Kenny sees the pub. Gold leaf climbs up to the middle of the outside wall, and large windows reveal a long, gleaming wooden bar and lots of customers enjoying meals as they talk and laugh like in a magazine advertisement. A large dark green awning, edged in deep crimson, hangs over the sidewalk. As they step inside, it has the feel of a museum, with glowing hardwood floors, ornate mirrors, polished wooden rails and large, engraved glass screens separating several of the tables from one another. A forest of marble pillars rises from the floor. Once they are shown to their table, Kenny looks up to see that the ceiling is divided by gleaming wood beams into a dozen squares, each containing a different mural. She says, "This place is amazing, Jamie."

He looks around thoroughly. "It is, rather. Isn't it?"

"Yeah," says Becca. "It's almost overwhelming—in a good way."

After they order drinks, Jamie looks at Kenny. "I'm sorry your family has to go through this. My father told me about the case so I'd understand what was happening at the deposition. It must be terrifying to face the possibility that the dim-witted, imbecilic, doltish young man might actually win."

She laughs at the perfect string of adjectives. "Actually, Dean is all of those things. The only intelligent thing he's ever done was choose my older sister, Marietta, to be the object of his obsessive love. She thinks he only likes her because she's the only girl who says no to him."

"If Marietta is at all like her younger sister, I can see his point." Jamie quickly looks away.

Kenny is caught off-guard, not sure how to respond. "Excuse me, guys, I need to visit the ladies' room."

When she gets back to the table, Jamie says, "Kenny, I'm sorry. I'm an idiot. I didn't mean to offend you."

"Oh, I wasn't offended. I was just in shock. See, boys don't usually compliment me and Becca."

"Why ever not?"

"We're not in any of the right cliques."

Jamie shakes his head quickly, as if to clear it. "Well, that's rubbish. You are both lovely, interesting, women. Any of my mates would be thrilled to go out with either of you."

Kenny rolls her eyes.

Becca says, "Thanks."

"Do you know what I think will happen?" says

Jamie.

"What?" Kenny asks.

"When you go off to university, you'll see that I'm right. You've been with this same group since when? First grade?"

"Most of them. The others, for the first three years of high school," Kenny says.

Jamie leans back in his chair and raises both hands in an I-told-you-so gesture, "See. That explains it. You don't happen to have brain-bucket reputations, do you?"

"Pretty much," says Becca.

"Believe me. That won't be a negative at university."

"And how do you know this?" Kenny asks.

"I just keep my eyes and ears open."

"Cool," says Becca.

Kenny is feeling pretty uncomfortable about the direction the conversation is taking, so she just smiles. After they study the menus and order fish and chips, she pulls her list of tourist sites from a small backpack and lays the paper out on the table. "So, Jamie, how should we go about seeing as many of these as possible? We just have this evening, tomorrow, and Wednesday until around three p.m."

He leans over the list to study it, and Kenny grins at Becca over his head. They can both already tell—this is going to be a boatload of fun.

To see in London:
1. Big Ben
2. The London Eye
3. The Tower of London
4. Westminster Abbey
5. St. Paul's Cathedral

6. Harrods

7. The Science Museum

8. The Natural History Museum

9. Shakespeare's Globe Theatre

10. Number 10 Downing Street

11. Buckingham Palace and the Changing of the Guard

12. The Houses of Parliament

13. Trafalgar Square

14. The British Museum

15. The National Gallery (which Kenny has already put a checkmark by).

Jamie takes his time studying the paper. "There's a lot here. Is this in the order of importance to you?"

"Oh, no," Kenny says. "It's just everything we could think of."

Becca adds, "Yeah. We don't want to run out of sights."

Jamie laughs, and his eyes crinkle as he tosses his head back. Then he gets serious. "Ladies, I can absolutely assure you that you will not run out."

"Did we overdo it?" Kenny asks.

"Not at all. It's a brilliant list!" He's looking at her and she notices how blue his eyes are. *Jamie is a nice-looking bloke…as they would say here.*

"Let's arrange it in the order of importance to you, shall we?"

"Sure," says Becca.

"Then I'll group the ten most desired sights in an efficient way so we'll be sure you get to see them all. If time permits, we'll squeeze in the last four after that. Agreed?"

"Perfect." Becca and Kenny say at the same time.

Many of the sights are closing by then, but they manage to jump on a tour boat, just before it leaves the London Eye Pier for an amazing Thames cruise which passes under four famous bridges. Then they meander for a couple of hours, ending up in Soho, which is crammed with interesting boutiques, theatres and restaurants. They share a huge vegetable paella in a Mediterranean restaurant before Jamie walks with them back to their hotel. Kenny is so psyched about spending the next day with Jamie that it takes her an hour to finally drift off. It's the first time in months that her insomnia isn't about the zoo.

Chapter 24

Jackie

Jackie's sure Nigel senses her elation with how well the deposition went. They walk quickly and talk about some of the contentious exchanges, all of which ended up scoring more points for the defense. As they approach her Tube station, Nigel asks if she can make time to join him for lunch. She thinks for a moment about all the work she still needs to do for the trial, but he really has been invaluable, and she's definitely in a celebratory mood. "All right. I can spare some time to relish our victory."

"Brilliant." He smiles and she notices what lovely blue eyes he has.

"I know a spot not far from here with a courtyard. It's basically a garden restaurant."

"That sounds perfect."

As they walk the three blocks to the bar and grill, they continue to talk about the case. Jackie tells him it's really important to her to win—if she can't get a settlement, which would be fine, as well. She also tells him something she's just realized. The Warrens have become like family to her—probably not the best attorney-client relationship.

The façade of the restaurant is simple, dark brick with white wood trim. As they enter, Jackie's eyes haven't adjusted to the dimness of the interior area by the time they reach the door to the patio seating. She's met with a blaze of color as they emerge from the darkened building. Flowers ring the courtyard and grow in abundance in the center area, around a goldfish and turtle pond. Tall, rotating fans keep the air moving softly. There are no other diners.

They're led to a corner table, and each orders water and a glass of wine. Jackie admires the set-up and gets up to take a quick peek at the turtles. By the time she sits back down, the drinks have been served. Nigel raises his glass, "To your defense of the Warren Family Zoo."

"Cheers," says Jackie as their glasses meet. They ignore the menus and sip their chardonnay.

"Tell me, Jackie, do you have a family?"

"Just my mom and dad." As soon as the words leave her mouth, she realizes he's asking if she has a husband or children. "I'm single. No kids."

He smiles at her, then takes a sip of his wine. "That surprises me. You rather strike me as a wife and mother—as well as an accomplished trial lawyer."

"I'd say thanks, but I'm not sure if that was a compliment…or something else."

Nigel laughs. "Oh, it was definitely a compliment." He sighs. "I suppose I tend to view the institution from the vantage of one who once found great happiness being married."

"Does your use of the past tense suggest you're divorced?"

"No. Actually, my amazing wife passed away…four years ago." He looks away for a moment. "Cancer."

"I'm so sorry. What was her name?"

"Mary. You see, she was beautiful and brilliant, like

you. In fact, you remind me of her a bit."

This isn't the usual conversation Jackie has with expert witnesses after their depositions. But Nigel is so relaxed and open she feels she's being invited in. "How have you coped since then?"

He looks at her intently. "Do you want to know the truth?'

She nods.

"I still think of her every day. But I've finally reached my favorite stage of the grieving process—acceptance. Now, it mostly makes me sad she isn't here for Jamie. I'm a firm believer that children need both parents. I think mums and dads provide different things."

Maybe Jackie is still in an argumentative mood from the deposition. She also knows that her ten years as a litigator have made her more confrontational in general. For whatever reason, she says, "Isn't that a little bit sexist?"

"Is it?"

"I'm no expert, Nigel, and I've never raised a child. But aren't both parents just humans, with distinct talents? Don't they simply provide different ways to guide a child, hopefully complementary with what the other offers? Isn't it just because they are two different people, rather than because one is called 'dad' and one is called 'mum?'"

Nigel smiles and his expressive eyes crinkle. Then he nods his head slightly. "Good for you."

"What does that mean?"

"I appreciate being challenged. Some might think it impolite to contradict such a benign statement as the one I made."

"Wait. Are you accusing me of being impolite?"

Jackie tries to sound amused because she isn't sure if she should be insulted.

He thinks for a moment before speaking. "I've often been accused—quite fairly—of speaking too bluntly. What I meant to say is that I love that you are a truth-teller. I find truly frank discussions are hard to come by. There are as many yes-men—forgive me, yes-people— in the scientific community as in the corporate world. It always disappoints me when the politics override the free exchange of ideas." Jackie nods, but doesn't say anything. "So, when I think about your take on the mum/dad dichotomy, I believe it actually makes more sense than my declaration. On reflection, my statement was riddled with stereotypes."

The waiter interrupts to take their orders. They quickly peruse the menus and both choose the special, salads with cups of clam chowder. Jackie says, "Well, good."

"I have an idea," he says. "Let's agree to be perfectly honest with each other for the duration of our lunch."

"Suits me."

"The fact we'll never see each other again, gives us a rather unique opportunity, wouldn't you say?"

"That's true, I suppose. I'm in, Nigel." She smiles at him. "But it won't really be that unusual for me. As you observed, I'm pretty much a truth-teller—even at the expense of some opprobrium."

"You tell the truth to yourself, as well as others?"

This catches her off-guard. How does he know? "I'll admit it. That's a lot harder."

"Yes. I quite agree."

Hoping to change the direction of the conversation, she asks Nigel to tell her about his childhood.

"I grew up in the country, just outside of Malvern."

She raises her eyebrows.

"A three-hour train ride west of here."

"Ah."

"As I mentioned during my deposition, my parents owned a small zoo. My older sister and I lived our entire lives, up until each of us went off to university, in a house adjacent to the zoo grounds. We had zookeeper chores every day."

"Kind of romantic though, right?"

"Only if your definition of romance is the relationship between animal feces and a broom." He chuckles.

"So, you were like Kenny and Marietta."

"Exactly. The terrain in that part of the country is gorgeous, Jackie. Rolling hills, charming cottages, white stone fences winding about in every direction, and sheep dotting the grassy countryside. It was quite idyllic."

"How many animals did you have?"

"That was interesting. Most zoos build up the numbers of exhibits, for publicity purposes, with lots of smaller mammals. But Mum and Dad wanted to keep just a small number of larger and endangered species, so over the years, we had elephants, chimpanzees, jaguars and leopards, rhinos and hippos, and lions and tigers and bears."

"Oh, my!"

"Yes. Like in the movie—but our lions definitely were not cowardly."

"You testified you had eight tigers in your family's zoo. What a great way to kick off your career."

"That's true. Of course, there's a good chance I would never have had a career studying tigers had I not been immersed in them as a child. You know, I really did get to know ours fairly well—as individuals."

"Nigel, you testified about your family's white tiger."

"That's right. Our Tony."

"I've been wondering why white tigers are white? I'm pretty sure they're not albinos since their eyes are blue."

"That's right. They're not really a separate sub-species or type of tiger. They're simply a rare form of Bengal tiger—roughly one in ten thousand. The coloring is just the result of a color mutation that occurs naturally, but infrequently. Our Tony was called a Royal White because he was white with black stripes. Of course, he had the typical blue eyes and pink nose. There's also a Snow White, which is either all white, or white with ghost stripes."

"Ghost stripes?"

"Barely visible. All of the Whites tend to have short lives in the wild since their coloring means they are poorly camouflaged. Like all Bengals, they do exceptionally well in captivity."

"Frankly, I feel a lot better about zoos now that I've learned how challenged the poor animals are in the wild. Since humans are destroying their natural habitat, it seems like the least we can do is keep the species alive in captivity."

" 'The least we can do' is a good descriptor. But the least is woefully insufficient, Jackie. Tigers born and raised in the wild are vanishing, and captive tigers are only a very poor substitute."

"Sure. I get it. You testified that tigers born in captivity can't really survive if they're sent out to live in the wild." She thinks about it for a moment. "Wait. Are you saying that breeding Bengals in captivity might have an unintended consequence attached to it—assuaging our guilt about letting them go extinct in the wild?"

"I hadn't really meant it like that. But of course, it's a possibility."

"Unfortunate for the wild tigers."

"Yes." Nigel grimaces. "Would you like to know what's really going on?"

"Well, you just testified about it for almost two hours." She pauses. "There's more, isn't there?"

"Of course. Conservation wasn't really the point of my expert opinion for the trial, so I kept it quite basic."

Jackie nods, suspecting she's about to see another glimpse of the explosively passionate Dr. Lucas, the one Hank detonated with his last question at the deposition. "Absolutely. How is conservation going...out there?" She raises her hand to gesture toward the east.

Nigel leans toward her and keeps his eyes fixed on her as he speaks. "Let me use China as an example."

"Are there wild tigers there?"

"That huge country has only a few dozen tigers remaining in the wild. Certainly, urbanization and careless development have meant habitat loss, but something much more nefarious is happening."

"Poaching?"

"And worse."

"What could be worse for tigers than poaching to get our grubby hands on their body parts?"

"Let me tell you the story, Jackie. One of the primary reasons was the publication of a book."

She tries to make sense of it. "So, it must've been a book about the monetary value of poached tiger. Right?"

"Basically. It was 1979. The book was about the curative properties of tiger bones—how they've been used in traditional Chinese medicine for over 1,000 years. You spoke of unintended consequences. A well-intentioned government reaction to the success of the book was to encourage the breeding of tigers intended for slaughter, so the wild ones would be left alone."

"Ouch. Isn't that a bit like if Abe Lincoln had said in the Emancipation Proclamation that all black people would be freed, but we'd make up for the loss of free labor by enslaving all blond people?"

"Precisely. And, of course, it didn't work. Once the tiger was officially commodified by the government, many tiger farms popped up and their owners earned tens of thousands of dollars for parts of the butchered animals. But all of the attention simply increased demand, and poachers accelerated their efforts to shortcut the process by murdering the wild tigers. In 1993, China did outlaw domestic trade in tiger bones. The 'farms' were supposed to become conservation areas or zoos, but the requirement hasn't been enforced. Finally, in 2007, an international authority—but one with little power of enforcement—banned all tiger farming for commercial purposes."

"Good."

"Yes. But as I said, there were no teeth in the decree, so not a lot changed. The issue was back in the mainstream news in the fall of 2018, when China took a big step backwards and legalized trade in tiger parts for medicinal use. Fortunately, there was an international outcry, and the government quickly backtracked on that. But—"

"Let me guess. The trade still flourishes under the

radar."

"It certainly does. Chinese customers now zip over to Laos or Thailand, thrilled to pay $200 for a tiger claw, or even $30,000 to as much as $50,000 for an entire tiger corpse. Have you heard of pink tiger bones?"

"No."

"It's been reported by a couple of reliable sources that the bones of live tigers are being harvested to produce the pink hue—for jewelry."

"How in the world...?"

"Apparently, the animals are anesthetized then butchered while there is still blood flow."

"Good God! That's barbaric."

"Yes. It makes my blood boil. And we know for certain that in Laos, like a couple of other countries, the government goes far beyond turning a blind eye to the tiger farms. Many officials are, themselves, actively engaged in enriching themselves at the expense of the tigers."

Jackie is stunned and her stomach turns. "So, to say we haven't been very good stewards would be a gross understatement."

Nigel sighs. "Rather like saying World War II was a bit of a dust-up."

They both become quiet and, Jackie thinks, ready to talk about something more pleasant.

"So, you mentioned you have a sister. Where is she?"

He smiles. "My dear Susan has been in Australia for a couple of years now. She works in wildlife conservation."

"Good for her."

"She married an Aussie. It's quite beautiful where

they live, and not far from access to one of the coral reefs which hasn't yet been bleached out of existence."

"A good excuse for you to visit Australia, then."

The food is presented in an attractive display, the steam rising from the chowder carrying a rich, earthy aroma. Jackie realizes there are numerous topics about which one could have a fascinating conversation with Nigel, but since her time with him is limited, she most wants to know what made married life so satisfying for him. After enjoying several spoonsful of the piping hot stew, she says, "As a person who's never been married, I'm wondering what it was about your marriage that made it so gratifying for you."

"I think it was all about choosing the right person."

"Of course. But how did you know Mary was the right one?"

"There were lots of objective things. We were both interested in zoology and the preservation of nature. She was a kind person, but she didn't shy away from challenging me. We tended to laugh at each other's jokes. And she was quite beautiful."

"I see. But, frankly, a good friend could be all of those things. Right?"

He thinks for a moment. "I suppose you're right. We did fall in love." He pauses. "But I think you're asking me why we did."

"I'd love to know."

Nigel stares into space before speaking. "She made me better than I was."

"Do you mean she made you want to improve yourself for her?"

"No. I was actually a better person because she was in my life." He glances at the fountain. "I can't think of any examples, but I knew it with great certainty, and I loved it. And I loved her."

"Wow. That's different."

"Is it?"

It occurs to Jackie that as much as she'd like to hear Nigel's answers, of course he'll expect her to reciprocate. "No. What I meant to say is, that's really lovely." She tries to keep control of the trajectory and asks him another question. "How many years did you have together?"

"Fifteen. Mary passed away in 2015. We married quite young, both only twenty-three. Then Jamie came along two years later. It was rather uncharacteristic for me—diving in so precipitously. But we were so much in love. And, looking back, knowing now I'd have her for only fifteen years, I'm so glad we did."

"Your marriage remained idyllic for all those years?"

"Oh my, no."

"What happened?"

Nigel grimaces. "I suppose it's too late to opt out of our honesty pledge?"

Jackie smiles. "Yes. Too late. Anyway, it was your idea."

"Well, we never fell out of love. Actually, I was the problem. Specifically, I was rather too in love with tigers. My studies and work took me away from home for months at a time. As you know, I got my advanced degrees in India. And I frequently needed to be out in the jungle to observe the tigers and monitor the conservation work. It wasn't especially dangerous. The fact is, I was more likely to get shot by a poacher than attacked by a tiger, but Mary wanted to keep Jamie safe and in school, so they never joined me in India. She didn't seem to be angry about it—just sad. Regrets aren't terribly helpful, but I really do wish I hadn't put my work ahead of my family. I've thought about it over the years—how I could've taken a different path." He sighs. "There's little use speculating about it. I did what I did. We survived as we survived."

Jackie takes some time to digest all of it. "Honestly, I don't know what to say. You seem to be an especially decent person. I think we all just try to make the best decisions at the time we make them. It seems to me that you've had a wonderful life." With those last two words, it strikes her that Nigel actually looks quite a bit like the movie star.

He pushes his plate away. "Enough about me. Let's talk about you."

She laughs. "Sadly, we've finished our lunches. So, I guess we're out of time."

"No." He shakes his head. "You shan't get off that easily. We'll have coffee. Would you like a dessert?"

"I'd love just a bite of something sweet. Would you like to share one?"

"Excellent." Nigel motions for the waiter, and they order two coffees and a piece of cherry pie. "Jackie, I've been wondering since you said you're single. Why is that?"

"Excuse me?"

"You're beautiful and accomplished, kind—"

"How could you know whether or not I'm kind?"

"Perfect." He smiles. "Well, it just so happens that you told me why Kenny and Becca would be in London with you. Furthermore, I saw you slip your credit card to Kenny."

Her mouth falls open.

"You're not the only one who is observant."

She sighs. "Thank you for all the compliments, Nigel. But the answer to your question is simple. I'm single because I want to be."

He puts his elbow on the table and rests his chin on his fist, wrinkles his brow, and says, "Why?"

"Why do I prefer to be single?"

"Yes."

"Let me ask you something. Would you ask a male lawyer that question?"

He thinks about it. "Probably not."

"Then isn't it a sexist question?"

"You caught me again."

She shrugs.

"But," he continues, "I'd still like to know the answer. Remember our agreement."

"Fair enough. Let me do it this way. I'll give you all the answers you'd probably readily accept from a guy. They all apply to me as well."

"All right."

"I like living alone. My career is important to me. I can hang out with friends and relatives when I want. It wouldn't be fair to stick a spouse with a workaholic. I don't lack for male companionship—and sex—when I want it. But I keep it uncomplicated. My partners know exactly what the deal is."

"And children?"

"Same premise. Think about how this would sit with you if I were a man saying it to you: I've never longed to be a parent. I tutor at the YMCA on many Saturday mornings, and can bond with the little ones there, if I choose to. I live a full and meaningful life without a spouse or children."

He looks away for a moment, then says, "Maybe I am sexist, Jackie, although I always try not to be. Please understand me. I'm not saying a woman could not find the happiest possible life without marriage and family. I firmly believe she could."

"Good."

"At risk of getting in trouble again, what I'm trying to say is something quite different."

"Go on."

"Maybe I'm just a terrible judge of these things, but I have a feeling you're not at all the type of woman you just described."

Jackie's mouth goes dry and she begins to perspire. She has to get out of this conversation. "Listen, Nigel. I've enjoyed having lunch with you—very much. But I've really got to get back to my hotel to work on the trial."

He purses his lips. "I think you are reneging on the rules of our lunch."

She stands as she responds. "I can't help what you think." She reaches down for her briefcase, assuming that looking as though she's about to leave will bring the waiter on the run. It does, and she says, "Two checks, please." She has to sit back down to await her bill. Nigel doesn't say anything, so Jackie changes the subject. "I'll send you an email to let you know how we do with our grudge tiger defense."

He appears to give up on her. "Thank you. I'd really like to hear how the Warrens make out."

They pay their respective bills with cash and leave the restaurant together. Jackie is desperate for a quick getaway and willing to pay for a cab. Fortunately, one is idling just down the block. As they part at the curb, they shake hands. Nigel holds onto hers a few beats longer than is customary. He looks into her eyes. "It's been my great pleasure to have met you, Jackie."

Jackie says, "Me too," and flushes with embarrassment at the way she ended their lunch.

****

Jackie jumps out of the cab at her hotel and hurries through the lobby and up three flights of stairs to their little suite. The girls are out for the day with Jamie, so she has the quiet she needs to work on her cross-examinations, but the tsunami of memories won't let up. They wash over her as she throws her briefcase on the couch and slips out of her blazer. She takes a quick, hot shower to try to rinse them off, but they cling—determined to distract her from her work. They are ever present after she dries off and puts on her sweats. She finally just gives in, climbs into her bed, and lets them have at her.

She is twenty-four and fresh out of law school. She spends that summer working at a book shop and studying for the July bar exam. After having aced her law school classes, it seems to her both anticlimactic and dreary to memorize statutes that any decent lawyer would look up, once in practice. Finally, the big day comes, and she's pleased with how it goes.

Jackie and a friend agree to meet the next evening, a Friday, to celebrate at a Rush Street bar. The place has an Irish name and a reputation as a great place to party, though she doesn't know it from personal experience as she's done precious little partying in law school. She arrives shortly after nine p.m. and thinks she was misled about the place as it isn't crowded at all. Sarah hasn't arrived yet, so she sits at the bar and orders a beer. She asks the bartender, a thirty-something redhead, why it's so empty on a Friday night. The woman says, "It doesn't get busy 'til eleven o'clock or so. Most people wouldn't show up this early—except maybe tourists." Jackie just nods, embarrassed at her ignorance of bar culture.

A young man with a very short haircut sits a couple of barstools from hers, and must've heard the exchange. "Damn. I didn't know that," he says to the waitress, who smiles at him. He's wearing blue jeans and a light green cotton pullover, and he is very nice-looking —as far as Jackie can tell in the dim light of the bar. He looks at her and says, "Do you mind if I join you?" He indicates the bar stool next to hers.

"Not at all. But, apparently, I'm a nerd about bars."

He smiles and points at himself with both hands. "Me too." He pauses, then looks at her and asks, "So, what brings you here?"

" 'Here' meaning Chicago? Or 'here' meaning my early-bird appearance at this bar?"

"I'd love to hear both."

She smiles. "I'm from southern Illinois. I came up to Chicago for undergrad and law school. I just took the bar exam, so I'm celebrating being finished with that horror."

"Celebrating alone?"

"Oh, no. I'm not quite that pathetic. My girlfriend is supposed to meet me here."

"Cool."

"I'm Jackie."

He reaches out his right hand to shake hers. "It's nice to meet you, Jackie. I'm Sam."

She's no kind of romantic but swears her hand

tingles when he touches it. "So, what are you doing here, Sam? That is, Chicago, as well as this bar."

He gives her a soft, close-mouth smile. "I worked construction at home in Indiana after high school to earn money for school. Then I moved to Chicago for college, and after that did another year of construction. I was ROTC, and now I've just finished my stateside training. My unit's being deployed to Afghanistan in mid-September."

"ROTC means Army, right?"

"Yeah. Army."

"So, you're an officer?"

He salutes. "Second lieutenant, Samuel Ames, reporting for duty."

"What will you do in Afghanistan?"

"We're a construction detail. So, I'll be doing what I used to do on the North Shore, except the buildings will be shorter, and less luxurious."

"Will there be fighting where you're going?"

"Of course. You may not have heard, but there's a war going on there."

Jackie feels herself flush with embarrassment but hopes he doesn't notice in the dim light. "Sorry. I admit to complete ignorance of exactly what we're doing there. I guess I just thought some soldiers might get to stay in safe places." She ventures, "Like in the Green Zone?"

He smiles. "I don't know about that. But we could definitely come under fire."

She frowns. "May I ask you something?"

"Sure." He catches the bartender's eye and points to his beer glass. Jackie's is still mostly full.

"Why do you want to do that?"

"Order another beer?"

"No." She rolls her eyes. "Go to a place where people will be shooting at you."

He just sits thinking for a moment, and then says, "ROTC was a way to pay for school. I carefully chose that out of the zero other scholarship offers I had. Right before college graduation, my dad died."

"I'm so sorry."

"Thanks, Jackie. So, the Army let me defer my training for a year after that so I could earn some extra money to help my mom out. Now that my grace period is over, I need to make good on my commitment."

"What will you do for the next two months?"

"I'm on leave until deployment. Apparently, the leave is usually a lot shorter, but some timing issue is delaying us until mid-September. So, I got my old construction job back for the next couple of months."

"Are you celebrating something tonight, Sam?"

"As a matter of fact, I am."

She waits a moment, but he doesn't elaborate. "Is it a secret?"

"I could tell you, but then I'd have to kill you."

She laughs. "It's your birthday, isn't it?"

"Wow. You're good. Are you always this intuitive?"

"I've never been right on an intuition before in my life."

"Then that's something else to celebrate."

"Wait. You're celebrating alone, Sam?"

"As I recall, when I asked you that question, you said, 'I'm not quite that pathetic.'"

She grimaces. "Yeah. I believe I did."

"I, on the other hand, am just that pathetic, Jackie."

"Seriously, don't you have college friends around here?"

"A few. It's just that I didn't realize I'd be released for my leave quite so soon. I just got up here this afternoon and haven't had time to reach anybody."

"Well, soldier, happy birthday!" Jackie lifts her beer glass to tap against his. "And you definitely shouldn't be alone on your special day. Why don't you join me and Sarah? She should be here soon."

After they chat for a few more minutes, Jackie checks her phone for any word from Sarah. She grimaces, then looks up at Sam. "Sorry. Sarah can't make it. I guess I'll just head home."

"Are you sure? We could hang out for a while. At least long enough to see what this place looks like when it comes to life."

She has to think about it since she has a thing about picking up guys in bars—as in, she doesn't do it. Still, it is Sam's birthday, and she kind of wants to celebrate getting through the long-dreaded bar exam. She smiles at him. "All right."

"Great! Would you like to dance, Jackie?"

She says yes.

When they start dating, it's heaven: dinners at his apartment or hers, walks through Old Town, picnics in Grant Park, and running together along the Lake Michigan shoreline. In time, something happens to Jackie that she never really believed could—she falls in love.

When Sam ships out for Afghanistan in the middle of September, he takes her heart with him. Maybe it was the brevity of the romance that made it so intense. That little September date circled in red on her calendar always pressing up against them. But even in that short time, she developed a new sense of being. Loving Sam makes her a better version of herself.

Sam is able to call Jackie for a brief phone visit every couple of weeks. He tells her he has to wait in a line for three hours to make a ten-minute phone call, so he alternates them between her and his mom. Jackie finds the calls to be awkward as hell. She generally just hears a simple version of what he's been doing, and if he's been well. Then they exchange a few words of love and longing. Sam was a pretty light-hearted guy when they were together in Chicago, but no lightness transmits through the phone. However, there is one thing she absolutely adores about the calls. Just hearing Sam's voice releases a flood of memories that restore her—at least for a day or two.

It's in early November that Jackie's yearning for Sam has a reason to crescendo.

She's always had irregular periods, so she thinks nothing of it when she doesn't menstruate in late August, or even by October. She feels a bit nauseated in the mornings for a while, so at first, she assumes she has some kind of low-grade flu. Then one day, it hits her. In spite of the fact that they used protection, she is probably pregnant. She's working for a medium-sized law firm, and has recently begun to take a lot of depositions. The one she takes that day goes from two to four thirty p.m., and as soon as it ends, she walks to a drug store on Washington Street to buy a home pregnancy test.

Jackie doesn't want to find out in a law office restroom, so she marches right into the Daley Center, which she knows will be pretty empty at this hour. She chooses a floor at random and goes straight into the ladies' room, where she rips the package open and reads the directions carefully. They recommend using her "first morning urine," but there's no way she can wait until the next morning. She places the little strip in front of her as she sits on the toilet and tries to relax so her urine will flow. She hasn't had time to run to a restroom since before the deposition, so flow it does. The little "x" appears, just as she knew it would. She throws away all of the paper products and walks over to the sink to wash her face and hands. Jackie is pretty sure she's flushed from the suspense and all the hurrying, but then again, it could be pregnant-woman-glow. Elated, she can't wait to tell Sam, but eventually decides to save it for a Christmas surprise.

Three days later, at her first pre-natal doctor visit, she learns she is almost eleven weeks pregnant, and her due date is April 28th. She hopes Sam will be as thrilled as she is, and carefully plans how she'll share the news during their Christmas call. And she imagines the moment when she'll see him again, and he'll meet their baby. Although she's over the moon with joy and excitement, Jackie tells no one, and actively conceals her pregnancy. She certainly can't share the news with anybody else before she tells Sam. She makes it through Thanksgiving with her folks in southern Illinois without spilling the beans, although her mother comments a couple of times about how preoccupied Jackie seems.

It's on December 10th, a day she'll never forget if she lives to be a hundred, that Jackie receives a phone call from Sam's mother, a woman with whom she's never before spoken. It's in the evening, shortly after she gets home from work.

"Hello. Is this Jackie Bauer?

"It is. Who's this?"

"Hello, dear. This is Elizabeth Ames, Sam's

mother."

"Oh, Mrs. Ames. I'm so happy to meet you...by phone, I mean." She is flustered, and suddenly worried.

"Yes. Sam left your name and number with me. He said you were a very special friend." Jackie doesn't have time to digest this description because Sam's mother's next words slap her in the face.

"I'm sorry. I have very bad news."

"No!" Jackie shouts it, then apologizes through her tears.

"No, dear. You're right. We've lost Sam."

The word confuses Jackie. Is he just missing? "Mrs. Ames, please tell me."

"He's dead. An accident on his base. They said a Striker was returning from a patrol and ran into Sam's Humvee. I think I got it right. Anyway, I guess it crushed Sam's vehicle." Mrs. Ames stops, then chokes out, "He died instantly."

Jackie cries hard, and so does Sam's mother. Finally, Mrs. Ames interrupts her sobbing to whisper, barely audibly, "I'm sorry, Jackie, I'm feeling weak. I think I need to lie down. I'll call you with the arrangements."

Jackie whispers, "Thank you." Of course, she should have consoled Mrs. Ames for her loss. First her husband and now her beautiful son. But Jackie's feelings of shock and devastation are overwhelming.

She flies to DC for his funeral. Apparently, Sam never expressed a preference, and his mother insists on Arlington National Cemetery, with full military honors. Jackie doesn't speak to anyone except Mrs. Ames, whom she greets briefly. Sam's mother is gray-haired, sweet, and elderly. Or maybe she just looks ancient from the toll her two losses have taken. The woman takes both of Jackie's hands in hers. "Just before he left for Afghanistan, Sam told me he'd fallen in love. I can't tell you how much it means to me that you gave him that." They hug and cry until someone interrupts them because Mrs. Ames is needed with the family. Of course, Jackie doesn't tell her she's pregnant with Sam's baby, since it would be a major distraction from her focus on her son. She doesn't attend their family gathering after the burial since only Sam's mother even knows she exists.

Jackie is so numb that only portions of the ceremony sink in; the chapel where literally hundreds of soldiers in full dress uniforms gather, and the procession to the gravesite led by soldiers on horseback, with one horse having an empty saddle with boots turned backwards in the stirrups. But the image that sears itself deeply into her memory is the young bugler, who shockingly looks a bit like Sam, playing the melancholy strains of Taps.

The last two weeks of December are a complete blur. In early January, Jackie awakes in the middle of the night with a piercingly sharp pain in her abdomen with almost continual cramps, and only seconds of relief between the jolts of stabbing pain. When she pulls back the covers to try to get up, she sees that her nightgown and the sheets are soaked with blood. She just manages to call 9-1-1 before she faints.

Jackie awakes in a bed in Rush-Presbyterian Hospital. A nurse alerts the doctor that she's woken, and the woman comes in and explains that she's suffered a miscarriage. The baby was a girl. The doctor says she's very sorry, and that someone will stop by later to discuss arrangements for handling the baby's body. She adds, "You'll be fine. From what I can see, you should be able to carry a baby to term in the future."

Her tiny daughter is cremated. She takes the little urn with her when she moves back to southern Illinois a few months later. She finds a beautiful place for her daughter to rest in a peaceful spot not far from the courthouse.

****

Jackie's never forgotten the doctor's phrase—that she'll "be fine." Never before or since have such untrue words been spoken to her. Having relived the best and worst moments of her life in her London hotel room, she falls into a deep sleep.

She works late that night and most of the next day, while the girls again tour with Jamie Lucas. Around seven p.m. on Tuesday, her cell phone rings. Since she doesn't recognize the number, she thinks she'd better pick it up since it might concern the girls.

"Hello."

"Hello, Jackie. It's Nigel."

"Oh. This is a surprise."

"Jackie, I'd really like to speak with you for a few minutes."

"Okay. Go on."

"No. I mean, in person."

"I'm sorry, Nigel. But I'm working tonight."

"It won't take long. I'm standing in front of your hotel."

"Wait. How did you find my hotel?"

"Jamie gave me the address."

"Oh."

"There's a quiet neighborhood bar on the corner. Could we just have a beer? There's something I want to tell you."

"Please, Nigel. Just tell me on the phone."

"I'm sorry. I can't do it that way."

Since he didn't mention anything about the girls, she wonders if it might be about her grudge tiger defense and decides she'd better see him.

"All right. I'll be down in a minute."

Jackie jumps into her blue jeans, a sweatshirt and sneakers, and takes the stairs to the lobby. As she walks out the front door and sees Nigel standing there with his hands in his jeans' pockets, she's reminded of how attractive he is.

"Thanks for coming down, Jackie."

"Sure. So where are we going?"

He points to a building kitty-cornered across the street. "Just there. I peeked in. They have quiet booths."

"All right. I'll have a cup of tea, though. I still have work to do tonight."

He smiles very tenderly, then takes her arm to cross the street like she's his fragile charge.

Once they are situated in a booth, he surprises her by reaching across the table and taking both of her hands in his. "Jackie, I just want to apologize for my behavior yesterday."

"Okay. What behavior, specifically?"

"My presumptuous insistence that you are a woman who would want to be a wife and mother. My refusal to accept your explanation of the lifestyle you want. And my inexcusable suggestion that you weren't telling the truth, per our 'agreement.' "

"Oh, that." She nods.

After their drinks are served, she says, "Actually, I think you were onto something with your idea we could be perfectly honest with each other since we'd never see each other again."

"It was a stupid game. I'm an idiot."

"No, it wasn't. And you can't be, since I don't retain idiots as my expert witnesses."

"I'm just so sorry."

She puts down her teacup. "Nigel, stop apologizing." It's quite intimate in the small booth with the narrow table between them. They're seated facing each other, so basically looking into each other's eyes.

"All right."

"I'm glad you came by. I need to tell you something, too."

He nods his head slightly and keeps his eyes on hers. Jackie tells him about Sam and Gloria. By the end of her story, tears are streaming down her cheeks. He hands her a paper napkin and she dabs at her eyes.

"I'm so sorry, Jackie. What you went through must've been completely devastating."

"There's more. You're right. I was devastated— barely able to keep going. Over time, I realized I had to find something to help me to keep putting one foot in front of the other. I thought about therapy or meditation. I even seriously considered drug or alcohol abuse. But what I settled on was work. For the past ten years, I've been a robot. I programmed myself to appear cheerful, friendly, creative…efficient. But the truth is, I'm just a lawyer-machine."

"You do know that's not right, don't you?"

"The thing is, I don't want a new love. I want Sam. I don't want to have a baby. I want my baby. My heart was broken—twice. I'll never get past it. So, I am what I am, a machine."

"But you're not a machine. You are a human being.

You need to stop thinking that way."

Jackie smiles because she knew he'd say this. "It's been ten years, Nigel, and I haven't told a soul until now. There's nothing to be done, so why burden others? I can't help it and no one can help me. It's just the way the balls broke for me. So, please don't try to help me. I'm not even in here anymore."

"You are. You're deeply and beautifully 'in there.' "

"Not really. By the way, you were right about your game. Here I sit, telling you the absolute truth. If I weren't flying home tomorrow, I'm sure I couldn't have told you, but I know it won't be a terrible burden for you because you don't really even know me. See, there's no one to know."

"Oh, Jackie. You really must get help with this. I didn't have the pleasure of knowing Sam, but I can't imagine you really believe this is what he'd want for you."

Jackie stops to think about what Nigel said. "You're right. Of course, what you're saying is logical. I guess I'm afraid to lose my grief because it would be like losing Sam and Gloria for good."

"Listen, I can see why you might fear that, but trust me, it doesn't work that way. In fact, I feel closer to my Mary now than when I was in the early phases of my grief." He pauses. "I'm having a hard time understanding how you haven't told anyone before today. Quite frankly, I can't imagine how that's even possible—that anyone could hold such grief inside for ten years without seeking help from a single soul. Have you thought about reaching out to Sam's mother?"

"It's been ten years."

"Can you imagine that her grief is any less fresh than

yours?"

Jackie realizes she's given no thought to Mrs. Ames since the funeral. It makes sense. She's probably the only person in the world who feels Sam's absence as much as Jackie does. "It's a thought. Perhaps I will."

"And what of your own mother? Are you close with her?"

"She'd like us to be, but I resist. She's always been very supportive, but after I left home for college, I clung to my independence."

"From what I've learned about you, it seems you've achieved that. Why not try a bit of the other?"

"Talk to my mom about it?"

"Worth considering?"

"Maybe. I'll think about that, too."

"Then again, I think sometimes it's easier to talk with a virtual stranger—like me. I hope you'll consider finding a therapist you like."

"I might."

"Seriously, try thinking about what you would've wished for Sam, if you were the one who'd died and he'd lived."

"Now you're making too much sense, Nigel."

He smiles.

Jackie is thinking through his suggestions as she looks down at her lap. She happens to glance at her watch.

Nigel says, "I know. You need to get back to work. But you can trust me on this, Jackie. Talking about it will help. It has made all the difference for me. It's a long process. I expect my grieving will never end, but I did get my life back. And I really believe you can get yours back by working through it with someone."

She stares at her lap again, for what seems like a few minutes. Then she looks up and says, "Actually, I do believe you."

"You do?"

"Yes. Because I can feel it already working…as I sit here. I suppose I have kept it bottled up long enough, I'll think about trying it your way."

"Really?"

"Yes. It's probably time."

"Please do, Jackie. You are one of the least robot-like persons I've ever met. I think you will surprise yourself."

She smiles. "Thank you."

As he leaves Jackie at the front door of her hotel, he gives her a very tender hug—long and gentle. She is swept up in the warmth of his face pressed against hers, and her ice barrier begins to melt. It's the first time she feels genuine tenderness toward a man in ten years, and she's shocked that it's still possible. She kisses Nigel on the cheek and is seriously tempted to move on to his lips. But it isn't the right time. Just knowing how she feels toward him gives her hope.

Maybe she can find a therapist she'll like. Maybe she can have a normal life. Maybe her evenings can be filled with something other than work. Maybe. But not until after she wins the Alcott case for the Warrens. She's always been an OCD-level tenacious person, and she needs to win this particular case more than any she's ever handled.

Chapter 25

Kenny

Kenny has to admit to herself that what her sister had called her "brilliant plan" was actually inspired. It's on the long flight home from Heathrow on Wednesday night that she has time to review it all. Reliving it takes her into what feels like a lovely dream.

At one of their first stops on Tuesday morning, Big Ben and the Houses of Parliament, the three of them mainly marvel that they really are standing in front of the iconic spots. Big Ben still has some scaffolding hanging off of him, so they continue to look for the perfect selfie back-drop. While they stand in line at the next attraction, The London Eye, Kenny and Becca describe their school, and also admit to how isolated they are from the other students. Jamie tells them funny stories about things that happened in his high school. It's one of those "public" schools, which means "private" in England. It's all-boy, and he had to wear a uniform. Then he makes a suggestion which absolutely transforms the rest of their time from merely interesting and educational to hilarious and liberating. He says, since they'll never see each other again, they should all tell the absolute truth, without embarrassment or holding back. He explains it's a game his father told him about, and that it will make their time together way more interesting.

Becca says they must pinkie-swear to it or someone might cheat. So, there in one of the huge enclosed passenger capsules of London's famous Ferris wheel, they all three make a pinkie-swear. They have to do it quickly because they don't want to miss taking pictures of all the famous London sights in clear view. As they gaze upon Kenny's new favorite city, she feels weightless, suspended over the Thames. Jamie tells them that, on a clear day, a person can see twenty-five miles from the ride.

When they walk back over the bridge near the Ferris wheel, Kenny turns her back to the rail, then tosses a coin with her right hand over her left shoulder into the Thames. After she tells Becca the legend of the Trevi Fountain in Rome, Becca does the same thing. Kenny knows the story from one of her mother's favorite movies. It will ensure their return to London—if the Thames works like the Trevi Fountain. There's no harm in hoping. Jamie says he loves her optimism and asks Kenny if there's a legend which will ensure he'll get to the states someday to visit the zoo. Kenny wishes there were, but admits that nothing comes to mind.

The two churches they visit, Westminster Abbey and St. Paul's Cathedral, are so steeped in history Kenny's read about that she actually feels her heart expand. Walking through them and listening to the audio connects the marvelous things they're encountering with events that only existed for her in books or on TV. It's hard to believe that the spectacular pageantry of thirty-eight coronations and sixteen royal weddings took place right where her feet are pressed against the stone floor. She's read that Princess Di was married at St. Paul's Cathedral, and Meghan Markle at the much more intimate St. George's Chapel in Windsor Castle. But Kate Middleton's wedding day pumps stepped on the exact spots where Kenny stands in Westminster Abbey. She leans over to touch the floor, since she doesn't like that the soles of her shoes bar direct contact with the surface upon which famous feet walked. And she doesn't think the guards would appreciate her going barefoot.

St. Paul's Cathedral is so majestic and gorgeous, Kenny can see why elegant Princess Di wanted to have her wedding here. She does wonder whether she really got to choose, though, based on what she's read about her tough life as a "royal." After touring the main floor, they squeeze themselves up the claustrophobic 163-step spiral staircase so they can experience the Whispering Gallery. Kenny leans into the wall and says softly, "Hi Becca. Lunch soon?" Becca hears every word on the other side of the open galley, 107 feet away, a second later. The whispering thing gets them talking about secrets. As they make their way out of St. Paul's and into the bright sunlight, the conversation goes straight to sex. Jamie admits to having a crush on one of his neighbors, a girl four years older than him who already finished university and is doing service work in Africa. Kenny asks if he knows of anyone who has a crush on him. He says there was a boy at school. Jamie didn't know how to handle it, so he mostly avoided the guy. But, not wanting to seem like a homophobe, he tried to be as pleasant as he could when they did run into each other. When he asks if they have crushes, Kenny and Becca look at each other for a moment and then burst out laughing.

"What's so funny?"

Kenny says, "Duh! It's Dean."

Becca jumps in. "But we don't want to talk about it because that stupid crush is what got us in the mess we're here to try to forget about."

"Of course," says Jamie. "Sorry. Better question: Do you know of people who have crushes on you?"

They both crack up at his ludicrous idea. Jamie shakes his head. "You girls are crazy. I'll bet lots of boys do. They just don't want anyone to know—because they're boys."

They laugh again at his absurdly positive view of their lives. After a long walk, they all push their way through the revolving door of the "world's largest, most upscale and expensive mall." It has over three hundred departments, all selling only luxury brands. Most of the people in there seem to be tourists like them, because they are taking pictures like crazy, and Kenny wonders if the place ever makes any actual sales. They basically run a mad dash through the store, and up and down the escalators. The image that will stay with Kenny forever is the gourmet meat department which has all kinds of former animals hanging upside down and laid out in refrigerated display cases. Kenny says it's enough to turn any remotely compassionate person into a vegetarian. Jamie winks at her and says she's very empathetic. He adds that maybe it's because his father was brought up in a zookeeper's family, but the only meat he feels comfortable eating is fish. It's funny that Kenny hadn't made that connection before, but she's intrigued by his explanation and watches him intently—which she tends to do—as she listens. She says, "I'm also a pescatarian and, now that I think about it, it probably is because I work with animals."

Jamie smiles at her.

Kenny and Becca are both dying to see the Science Museum and the Natural History Museum, and they agree that Jamie will lead them directly there after a quick lunch. The place they find to eat is like a diner, and they sit in a little booth with red vinyl seats to eat grilled cheese sandwiches and chips, the British version of french fries. Jamie, who sits across from them, keeps glancing at Kenny, even when she's not speaking. Once she wipes her napkin across her mouth to make sure she's not wearing anything there that shouldn't be there, it hits her that he likes her a little. Of course, that makes her feel amazing. Neither Jamie nor Kenny goes beyond glances, smiles, and ever-so-slight brushing-up against the other since it would be mean to leave Becca out.

Once they arrive at the Science Museum and look over the sign listing the exhibits, Kenny realizes she could happily spend the rest of her life there. The Launch Pad Gallery and the actual Apollo 10 capsule leave her feeling she'll almost definitely have to become an astronaut. But then the huge display of the history of robots pretty much convinces her to go into AI or robotics.

It's getting late, and they still have tons of things on their list, so they tear themselves away. At the Natural History Museum, they make an aggressive fast sweep, which is fantastic but yields no additional career urges. They're all dying for a break, so they find a cafe and have hot tea and biscuits, known in the U.S. as cookies, to keep them going until dinner.

Kenny realized early-on that the whole trip would be like a sneak preview of London. But both she and Becca prefer to see a little bit of everything they can, rather than spend their time at just one or two museums.

After Natural History, they take in the Tower of London, which is actually like a mini city of twenty towers. The Bloody Tower is a horrifying torture-chamber. The Armouries include Henry VIII's suit of armor, which would make any sane person feel sad for Henry's horse, who carried not only the armor-wearing fat man, but also its own suit of armor. Becca goes gaga over the crown jewels, but Kenny can't tell them from costume jewelry.

Kenny's favorite spot is the room where the Royal Menagerie was kept. From what she sees and reads, the royal attendants weren't especially good at safety precautions. But the very idea that there were once lions and tigers within those walls is pretty fascinating, at least to a zookeeper. As their time dwindles, Jamie tells them the bad news—they'll need to do some culling. After wrestling with the pros and cons, Kenny and Becca finally agree to save Shakespeare's Globe Theatre and Number 10 Downing Street for another trip. They have dinner together, then walk through a number of lovely parks before time to head back to the hotel.

On Wednesday morning, Jamie meets them outside the hotel so they can get an early start. Jackie told the girls that they need to check out of the hotel at three p.m. to be sure they have plenty of time to navigate Heathrow for the trip home. The three make it to Buckingham Palace early and are able to get a great viewing spot for the eleven a.m. Changing of the Guard. While they wait for the ceremonial stuff to begin, they each tell their earliest memory. Jamie's is sweet. He remembers standing on a stool at the kitchen counter making Christmas cookies with his mother. His father had been away for work for several weeks. A heavy snow began to fall when his dad walked through the front door, carrying a suitcase and a briefcase. Because his father was coated with snow, Jamie's pajamas got soaked when they hugged, but it didn't bother him a bit. He figures he must've been around five years old. Jamie says he isn't positive it's his absolute first memory, but since he loves it so much, he's sticking with that one. Kenny says it's the sweetest thing ever, and Jamie smiles at her.

Becca shakes her head like she's trying to rattle her memory into position. She was around four years old when she had a dream in which her mother kept insisting that she at least try to go potty before a car trip. Becca tried so hard that she actually peed in her bed, and her parents both scolded her. What stuck with her was how unjust it felt since she was just trying to do what she was asked to do. Jamie and Kenny groan and agree she was wrongfully convicted and that her parents should've listened to her explanation of the extenuating circumstances.

When it's Kenny's turn, she realizes she has much more interesting memories than her earliest one. But she pinkie-swore to tell the truth, so she shares with them her very first one. She was sitting on her mother's lap in a rocking chair, and her mother kept falling asleep while reading to her. Every time she did, Kenny would jab her little elbows in to wake her mother up. She didn't get angry or anything, but she kept dozing off, so Kenny had to keep jabbing. Becca says she isn't sure what to make of it. They all agree to psychoanalyze each other's first memories, but the guard-changing ceremony begins.

What is probably routine for Londoners is like a fairy tale for Kenny, so she tries to really focus on every moment of it. Next, they stroll around Trafalgar Square, the official "Center of London." Planting themselves before the 168-foot monument of the great Admiral Nelson, they take tons of pictures, but Kenny thinks the one of a pigeon sitting on Becca's head is the most fun.

They grab sandwiches near the busy square, then dash to the British Museum for their remaining hours. The architecture of the place is brilliant—a huge glass roof over the museum's courtyard, and absolutely everything Kenny sees amazes her. The Egyptian mummies and the fragments of the Seven Wonders of the Ancient World pull her back in time in an extraordinary way she's never experienced before. But the absolute high point is seeing *the,* undeniably legit, Rosetta Stone. It dates back to 196 B.C. and holds the key to understanding Egyptian hieroglyphics, a written language made up of small pictures that died out in the fourth century. No one knew how to read it, so it was a totally lost language until the stone was found. Although the back of the thing is rough, its front is smooth and completely crammed with words—in three different languages. So, using the Greek, which they knew, scholars were able to decipher the hieroglyphics and miraculously, how to read the lost language. The story reminds Kenny of the way it will go for endangered animals if we're stupid enough to let them slip out of existence. Zoos like hers can breed tigers, but it's not the same since tigers bred in captivity can't go back into the wild. She can't understand why we humans—sort of the natural world's zookeepers—are letting the wild ones die out. Once they're gone, there won't be a Rosetta Stone to bring them back.

When it's time to head back to the hotel, they take turns asking really tough questions, since the truth-telling adventure is about to end. What she learns is that the saddest thing in Jamie's life is missing his mother. He's a virgin. And his favorite thing in the world is hanging out with his dad. Jamie probably already figured out that Kenny and Becca are virgins, so he doesn't ask that obvious question. But Kenny does have to own up to her saddest thing—missing her father. And her happiest thing—studying science. The others groan at that one, although Kenny happens to know that Becca also loves science. Becca says she's sad there aren't any other Asian families in Heartsville, and her happiest thing is daydreaming about moving away for college. They are all getting bummed out by telling their saddest things, so they call an end to the game. They exchange contact information before Jamie leaves them at their hotel. Of course, they can keep in touch, but Kenny is saddened by the knowledge they'll probably never see Jamie again.

While they're standing in line to board their flight, Becca leans toward her friend and whispers that she thinks Jamie "likes" Kenny. Kenny pooh-pooh's it but feels an impossible combination of excitement and serenity after that.

Kenny also knows her sister's idea will work. Whatever crap is dumped on her because of what comes out at the trial will hurt less because of London. Heartsville, Illinois is just a tiny speck on the globe. College will be wonderful not just because Kenny knows she'll find the academics exciting, but also because she now realizes that some boys there will probably like her, and she'll probably like one of them back. It's not as hard to keep your eyes on the prize once you can visualize the prize. She owes her brilliant sister a huge thank-you.

Still, as the tiny airplane on her TV screen displays

their progress toward the US east coast, her heart sinks at the idea that her mother could lose the zoo. She doesn't know if absence makes the heart grow fonder, but Kenny can't wait to get home to all her babies. It's true that some of them weigh over six hundred pounds, and quite a number have what you would never call classically beautiful faces, but they are all precious to her. She's convinced they all understand more than most people think. She's taken care of them for the past ten years— more than half her life. She knows them, and a lot of them know her. Several are definitely imps, but she thinks she has a lot of "impathy" because they are all innocent children to her. The truth is, she adores every one of them. She can't help wondering. If having to wait a few more hours to see them makes her this anxious, how would it feel to lose them?

Chapter 26

Jackie

During the three weeks following her return from London, Jackie is consumed by her work on the Warrens' defense. Fifteen-hour-days segue into twenty-hour days, with her usual trial all-nighters looming on the horizon.

Although the trial isn't set to begin until Monday, Judge Marcus orders the lawyers to appear with their clients at four p.m. on the Friday before that so she can announce her rulings on pending motions, and then conduct a final pretrial settlement conference. Jackie and the Warrens arrive early, and she asks them to take seats at the table on the left, at the front of the courtroom. Jackie remains standing as she pulls a legal pad and pen out of her briefcase. As she hears the main door open, she turns to see Hank arrive, gives him a smile, and receives a nod in return. Hank stands back to hold the door for Dean, who enters on crutches. As he steps through the doorway, Dean pauses to scan the area before continuing on one leg and the two wooden sticks toward the plaintiff's table. Hank scoots around Dean so that he can hold the wooden gate open as his client reaches the front section of the room.

Since Dean is looking at the floor, Jackie feels comfortable watching him. He's lost weight since she last saw him, but not so much that he isn't still exquisite. Once Dean is seated, and his crutches are propped against the table, Jackie sees him glance at the Warren table, where his eyes meet Marietta's. They both quickly look away as though the appearance of the other causes immediate pain. She keeps an eye on the two of them, and doesn't see another exchange between them for the duration of the hearing and conference.

The elderly bailiff announces that Judge Marcus will be on the bench in a short time, but it's over twenty minutes before she appears. Everyone rises and remains standing until the judge is seated. She studies her papers for a moment before looking up, which prompts the bailiff to loudly call out the name of the case, as if everyone present doesn't already know why they are there.

The judge speaks loudly and clearly. "I've considered all of the pending motions and have read the supporting briefs. I will not allow further argument. Counsel may remain seated." Jackie glances at Hank, who shrugs his shoulders barely perceptibly. "As to the cross motions for summary judgment regarding the provocation defense to the Animal Control Act, I deny both the plaintiff's and the defendant's motions. Mr. Perdue has also moved to bar the so-called 'grudge tiger' defense. Because failure to have provoked is a necessary element of plaintiff's claim, I will allow Mrs. Warren to present the defense to the jury." Jackie smiles to herself, then glances at Hank, who tightens his mouth, just short of a scowl.

"The rulings on the remaining pending motions were released yesterday. I assume you've both read them." She looks from Jackie to Hank.

Jackie stands and says, "Yes. Thank you, your honor," followed by Hank doing the same.

"Are there any questions about the rulings, Counsel?"

"No, your honor," say Jackie and Hank at the same time.

Hank says, "Your honor, at this time, plaintiff moves to withdraw Count I of our complaint, the negligence count."

Jackie nods to herself as she processes Hank's move. Judge Marcus looks at Jackie. "Counsel?"

"No objection, your honor."

"Very well. This case will proceed to trial on a single count, plaintiff's action under the Animal Control Act." The judge looks at Hank and then Jackie. "If there's nothing further, this hearing is adjourned. I'll give counsel fifteen minutes to discuss the import of my rulings, and the withdrawal of Count I, with your clients. Then I'll conduct the final pretrial settlement conference in my chambers. The bailiff will instruct you as to how I'll proceed." Judge Marcus stands and everyone rises as she leaves the courtroom.

Jackie huddles with Carolyn, Marietta, and Kenny at their table. "First, it's great news that the court is allowing our grudge tiger defense—for the obvious reason."

"Because provocation is our only defense," Kenny says.

"That's right. Of course, I could also argue the defense of trespass. But I've weighed the evidence and still don't like our position for a number of reasons. We've developed our provocation defense very well. If the jury believes Dean was attacked because he provoked

Ms. Benni, we win. I'd like to make that fact as easy as possible for the jury to understand. I think we can accomplish that best by presenting just our strongest defense."

"Do you think Hank was surprised that the judge will let you go ahead with it?" asks Marietta.

"Not at all. We both knew she'd deny our cross-motions on it. It's a fact question, and those are for juries, not judges."

"I'd like to know what you think of Hank withdrawing Count I," Carolyn says.

"It makes sense. He obviously realizes Dean would be found more than fifty percent the cause of the accident, which means he loses that count. And he really doesn't want me going on and on to the jury about Dean's negligence—which is now a non-issue. Basically, he wants to accomplish the same thing I do— show the jury that, in spite of all the witnesses and expert witnesses, this is actually a pretty simple case. The main difference is that Hank will be dismissive of our grudge tiger defense, while I'll hammer it."

"What about the settlement conference?" Carolyn says.

"My guess is that Judge Marcus will try to persuade them to accept the insurance money. I suspect it's Dean, not Hank, whom she'll have to convince."

When the bailiff returns, he invites Jackie and Hank to follow him through the hall behind the courtroom to Judge Marcus's chambers. The two attorneys take seats in front of her large mahogany desk, and Jackie explains that her insurance company client, Helen Huffer, cannot be present due to a scheduling conflict, but is available by phone.

"I remember Helen," says Judge Marcus. "That's acceptable. Where do settlement negotiations stand, Ms. Bauer?"

"Although we do expect a defense verdict in view of the evidence we'll be able to present, and the irrefutable conclusion of our tiger expert, Ms. Huffer offered the entire policy limit, $500,000, to Mr. Alcott to resolve this. He declined, so she withdrew the offer, and asked me to prepare for trial."

"Is the offer still available?"

"My client instructed that she will reluctantly reinstate the offer if Mr. Perdue tells you that it will settle the case."

"Mr. Perdue?"

"With all due respect to Ms. Bauer, the offer's a joke. That won't even cover my client's medical."

"Although the jury could find the defendant not guilty," says Judge Marcus.

"Again, with all due respect, not likely." Hank folds his arms and stares at Jackie.

The judge looks between the two lawyers. "Mr. Perdue, please bring your client in. I'd like to speak with him. Ms. Bauer, please give us a moment."

Hank hurries back to the courtroom, and then escorts Dean as he slowly makes his way back to chambers, passing Jackie in the hallway. She smiles at him, but Dean's eyes don't leave the floor. Jackie returns to hopeful looks on the faces of Carolyn, Marietta, and Kenny.

"I gave the judge the background on settlement negotiations. Now she'll try to convince Dean he could very well lose the case and would be wise to take the sure thing—the $500,000."

211

"Do you think she'll convince him?" asks Kenny.

"She might convince Hank. But it's Dean's decision, and I haven't a clue what he's thinking right now."

"Me neither," Marietta says. "Although the judge seems like she could be pretty forceful."

"Yes. I've seen her persuade plaintiffs before."

Carolyn asks, "What if Dean says he wants the insurance money *plus* something from me?"

"That could happen. But it's more likely if $500,000 isn't enough, $600,000 won't be either. Some plaintiffs try to get the big verdicts, even ones that aren't collectible, simply for the vindication. So Carolyn, what would you like to do if he does demand something above the insurance money?"

"The most I could possibly come up with—and I'd have to take out another mortgage—is $100,000."

"Do you want me to let the judge know?"

"Not unless Dean says that it will definitely settle the case."

"Understood."

Another half hour passes, and the bailiff returns to summon Jackie back to chambers. Hank and Dean are seated in front of the judge as Jackie enters the room. Judge Marcus says, "You won't need to sit, Ms. Bauer. The settlement demand is now $3.8 million dollars. Mr. Alcott refuses to negotiate down from that. Do you need to call Ms. Huffer?"

"No, your honor. I have no authority beyond the $500,000. Mrs. Warren has instructed me, as well. We're prepared to proceed to trial."

"Very well, Counsel. Monday morning, ten o'clock."

Upon her return to counsel table, Jackie lets the Warrens know what happened in chambers. Carolyn puts her head in her hands, and her daughters lightly pat her back. Jackie says, "Carolyn, we couldn't be more ready for this trial."

"I'm not sure I can do this," Carolyn says.

"But you can," Kenny says.

"And you will, Mom," Marietta says.

Carolyn bites her lower lip but says nothing.

As the women file out of the courtroom, Kenny grabs Jackie by the arm and whispers, "What about the state's attorney's lawsuit? Will that be part of the trial?"

"They're separate, Kenny. And we're only at the early stages of that one. Hopefully, the judge will rule soon on my motion to dismiss."

"Okay. Thanks."

Chapter 27

Marietta

Marietta is devastated that the pre-trial conference didn't end with a settlement, and the trial will begin in two days. Through no fault of her mother's, she's being pushed against a wall. All of Carolyn's unflinching courage and resourcefulness are no match for a law that blames her when she did nothing wrong, and a civil court system that could so easily award her beloved zoo to Dean. Marietta both admires and loves her mother more than anyone she knows. When she was little, Carolyn made her feel equally adored and included when darling baby Kenny came along. She was the glue that held their household together when Marietta's dad fell into his well of depression—which happened a lot over the years.

She was the one who kept everyone moving forward when he was diagnosed with brain cancer, through three surgeries and his diminishment that followed each. She took nothing for herself as she marched on—the good soldier. Marietta acknowledges that, sometimes, her mom performed her nurse duties so coolly that an outside observer might've questioned whether she did them out of love or duty. But Marietta suspected the shell was something her mother created to keep it from hurting unbearably when she would lose her husband—as the doctors assured her she would. Of course, Marietta doesn't know this for certain. Does a daughter ever really know her mother as a woman? Marietta can only attest to what her mother is to her, a woman with an intuitive acumen about what to do and what not to do with her daughters, the zoo animals, the staff, and the public—a woman who holds everything together. The classic unheralded hero.

Beginning when Marietta was quite young, she realized that her mother would never let others catch a glimpse of whatever pain or fear she felt—so much so that, until her dad's funeral, she'd never seen her cry. Now, Dean's lawsuit resurrects that isolated memory. She knows her mother is a mess. She's actually been drinking Marietta's chardonnay, which is almost comical in how out-of-character it is for her. The juice glass in the sink with a residue of white wine and a straw still standing upright would make Marietta laugh if it didn't make her cry. *"How could this happen to us?"* is a moronic cliché. It doesn't matter how it happened. All that matters is how it will end. Logically, she understands the situation isn't really her fault, yet when it dawns on her that she may hold the key to saving her mother, she feels compelled to act. Marietta knows she shouldn't approach Dean without Jackie's knowledge. The problem is, if she reveals her plan, Jackie will try to stop her.

So, around nine p.m. on the Friday of the failed settlement conference, Marietta sits on the corner of the bed in her small, terribly neat bedroom, and rings his number. "Hi, Dean. It's Marietta."

"Really?"

"Yeah. It's me."

"What do you want?"

"I want you to take the insurance money and leave my mom alone."

"Why should I do that? I wouldn't mind owning a zoo."

"Liar."

"You called me up just to call me a liar?"

"No. Sorry, Dean. For some reason, I'm a little touchy about anyone trying to take my mom's business."

"So, what do you want?"

"I was wondering if it might help if I stopped by to see you—to talk it out?"

"You never wanted to see me before."

"I know."

"But now that you want something from me, you're willing to spend a little time with me."

"I know it looks bad, Dean. But the truth is, I've been feeling awful ever since your accident—about not visiting."

"Mmm-hmm."

"Our lawyer says I shouldn't talk to you."

"Right. So how come you can talk to me now?"

"I can't. I mean, Jackie would kill me if she knew. But I feel like I have to take that chance."

"Marietta, I'm tired…and my leg hurts. Let's get down to it. What will you do for me if I do what you want about the money?"

"What would you like me to do?"

"Dad will be out making deliveries tomorrow morning. You can come over any time after nine a.m."

"Okay. Good."

"Marietta, I'm not inviting you over for conversation. Remember what you said—that Jackie would kill you?"

"What then?"

"If you can make me feel good enough, I may be willing to consider what you want."

"Wait. What do you mean?"

"Good night, Marietta." The line goes dead.

She wonders how Dean can feel up to having sex, since Jackie reported that the wounds in his leg and arm aren't yet healed, which was confirmed by the way he limped into the courtroom. Then it hits her that the proposal isn't for mutual enjoyment. Marietta isn't a virgin, but she's never done what Dean is asking for. It's obvious that he hates her for what she said to him, and he probably blames her for his injuries. He wants revenge and demeaning her—having the power to get what he wants from her—will be his retribution.

Marietta spends the night wearing a path in the carpet trying to decide what to do. By the wee hours, she's imagining complications so bizarre they never would've entered her pre-exhaustion consciousness. Her sleep-deprived, demented mind sees a video being made, blackmail for sex, and a lifetime of sexual servitude. She finally collapses onto her bed at six a.m. and has slept only a couple of hours before it's time to leave for Dean's.

The way Marietta sees it, she's on a mission, a crusade for her mother, and she'll use the best-suited weapon in her arsenal, her desirability. She's decided she owes it to her mother to save the zoo, so she'll do it the only way she can. Once she showers, shaves her legs, and applies bath-powder and make-up, there are hardly any traces left of the sleep-deprived nut who dreamed up fall-out far beyond what is realistic to fear. She dresses quickly in a knee-length blue jean skirt, sleeveless white cotton sweater, and flip-flops.

Without pausing for breakfast, she drives to Dean's house. There's no sign of Mr. Alcott's pick-up truck, so she walks to the front door and knocks. Hearing a muffled sound from within, and not wanting Dean to have to drag himself to the door, she tests the doorknob. Just as she hopes, the door opens. She raps lightly again as she sticks her head inside the door. "Dean?"

"Yeah. Come on in, Marietta. First door on your left."

She enters the room and sees Dean sitting up in bed. He's always been all about his physicality and seeing him bandaged and essentially immobile is jarring—just as it was when she saw him walk into the courtroom on Friday on crutches, very slowly and deliberately.

"I'm so sorry you got hurt, Dean." She stands at the end of his bed.

"Marietta, Marietta." He shakes his head. "You never wanted to talk to me before. So don't insult my intelligence by starting now."

She flushes with embarrassment. "Okay."

"Just come over here and give me a kiss."

She hesitates for a moment, then walks toward the head of the bed, leans over and kisses him softly on the lips. His creamy smooth lips taste of toothpaste. He doesn't kiss back. She swallows hard and sits down next to him on the bed.

"Now, take off your top."

She reaches down to pull her sweater over her head. "Stop."

Marietta quickly pulls her sweater back down. "What's wrong?"

"You are. Now get out of here, Marietta. You've just

managed to do something you tried and failed to do for years."

"What?"

"You cured me of being in love with you."

"I don't understand, Dean."

"Come on. You're supposed to be smarter than me. You told me I only wanted what I couldn't have. I've had a lot of time to think about it since that day. You were wrong. What I wanted was a girl I respected."

It doesn't make sense, and Marietta can feel her forehead wrinkle. "But, Dean, I was a jerk in high school. Why did you respect me?"

"For not falling all over me like all the other girls."

There it is. And now she's joined their ranks—for a perverse reason. She knows there's nothing she can say to defend herself since her actions have already spoken. She rises to leave. As she gets to the doorway, she turns back to Dean. "What about the zoo?"

"My lawyer says the jury will decide."

"I see."

"No, Marietta. You never did."

She steps through the doorway, and Dean calls her back.

"Yes?"

"Since I don't expect to be talking with you again, there's one more thing I'd like to say."

This raises her hopes a little that Dean isn't going to let her leave feeling like crap. "Sure. What is it?"

"You've always treated me like I was stupid. Like the way you reminded me the day I got mauled about how I graduated two years behind our class."

"Well..." She tries to sound kind, and says softly, "It is a fact."

"Yeah. I know. But I thought you might like to know *why* that happened."

"Not doing the work, I assume."

He smiles softly and shakes his head at her, like he's about to run out of patience with her lack of insight. "A while back, I got tired of being told I was stupid, when I know in my heart I'm not. So, I saved up my money from what you reminded me is my minimum-wage job and paid for a psychiatrist in St. Louis to see me. He told me I have dyslexia—both as to letters and numbers, and that I have a very high IQ. He explained that the school should have caught it. They should've taught me coping mechanisms. He couldn't understand why my parents didn't insist I get the IEP I was entitled to. I explained to him that my mom ran off when I was little, and Dad never expected much from me anyway. So, I told the doctor how frustrated I'd been that no matter how hard I tried, the letters and numbers never made sense to me."

"Oh, my God, Dean."

"He said it was criminal it hadn't been identified. I'm telling you, the guy was pissed. Anyway, a couple of months before my accident, he got me set up with an expert at the community college. The guy works with me once a week, and it's already starting to help. The truth is, I was pretty darned excited about it. That's why I wanted to take you out to the concert. I wanted to tell you about what I was working on, since it was really good news for me."

Marietta's mouth hangs open. "I didn't know. I'm so sorry I said no, Dean. I'm thrilled for you that you finally got a diagnosis and a plan. That's wonderful news."

"Yeah. Well. I'm taking care of myself from now

on. I just wanted you to know."

"Thanks." She nods and starts to walk out the door, then thinks better of it. She steps back into the room and stations herself at the end of his bed.

"What is it now?" says Dean.

"You just said you don't expect to ever talk to me again. Then you gave me your perspective on everything."

"So?"

"So, I want to give you mine."

"Can I stop you?"

"I don't see how."

"Fine. What?"

"Okay. First of all, you really shouldn't judge me for assuming you were lazy in school since the entire faculty and staff thought the same thing. I'm sorry they let you down, but that's not really my fault."

"Mmm-hmm."

"Second, I'm only here because I would literally do anything to help my mom, whom I love very much. I realize it was stupid, but maybe if you had a mom you loved very much, you'd understand."

"Thanks for reminding me of that."

"Sorry. But I'm trying to be honest here. Third, that day when we were talking, you admitted you've asked me out literally hundreds of times. I wasn't just trying to set myself free by telling you the truth about my feelings, I was also trying to set you free. You can think what you want—"

"Thanks."

"But it really wasn't a normal reaction for you to walk into a tiger cage over it."

"Anything else?"

"Yes. I honestly don't understand how you can do this to my mom. She's always been kind to you and your dad. How can it not bother you to put her out of business? And the zoo is way more than a business for her. I think you know that. I'm not just ranting, Dean. I really want to know how you can do this to her."

Dean studies the ceiling for a few moments. "I do like your mom, Marietta. But I think my reasons are solid. See, your mom has the skills of being a business person. Plus, she can always teach again. She won't starve. You've got a job with benefits and shit. You plan to finish college and get a better one. And Kenny. Are you kidding me? She'll probably earn multiple degrees and be just fine. You know all this."

Marietta stares at him, determined to try to understand his thinking. "So?"

"I'll never catch up. I'm functionally illiterate, learning at age twenty-two what I should've learned in second grade. I was strong enough to get an okay job doing physical labor. I can't do anything now, and the doc says I'll probably never get back to where I was. Yeah. I live in my dad's house, but it's not my dream situation. Look, Marietta, you live with your mom because you're saving money to get your degree. I live with my dad because I can't afford anything else, and with what happened, I may never be able to. The bottom line is that I need the money, and your family doesn't."

She takes a moment to digest his points. "You don't know what you're talking about. Running our zoo isn't 'being a business person' to my mother. She worked at a zoo in Milwaukee from the time she was fifteen years old until she finished college because she loved it. Our zoo is a dream she spent the last twelve years making come true. She works day and night to be sure the animals are all well, and well-fed, and their enclosures are clean, and the bills are paid, and the families are all thrilled with their visits. I don't expect you to have thought about this, but the truth is, her zoo means something to people. My mom gets that. In a way, it's like my job. I always remind myself that the folks on my flight may be celebrating an anniversary, or on their way to a wedding—or a funeral."

"So what?"

"So a part of their experience is in my hands. Everybody wants a pleasant trip, with a friendly, competent, and kind flight attendant. Maybe in the big scheme of things, it's just a speck, but to my passenger taking her little girl on her first flight, it's a big deal. And the experience of a family zoo trip is a big deal to the parents, and the kids who've waited a year or more for a chance to visit. And it's a big deal to my mom that the children enjoy a special day and create a beautiful memory. People come up to her all the time to tell her how much our zoo meant to them when they were little. It's not just a business to her."

Dean looks down when he says, "I guess she could get a job at another zoo."

"Seriously? She doesn't have a degree in zoology. In fact, she has no formal training at all, just on-the-job and self-taught. And she's almost fifty-six years old. Plus, there aren't any other zoos around here. The St. Louis Zoo is over two hours away. And what kind of job do you think she could get there? Sweeping out the bathrooms?"

"Yeah. Well, I'm sorry about that. But if I don't go for the money, I'll be the one sweeping the bathrooms."

He looks away and says nothing more.

"Just think about it, Dean." Marietta sighs softly, walks out of the room, and quietly closes the bedroom door behind her.

She starts to drive home but has to pull over in an empty parking lot to try to get a grip. Her throat is dry and seems to be swelling up, and her face is on fire. She needs water but didn't think to bring any. She knows she should be relieved that Dean let her off the hook on the sex thing, but only embarrassment bubbles up. After doing slow breathing for a few minutes so she won't hyperventilate, she laughs out loud as she realizes that she's just outdone her sister's mortification. Slap-happy from lack of sleep and stress, she bursts into tears. She is also hungry. She drives to the nearest town's only drive-through coffee shop and orders black coffee and a donut. She parks and eats slowly, focusing on each bite—and nothing else.

Once home, she hurries up the stairs, showers to try to scrub off the tarnish, and lies down for a long nap. At this moment she needs sleep. She has the rest of her life to worry about what she was willing to do, how badly the schools failed Dean, and her abysmal failure to shame Dean into abandoning the claim above the $500,000 against her mother

****

On Monday morning the parties and lawyers are all present in the courtroom, ready to begin. Carolyn, Marietta, and Kenny are at the same table with Jackie as on Friday, while Dean is at the other, seated next to Hank. Judge Marcus takes the bench and Marietta's heart does a flip-flop. "Good morning, everyone," says the judge. "I'm afraid a criminal speedy trial matter has come up, so I won't begin jury selection in Alcott v. Warren until after lunch. One o'clock." Judge Marcus stands and leaves the bench, and Marietta is able to relax a little.

When it's finally time, twelve people, none of whom Marietta knows, walk into the courtroom and sit in the jury box. More people file in and sit in the general spectator seating section. The judge asks each of the ones in the jury box all kinds of questions. Then Hank does, and finally it's Jackie's turn. Both Hank and Jackie kind of preview their versions of the case in the questions they ask, which must be normal since the judge doesn't stop them. Some potential jurors are rejected "for cause," which Jackie explains means they have some kind of conflict of interest or prejudice that could keep them from being impartial. Some are rejected by "preemptory challenges," for which the lawyers don't have to give a reason. Each time one juror is dismissed, a new person walks up and takes the same spot in the jury box. By five p.m. twelve jurors, eight women and four men, are empaneled and told what their job entails.

On Tuesday, Judge Marcus again has other court stuff early in the morning, so opening statements don't start until ten a.m. Marietta has watched probably over a dozen trials on TV and in the movies, but none of that has prepared her for what she sees that week. Hank's opening statement makes her angry because he lies his ass off, like saying that her mother is careless in how she keeps Ms. Benni, and that Dean was just as reasonable as he could be to walk into a tiger enclosure because he'd heard that others did it before without getting hurt. Finally, he totally makes up a story about the fine professional modeling career Dean was just about to embark upon when the rug was pulled out from under him by evil Ms. Benni and irresponsible Carolyn Warren. He even mentions the kicking thing but says it was just a "little tap." It's hard for Marietta to believe that a jury could fall for that when Jackie has a video recording of Dean hauling off and walloping at Ms. Benni's head. His whole opening infuriates her.

Jackie's opening statement seems very factual, well organized, and easy to follow. It has the added virtue of being truthful. She talks about Marietta, and her mother, and Kenny, describes the zoo in some detail, and tells how Ms. Benni came to the family. She explains in a way anyone can understand what Dean has to prove. Then she tells the story of how Ms. Benni has always been a grudge tiger, and how Dean's decision to kick at her head was the cause of the injuries he sustained two weeks later. It was an intentional provocation, which is a complete defense. She ends by saying she's confident that after considering all the evidence, the jurors will arrive at a verdict of not guilty.

Looking around the courtroom, Marietta realizes what a show this will all be. Hank has shown up without his glasses, wearing contacts tinted blue…probably to match his three-piece suit. Dean has a fresh haircut and no facial stubble. He wears a crisp white shirt and pale blue tie under a gray summer-weight suit. Only his right arm is in the sleeve of the suit jacket, which hangs loosely over his left shoulder since his arm is in a sling. Marietta guesses he has nothing on under his shirt except his tan so he'll be able to display his body while giving the jury a good look at his upper arm. She didn't expect he'd wear swim trunks under his dress pants so the wound on his thigh can also be viewed by the jury. But that is what he does, right after the lawyers finish their opening statements, when Hank calls him as the first witness.

Jackie seems also to have dressed to play a part. She has on a gray skirt-suit and heels, and she's pulled her hair up in a bun. It's also the first time Marietta sees her wearing lipstick and mascara. Taking all this in, she begins to understand why Jackie asked her to plan to give her testimony on Thursday afternoon dressed in her navy and white flight attendant uniform. And she, Kenny and Carolyn are supposed to show up, every day, in something a person might wear to church. Apparently, lawyers squeeze every bit of credibility they can out of dressing their witnesses. Even Judge Marcus looks prettier somehow. She wears the same black robe, but she's done something with her mousy brown hair so it looks sleeker. Marietta suspects the judge could look even better if she would ever smile.

Of course, Ms. Benni's prior owner, Eugenia Wilcox, and Jackie's expert witness, Dr. Lucas, will be appearing only through the playing of their video-taped depositions, so however they looked when they were recorded is what the jury will see.

Opening statements take so long that the judge calls a comfort break right afterwards. Following that, she says the first witness will testify. At the rate it's going, Marietta fears the trial will take weeks. Dean lays on the charm like he's going out for the high school play— something he definitely didn't do. He lies about barely touching Ms. Benni with his kick and blames his decision to walk into the tiger cage on the day of the mauling on Marietta for saying something really mean to him. She thinks she manages not to grimace. He explains he'd heard of two times when others had entered Ms. Benni's enclosure, and he exaggerates how close they had gotten to the tiger. He says he also heard that Ms. Benni seemed bored about both intrusions. He tells the jury how Marietta said she'd never date him because he isn't even average, and how that broke his heart. He manages to produce tears during that bit of the testimony, which she suspects Hank might have suggested, but which might be genuine—but, she thinks, probably not. He claims he threw his cell phone out of pure frustration and humiliation, and that it never dawned on him that Ms. Benni might attack him.

Then Dean lays out his tale of woe about how sick he got and how his pain was almost unbearable. Finally, he earnestly explains in detail his plan for a modeling career, and how all of his dreams were dashed when he was scarred for life—literally. Once he finishes giving his testimony, Dean takes off his shirt and strips down to his swim trunks to display his injuries. Everyone can see that his body was rather perfect before the two slices were made. All of the jurors keep their eyes glued to Dean during his entire testimony, but when he strips to his swimwear, Marietta thinks the women may fall out of the jury box. None of them seems the least bit embarrassed to ogle him.

Jackie does a great job of cross-examining him, but Dean is able to control his temper and act calm when she exposes his lies and exaggerations. He just gives bullshit answers, then smiles kindly at her. Marietta truly believed that Dean "wasn't even average," but now she sees he's a darned good actor—another career he can claim he lost out on.

Jackie asks, "Isn't it true that you pushed Marietta

to tell you the truth, once and for all, about why she always said no to dating you?"

"Yes. I did ask her that."

"Isn't it true you're in love with her—that you've been in love with her for almost ten years—and that you persisted in pursuing her after she'd made it crystal clear that she didn't want to date you?"

Marietta sees where Jackie is going with this. She needs to exculpate Marietta for her comments to Dean so the jury won't take the whole thing out on her through Carolyn. But Jackie is opening up a can that Marietta filled with worms on Friday night. Marietta sits straight up in her chair at counsel table, her eyes glued to Dean. She wants him to look at her so she can use her eyes to implore him not to tell the world what she did, but he just looks at Jackie.

"Everything you said is true except one thing."

"What?"

Dean sighs. "I'm not in love with her anymore."

Marietta stares bullets into Jackie's back trying to beg her by mental telepathy not to ask, *"Why not?"*

"I see," Jackie says.

Of course, Dean easily could have blurted out what she offered to do in his bedroom, but he chose not to, and Marietta is grateful.

"Mr. Alcott, you say that when the accident happened, you were on the verge of embarking on a career as a model. Is that correct?"

"Yes, ma'am."

"Can you tell the ladies and gentlemen of the jury the names of a few of the agencies you planned to apply to?"

"No ma'am. I didn't get that far when the tiger

attacked me and ruined my chances."

Jackie presses on. "Before the accident, did you prepare a resume?"

"No ma'am."

"Did you have a head shot, or any other photo made to use with your applications?"

"No ma'am."

Jackie appears to smile kindly at Dean. "Can you tell us the name of one male model you admire?"

"No ma'am. See, I was just about to do all of that when I got mauled."

"But you finished high school two years before this and hadn't done any of these things by the date of the accident. Correct?"

"That's correct. I wasn't in a hurry. I was just getting around to it when I got hurt."

"Can you tell the jury one single thing you did that shows you really planned to go into that line of work?"

"I told Jimmy."

"In sixth grade. Correct?"

"Yes. That's right, ma'am."

Dean ends his answers on the subject by grinning kindly at Jackie. It's the only evidence he has—a dazzling smile. But Marietta worries that it could be enough.

Hank puts the treating doctor and then a plastic surgery expert on the stand to explain how horrendous Dean's injuries are, how many surgeries he'll likely still need, how painful it will all be, and how much it will probably cost.

Plaintiff's next witness is an effeminate man, oddly-dressed in a black form-fitting suit and yellow bow tie, who raves about what Dean's prospects for a big modeling career would have been and guarantees the jury that Dean easily could have commanded $100,000 a year once he moved to St. Louis or Chicago—and even more if he'd moved to New York. This relocation is what Dean earlier testified was his exact plan.

Hank calls Dean's buddy Jimmy to the stand to lie about how Dean told him it was his definite plan to move to a big city to go after a modeling career. That's the reason, according to Jimmy, that Dean still lives at home. He's saving up his money for the big move. Jimmy explains that he and Dean never mentioned it to anybody else because it was the kind of career the guys would've made fun of. Marietta thinks Jimmy seems to be blushing, but it may just be that the redhead's freckles pop under the fluorescent light. All of his answers sound mechanical and rehearsed to her.

Jackie cross-examines all of Hank's witnesses really well, but by the end of the day, Marietta feels like shooting herself. After court lets out, Jackie reminds them that trials always feel like a see-saw ride. After plaintiff's opening, you're down; after your own opening, you're back up; at the end of plaintiff's evidence, you're back down. But she says tomorrow, when the defense evidence will start to go in, they'll all feel good again. Marietta takes her word for it since she doesn't have the energy to analyze it. She craves nothing more than sleep, and she can tell that her mother is also flat-out exhausted from the ordeal.

Chapter 28

Kenny

Mr. Perdue finishes putting on his witnesses on Wednesday morning. The last guy he calls is an expert economist to talk about the value of all of Dean's economic claims. He explains in detail how Dean's injuries will cause him to lose a total of just over $3,000,000 for medical bills and all of the fabulous money he can no longer make as a model. And on top of that, the jury can award whatever they want for Dean's pain and suffering, disfigurement, and loss of some physical ability. This expert is incredibly boring, and Kenny assumes it's because he has a weird way of talking without any inflection—basically, like a computer. She'd nod off if the numbers he threw around weren't so terrifying.

Jackie tells the Warrens that the guy's projections are reasonable *if* the jury believes that Dean's future life would have included a high-paying modeling career. So she just makes a few points and corrections, and gets the witness to admit the lower number that represents lost earnings if the jury doesn't buy the bright future as a fashion model. She only spends a few minutes on it though. It seems to Kenny that Jackie is putting all of her energy into getting a verdict of "not guilty" because Carolyn can't afford either number the economist projected.

Right after Jackie finishes cross-examining the economist, Mr. Perdue says that the plaintiff rests. The two lawyers go back to the judge's chambers with her to argue some more motions, as Jackie told them in advance that they'd have to do right after Mr. Perdue finished putting on his witnesses. Apparently, whatever the rulings are don't change anything since Jackie starts putting on the defense witnesses as soon as they come back to the courtroom.

They all give their testimony that afternoon. Her mother and sister go before Kenny. They are allowed to remain in the courtroom during each other's time on the witness stand. Kenny assumes it's because each of them is testifying about her own visit into Ms. Benni's enclosure, so it isn't like hearing her mother or her sister testify will change Kenny's version. Of course, Jackie also has each of them tell the jury—at length—how Ms. Benni has always been a grudge tiger.

When it's Kenny's turn to testify, she is literally shaking as she walks up to the witness box. Worse, her right hand visibly trembles as she raises it to swear to tell the truth, and she worries the jury might think it's a sign she's a liar. First, Jackie asks her to tell a little bit about herself.

"My name is Kenna Warren, but everybody calls me Kenny. I'll be a senior this fall at Heartsville High School. Then I plan to attend college in Chicago or St. Louis. For the last ten years, I've helped with my mom's zoo whenever I'm not in school." She looks directly at the jurors and tries to make eye contact with each of them to create a bond. It doesn't work out that well, since most of them react by looking away or at their hands, so she abandons the strategy.

The next questions she gets from Jackie are all about the episodes when Ms. Benni showed she's a grudge tiger. Kenny's nerves are calming since she loves to talk about their tiger. Then she has to tell the story of how she went into Ms. Benni's cage on Becca's dare. She emphasizes how she only went in a couple of steps before she hurried back out.

Jackie agreed ahead of time that she'd save the hardest stuff for last. They hope Kenny will be so used to talking from the witness stand by then that she'll be relaxed enough to explain the whole thing about how and why she took videos of Dean on her phone.

Jackie asks, "Have you, on one or more occasions, used your cell phone to create a video recording of Dean Alcott?"

Kenny freezes. Jackie knew she'd be scared to death to talk about it, so she and Kenny rehearsed this part probably a half dozen times. Kenny also asked Becca to come to court to give her moral support, so Kenny looks for her friend in the visitors' area of the courtroom. Her eyes land on Becca, who does something Kenny's never seen her do before. She winks at Kenny—pretty dramatically. It looks so comic that Kenny almost bursts out laughing. She coughs to cover up the giggles and asks Jackie to repeat the question. Now that she feels human again, she's able to answer this question and all of the rest. Kenny explains how and why she recorded Dean, and describes the two days when she got videos of him and Ms. Benni together. Since she'd begged Jackie not to, their lawyer doesn't question Kenny about who she showed the videos to. But Jackie did prepare her for how to handle that one if Hank would go there during his cross-examination.

Kenny gets the impression the women jurors are looking at her sympathetically during her explanation of the whole business of recording Dean. Of course, this would be a logical reaction for them to have, now that they've also seen Dean shirtless—and trouserless.

When Mr. Perdue cross-examines her, he doesn't ask about her stories of Ms. Benni being a grudge tiger. More surprisingly, he doesn't go after her at all about why she recorded Dean. Best of all, even though he knows from her deposition that she shared the recordings with Becca, he doesn't even ask if she showed the videos to anybody. What he spends his time on is that Kenny once stepped inside Ms. Benni's cage and that she told Dean about it. Although Kenny didn't expect that to be his only focus, she knew it would be a main one because that's what he went after with her mother and Marietta when he grilled them. She assumes he's trying to make sure the jury doesn't think that Dean provoked Ms. Benni simply by going into her enclosure.

Kenny feels like the three of them did fine, and that it really isn't all that hard to give evidence if you just stick to answering each question truthfully, and if you have your best friend in the courtroom making faces at you. Jackie told them ahead of time just to be honest, and she'd deal with any "fall-out." Kenny just has to trust that Jackie can handle whatever harm the truth is causing to the defense of the zoo.

Jackie's last witness of the day is Charlie, who confirms the grudge tiger stories and what they all said happened on the day of the accident. He also explains how Dean was able to get the code to enter Ms. Benni's area. On cross-examination, Charlie says the same things

Dean did about the day they worked together to remove the tree limb while Ms. Benni was locked up in her holding pen, and he admits that he and Carolyn could've changed the code once they suspected Dean had it, but didn't do so. By the end of the day Wednesday, the Warrens are totally wiped out. When they arrive home, all three of them just hit their beds, knowing that the trial will probably end the next day. They also know their lives as zookeepers might end then too.

They don't need to get up early since the trial isn't scheduled to start until eleven o'clock. Apparently, Judge Marcus needs the courtroom again for other matters in the morning. At ten forty-five a.m. on Thursday, they walk into the courtroom wearing their last-day-of-the-trial, Sunday go-to-church clothes. Jackie tells them that the jury will be shown the video-taped depositions of Eugenia Wilcox and Dr. Lucas. Then both attorneys will spend time with the judge in her chambers to present more motions and to argue over what jury instructions should be given. All of this will happen before closing arguments. The word "closing" gives Kenny hope the nightmare will soon be over. The jury will decide if it also means the real nightmare is about to begin.

Jackie has already told them that they won't hear any objections when the video depositions are played for the jury because the judge will have ruled on any that either lawyer made, and a technician will have cut out anything the jury isn't supposed to hear. Jackie said the judge overruled all of Mr. Perdue's relevancy objections, saying that everything Dr. Lucas has to say about tigers goes to his credibility as a tiger expert, and she reminded Dean's lawyer that he had been free to hire his own tiger expert. Also, the judge denied all Hank's motions to strike portions of the testimony of the two witnesses as unresponsive, even though Jackie thinks Mr. Perdue actually should have won a couple of those.

Jackie's helpers set up a 60-inch TV facing the jury, a smaller one for the judge, and one for those sitting at the two counsel tables. After they all take their seats and the jurors are brought in and seated, Judge Marcus looks at Jackie. "You may proceed, Counsel." The constant drumbeat of phrases like "May I proceed?" "May it please the court," and "May I approach the bench?" throughout the trial remind Kenny of the game, *Mother, may I?*

"Thank you, your honor," Jackie says. "The defendant's next witness is Mrs. Eugenia Wilcox, by video deposition. Your honor, shall I explain to the jury or would you prefer to?"

"Go ahead, Counsel," the judge says.

Jackie tells the jury she will be playing the video-taped deposition of Mrs. Wilcox, how it came to be, and that any objections have already been dealt with. She presses a button on a remote, and Mrs. Wilcox's sweet face fills the screen.

Both Jackie and Mr. Perdue are with Mrs. Wilcox in a conference room at the assisted living place where Kenny and her mother met Ms. Benni's prior owner, but the camera stays on Mrs. Wilcox the whole time. Kenny likes that the videographer does a close-up first. She guesses there must be premium lighting in that room because Mrs. Wilcox looks prettier than when they met and Kenny showed her the video of Ms. Benni. She seems grandmotherly, but also like a fairy godmother. That part is probably wishful thinking. Her hair is as pure white as a new bar of soap, and it looks freshly cut and styled. It's so perfect that not a strand moves out of position as she gives her testimony. But as frozen in place as her hair is, her rosy face is just the opposite. She uses her light blue eyes and drawn-on eyebrows really expressively. Kenny gets the feeling Mrs. Wilcox might have wanted to be on TV her whole life, and this is her big shot at it. She has a way of smiling, really slowly and dramatically, like the smile is creeping up on her and she has to release it carefully so it doesn't burst out. Once it reaches full throttle, it's as dazzling as Jackie's, but not quite as big. Kenny doesn't think Mrs. Wilcox seems to be acting. It's just the opposite. She comes across as a sincere person who loves animals.

The witness is wearing a baby-blue cardigan, closed only at the very top with one large pearl button. Under it, she has on a blouse of the softest cream color, which has a kind of mock-turtleneck collar with delicate ivory lace embroidered along its edges. Kenny thinks the way it contrasts with her pink neck is really pretty. Her large pearl clip-on earrings kind of go with the button—like she made an effort to match everything. Mrs. Wilcox is one of those people who uses her hands to help her express her thoughts, at least when she's testifying for a trial. Once she's sworn in and has given her name and address, Jackie asks her a little bit about her life.

"You said that you live here at Belden Acres, an assisted living facility, and that you are retired. Correct?"

"Yes. That's correct."

"From what type of work did you retire, Mrs. Wilcox?"

"My husband and I founded a safari park—where families could drive through the grounds and see animals in open, natural habitat. Our customers' cars could stop along the way, and the animals would approach for food which the visitors could purchase at the beginning of their tour and carry with them. Camels and zebras and many others would stick their heads right in the vehicles, which was a huge treat for our guests." Mrs. Wilcox is animated as she speaks, as though she's making a TV ad for her business. "We called our park Animal Kingdom."

"When was that?" Jackie asks.

"My husband Jack and I opened the doors almost twenty-five years ago. We operated at full capacity—roughly fifty animals—for seventeen years. But then Jack had his first heart attack, about eight years ago now, and it was too much for us. Neither of our children wanted to take over the park, so we sold off our treasured animals and put that part of our property up for sale. Then Jack and I just enjoyed our retirement until he passed away—just a few months ago." Mrs. Wilcox bites her lower lip.

"I'm so sorry for your loss, Mrs. Wilcox." Jackie pauses to give space between her condolences and getting back on track to talk about Ms. Benni. "Did you at some point own a tiger cub, which is now named Ms. Benni, and now lives at the Warren Family Zoo?"

"We certainly did. We called her Tubbles because she was so slender for a cub, and my daughter thought it was a cute name and kind of funny. Jack and I sold her to Mrs. Warren eight years ago, when we were forced to sell off our animals."

"When did Tubbles first come to be a part of your safari park?"

Mrs. Wilcox chuckles. "We only had that silly girl for two years. We'd never really envisioned including a tiger as an attraction. Of course, a tiger couldn't roam among our customers' cars, or with the other animals for that matter." She throws her hands up at that idea, and Kenny hears a couple of jurors laugh. She assumes it's the reaction Mrs. Wilcox is going for.

Jackie says, "How did you come to own Tubbles?"

"That part was a sad story. A friend of ours, a woman we'd run into several times at seminars, called us one day. She said a family in the northwest part of the state had been running a very small family zoo. They had bred their female Bengal tiger but hadn't given her all of the care she required once she was pregnant. The tigress died a couple of days after delivering her two cubs, a male and a female. There is a wonderful tiger rescue zoo not far from that family, but the gentleman who runs it had reasons why it wasn't possible for him to take on the cubs. You see, hand-raising a tiger cub is a tremendous amount of work."

"So she contacted you?"

"Yes. She said she had a home for the male, if he reached eighteen months. But what she needed was someone to hand-raise the two cubs until then, and to keep the female if another home for her couldn't be found."

"Did you and your husband agree to those terms?"

"Our friend needed an answer immediately." Mrs. Wilcox again throws her hands up—which Kenny suspects must be one of her signature moves. "If we'd had time to think about it, we'd probably have said no. But once we agreed, we had those two babies the next day."

"What did their care require?" Jackie cocks her head, watching the TV screen, as though she's interested in tiger care.

"Well, as soon as we got off the phone, we ran around preparing a room for the cubs."

"A room in your house?"

"Oh my, yes. You see, Ms. Bauer, they were little, tiny babies. The male was the larger cub, and we called him Henry. Tubbles was only the size of a small house cat. Because they lost their mother so young, we had to do things like spray an antibiotic on their little umbilical cords every four to six hours until the things dried out and fell off. We also started out feeding them every two to three hours to get them established on the rubber nipples. Henry needed one quite a bit larger than the one Tubbles used. We had to place them on their tummies, on our laps, when we fed them to keep them from overeating. And it was very important that they be weighed every twenty-four hours, with the results phoned in to the vet. Those first few weeks of hand-raising are very precarious—and exhausting." Mrs. Wilcox shakes her head at the memory and then lets out one of her sweet, slow smiles.

"And did you say the two cubs were kept in your home this whole time?"

"Yes. Certainly. We had an extra guest room—with hardwood floors." She raises her eyebrows to be sure the jurors catch what she's saying. "Of course, we couldn't keep a diaper on a tiger. The truth is, when they're tiny, cubs have to be stimulated to urinate and defecate after each feeding. This is done by massaging, near their private parts, with a cotton ball just slightly wet with warm water. This is to replicate what the mother would naturally do." She chuckles. "Well, not with a cotton ball." She seems to wait, as though she knows the jury will laugh when they view the video, then she continues. "We also rubbed their little faces with a warm cloth to wake them up and be sure they took their food. In nature the mother would do these things with her tongue. Once they started solid food, we only had to do the cotton ball procedure once a day. By the time Henry was eight weeks old, he was able to do his business without help. It took Tubbles until she was ten weeks."

"Did both of the cubs develop well?" Jackie asks.

"They did. Once they started walking, they needed space to run and climb. Fortunately, we had a fenced-in back yard from when we'd had a dog. So we set it up with objects for the cubs to climb on that weren't too high above the ground—for safety."

"Did there come a time when the tigers could not be kept in your guest bedroom?"

"Of course, dear. What an odd question. Does anyone keep a grown tiger in a guest bedroom?" Mrs. Wilcox laughs, and Kenny realizes she's having fun giving the deposition. "I'm sorry, Ms. Bauer. That just struck my funny bone."

"That's quite all right. Let me rephrase the question. How old were Henry and Tubbles when they became too big to stay in your guest bedroom?"

"Seven weeks. Tubbles could've stayed longer, but Henry needed more space, and we wanted to keep them together."

"I see. Please tell us about Tubbles's personality, when she was still small enough to live in your home, and as she grew?" Jackie's voice is kind and encouraging.

"Normally, she was a very sweet little girl. But she developed a quality that really stood out."

"What was that?"

"Well, this may sound strange. But the truth is, she was a very vindictive little rascal when she was upset with us for some reason."

"Can you give the ladies and gentlemen of the jury some examples?"

"My, yes. The very first time was when Tubbles was just six weeks old. We were just weaning her from the bottle. I was thrilled that she took the solid food. I say that so you won't think she was angry because she was hungry. What happened was because she was furious, not famished. It was to be her first day with no bottle at all. Now, Henry had no problem with this and seemed to be quite pleased with the little meatballs bathed in formula. But Tubbles jumped off my lap and ran around the room, sniffing everywhere. We assumed she was looking for her bottle with the rubber nipple. When she finished poking around, she walked right up to where I was sitting and urinated on my foot. Then she slinked over to where Jack was feeding Henry and urinated on Jack's foot. We really didn't think it was accidental, but we wanted to give her the benefit of the doubt that first evening. But when this same pattern went on for almost a week, we realized that Tubbles was not only showing her anger, she was holding on to it. Not, I may say, a good quality for tigers—or humans. Thank goodness, she finally let that one go, and life went on."

"Can you give us other examples of Tubbles' 'vindictive' behavior?"

"Heavens yes. You see, it was just who she was. I guess the best way to say it is that it was part of her personality."

"Can you tell us about the next time you observed

this?"

"I certainly can." Mrs. Wilcox smiles.

"Then please tell us."

"Oh. I'm sorry, dear. But I remember you told me not to volunteer information beyond what the question calls for."

"That's right. You have a good memory. Now, please tell us about the next time you saw evidence of Tubbles' 'vindictive' behavior."

"The cubs were about three months old. Tubbles and Henry had a holding area just outside the backyard play area. We kept them in the holding pen before and after letting them go out and play. But while they were in there, they could see their play area through the wire mesh fence. They always kept their eyes focused on us as we cleaned up and filled their water bowls, etc. Well, we'd had the set-up I told you about, with the little structures for them to play on, for about six weeks. Jack and I decided it was time to rearrange everything to make it more interesting for the youngsters. We also took the opportunity to hide their favorite toys under piles of hay so they could have the adventure of finding their playthings. Once they were allowed in, dear little Henry was as playful as a puppy, running around and pawing and sniffing at things. He really seemed to be energized by the new arrangement, which is what we were hoping for. But Tubbles walked around the area slowly, with her tail sticking straight up. Then she came out with a young tiger's version of a roar. Finally, she walked around the play area and slowly and methodically sprayed urine over all of the play structures and the toys Henry had excavated." Mrs. Wilcox shakes her head. "Now, that could certainly be understandable behavior. But Tubbles did exactly the same thing every time we let her out to play—for two solid weeks. By that time, she'd made her point and she resumed playing with Henry."

"After that episode, were there any others you can tell us about?" Jackie quickly adds, "And please do."

"Definitely. As I've tried to convey, it was just the way Tubbles was. There were many little things she did along those lines. The next really big thing happened when the cubs were three months away from their second birthday. By that time, these were large cats, living in their own enclosure a few hundred feet past our backyard. Well, the time had come for Henry to be taken to his forever home at a well-regarded zoo in northern Illinois. By this time, he was much larger than Tubbles, and more aggressive. So even if he'd stayed at our park, the two of them would've been separated for her safety. We made sure that Tubbles saw Henry being taken away, into the traveling pen and onto the truck. We didn't want her to be wondering, looking around, thinking he might be somewhere at Animal Kingdom. Of course, since she's a tiger, we didn't know if she understood this or not. But, wherever she sensed he'd gone, she knew for sure he was no longer in her enclosure, and she was not happy about it. As it turned out, we only had her for an additional two and a half months before I had to start selling off animals following Jack's heart attack. Tubbles stayed angry with us for that entire period."

"What did she do that led you to think she was angry with you?"

"I didn't just think it." Mrs. Wilcox nods emphatically. "I knew it. First, she ripped to shreds all of the toys in her enclosure. She chewed up her watering tub. And every time Jack or I went near the enclosure, she'd back up so that her bottom was up against the fencing closest to us and urinate. I felt sorry for her, so I ordered new playthings. She ripped those up too. She was so put out with us for so long that I honestly wondered if she'd ever let it go."

"So it's your testimony that she stayed angry with you for two months?"

"Yes. She did." Mrs. Wilcox sighs, and Kenny expects the memories of all of this will make her cry. But the witness goes on, dry-eyed. "After Jack's heart attack, I found a home for her with Mr. and Mrs. Warren. I suppose it was a blessing in disguise for me that I had to let her go. I knew it was a chance for her to have a new start with a family she wasn't angry with—yet."

"Did you keep tabs on Tubbles after she left your care eight years ago?"

"No. I would've liked to. But there was so much work to do, placing all of our animals in good homes, and of course, caring for my husband."

"Thank you, Mrs. Wilcox. Those are all of the questions I have for you."

Jackie pauses the tape and asks Judge Marcus if she should go ahead and play Mr. Perdue's cross-examination, and the judge nods. Jackie presses a button on the remote, and it continues to be only lovely old Mrs. Wilcox on the screen. But now it's Mr. Perdue asking the questions. When he introduces himself, Kenny can tell he's putting on an act to sound friendly. Then he tries to make Mrs. Wilcox look bad.

"Mrs. Wilcox, you say you live at an assisted living facility. Correct?"

"Yes. I do."

"So, you require assistance to live?"

"What do you mean by that crack, young man?"

Mr. Perdue clears his throat. "I was just wondering whether one of the things you need assistance with is your memory?"

"No. It's not. If you must know, I had a hip replacement recently. I have trouble walking, especially with stairs."

"You testified that you cared for Tubbles starting ten years ago, for a period of two years. Is that correct?"

"Yes."

"That's a long time ago."

"Is that a question?" Mrs. Wilcox narrows one eye.

"It would be easy to forget things that happened eight to ten years ago, would it not?"

"If you are suggesting that I do not remember my time with Tubbles, you are mistaken. It was quite memorable."

"But you would agree, would you not, that you employed a lot of supposition in concluding that Tubbles was an especially vindictive tiger?"

"No. I would not agree. She was vindictive."

"Hmm. Well, let me put it this way. You are not a qualified expert on tiger behavior, are you, Mrs. Wilcox?"

"No. I'm just an expert on Tubbles. Furthermore, I believe that there is a gentleman from London who will address tiger behavior as a 'qualified expert.'" Mrs. Wilcox is clearly not a fan of Mr. Perdue, and Kenny assumes he isn't too happy that he's getting nowhere.

"There's something I've been wondering about during your testimony. How can you be sure that Tubbles and Ms. Benni are the same animal?"

Kenny thinks Mr. Perdue is letting himself in for

another scolding from the formidable Mrs. Wilcox, who purses her lips and wrinkles her forehead, as though she's trying to assess just how to deal with the moronic question. Then she takes a deep breath and the smile creeps across her face.

"Young man, I can assure you I am not an idiot. By the time I had to sell Tubbles, I had one, and only one, tiger. You'll have to take it on faith that any respectable woman knows at all times just how many tigers she owns." Mrs. Wilcox pauses. Kenny suspects their witness knows she needs to give the jurors time to laugh…which they all do. "Mrs. Warren has said that she only owned one tiger. You see my point—"

"All right."

"Excuse me, young man, but I hadn't completed my answer. In addition, all tigers have unique markings. This is common knowledge. I know what my tiger looks like. And then, just a couple of months ago, I got to see a video of Ms. Benni—the film where that terrible boy kicked at her head. That was my Tubbles. When I watched that video, the first thing I said was, 'that boy picked the wrong tiger to kick at.' When I was asked what I meant, I said, 'She has a vindictive character.'" Mrs. Wilcox looks almost regal as she tilts her head and raises her eyebrows slightly, as though to say, *"Take that, you impudent young man."*

The camera remains on Mrs. Wilcox as Mr. Perdue says one last thing. "I have no further questions. Thank you, Mrs. Wilcox." Now his voice is friendly again, as though he didn't just accuse the elderly woman of having a degenerated memory and not being able to recognize her own personal tiger. The last image of Mrs. Wilcox is of her slow-burn radiant smile. Kenny expects "the end" to appear and the credits to roll.

Kenny feels fantastic after that. All the jurors were totally engrossed in the stories of adorable Tubbles and her "vindictive character," as their genteel witness put it. She can't imagine how anyone can still doubt that Ms. Benni is, and always will be, a grudge tiger.

Kenny watches the jurors as much as she can throughout the trial. Because there are twelve of them, it's hard to keep track of all their reactions to the various witnesses who are paraded before them. It helps her to categorize them by their appearances, so she mentally lumps groups of them together. She sees them as five older women (three white, two black), three young women, and four overweight middle-aged white men. She realizes she's being sexist to only notice the weight problems of the men, but it's just how they strike her. They're all pretty much inscrutable when Dean's medical and economic experts testify. It isn't just impossible to know what the jurors think, Kenny can't even tell if they are paying attention, or possibly writing short stories in their heads, which she sometimes does during a boring sermon in church.

But when Dean testifies, several of the women looked *besotted*—a word from one of her ACT vocabulary lists. It's as though they are hanging on every word he speaks, some with motherly looks, others definitely not motherly. No foreheads wrinkle in reaction to anything he says, including during Jackie's cross-examination on the modeling career thing. The four men look just the opposite. If Kenny were to guess, she'd say that Dean's incredible attractiveness somehow threatens their manliness, and they aren't thrilled about it.

Then when Jimmy testifies right after Dean, several

of the women are visibly disappointed, pursing their lips and sighing and things like that. It's like they want the trial to be all Dean, all the time. Of course, he is sitting at the plaintiff's table with Mr. Perdue all day, every day. So they wouldn't be all that Dean-deprived if they would just take their eyes off whoever is testifying and shift them about five yards to the left. But everyone, including the judge, would notice if a juror didn't even look at the person giving evidence. How embarrassing it would be to get reprimanded by Judge Marcus, as in, *"Will the juror please pry your eyes off beautiful Dean and give at least a modicum of attention to the witness."*

Kenny thinks it's hard to believe that all the women like Dean, and none of the men do. But the thing about Dean is, he's not just handsome. It's more like he's a magnet to females. There's some kind of invisible force going on. It reminds her of what she read in a teen magazine about the star of that Caribbean pirate series— how teen girls, their moms, and their grandmas all liked him.

The jury reacts to her mother and Charlie by paying attention. Kenny assumes they want to be respectful since those two witnesses are clearly respectable adults who answer all the questions put to them in a direct way. Marietta is a different story. It's basically a variation on the reaction the jurors had to Dean, in that a couple of the men seem to be besotted, and the younger women appear to eye her suspiciously. However, the five older women don't seem to care that she's beautiful, and they just pay attention with neutral looks on their faces.

Chapter 29

Kenny

Jackie told them it was Dr. Lucas's testimony that would make or break the grudge tiger defense. She decided to have his video played next, as the last witness of the trial. With the judge's permission, Jackie introduces the video to the jury and presses "play." When Dr. Lucas's face fills the screen, it instantly brings back all Kenny's memories of the magical trip, but she forces herself to put it out of her mind and focus on the trial.

Then the videographer lets up on the zoom, so the viewers can see Dr. Lucas's whole upper body above the table. Of course, he is dressed in the navy jacket, pale blue shirt, and a navy tie with tiny yellow dots that she saw him wearing in London. Kenny thinks it's very savvy of him to look right at the camera, as though he's telling that inanimate object a story. Then again, it's probably something Jackie suggested. It works. He's looking directly at the jury. His hands are folded and resting on the table. The first thing they hear is Dr. Lucas being sworn in to tell the truth. Then Jackie speaks from off-camera.

"Please state your name and occupation and describe your educational background."

"My name is Dr. Nigel Lucas. I study tigers." He is smiling, and his blue eyes shine so brightly, they almost seem to glow, the way a cat's do when it is caught in the light after dark. "I earned my undergraduate degree at Oxford—in England. Then I worked for a nature conservancy in London for a couple of years. We supported tiger preservation efforts around the world. I went on to earn my masters and my doctorate in wild animal studies from a university in India, the Indian Technical Institute. The reason I did my post-graduate work in India is—well, that's where the tigers are." Dr. Lucas smiles again and looks very relaxed and confident.

"I'm now working with another nature conservancy group, also here in London. In addition, I grew up a zookeeper's son, just outside Malvern, England. So I worked at a family zoo, rather like the Warren's, from when I was a chap just big enough to hold a broom until I left for university at eighteen. Over those fourteen-odd years I tended to the animals at our zoo, I had the pleasure of taking care of eight different tigers. We had such a large number because our zoo acted as the tiger rescue in that part of the country. I learned the tigers' behaviors, their likes and dislikes, and their personalities. Only one of our eight, Tony, was a revenge tiger—a grudge tiger." At this point, Dr. Lucas definitely has the jury's attention. Kenny thinks most people would enjoy watching a nature documentary on tigers presented by a handsome scientist.

"Thank you, Dr. Lucas, we'll get back to Tony later. Now, can you tell the jury whether you are being paid for your time, or receiving any money or other compensation whatsoever for being here to testify today?"

"No. I'm not being paid, or receiving any other compensation to give my testimony."

"Please provide the jury with an overview of tigers."

"The scientific name is Panthera Tigris. The genus, Panthera, includes only lions, tigers, leopards, and jaguars. You see, they all roar. Actually, the reason these four mammals can roar is that they have thickened folds below their vocal cords. Vibrations of those folds produce the roar, which is so terrifying to other wildlife that it can actually paralyze them."

He leans forward as he speaks, as though he's telling each juror something very important—information they'll want to focus on and remember. "Tigers are, by far, the largest member of the cat family. The word 'Tigris' denotes the species. Of course, there are subspecies of tigers. Sadly, three of the nine subspecies are already extinct. They will never again walk our planet. Also, one of the remaining six sub-species is already extinct in the wild. That one, the South Chinese, as well as the five other remaining subspecies, are all endangered. These include the Bengal. I hesitate to get ahead of myself, but you may wish to know that Ms. Benni is a pure-bred Bengal." Dr. Lucas grimaces. "It pains me to say it, but in the early 1900s, there were 100,000 tigers throughout their range. Today, only 3,000 to 4,500 still exist in the wild. Of these, the Bengal is the most numerous, at probably 2,500.

"There are two main reasons for the loss of our wild tigers. First is simply that human development efforts which haven't taken the tigers' habitat into consideration have left the animals with small and scattered spaces for their territories. But the more serious immediate threat is the illegal wildlife trade. The poached tigers are killed and used for status symbols, decorative items including clothing, and traditional medicinal cures. Their paws and penises are especially valued, and tiger bones can sell for over $115 a pound. India, in particular, has done a good job in attempting to protect the species from extinction. Closer monitoring using new technology, and stricter wildlife policies are succeeding at keeping the species alive in that country. Approximately 2,500 tigers, many of them Bengals, roam the dedicated preserves in India today. That's more than half of all of the world's tigers in the wild." He's spilling out a lot of details, but Dr. Lucas still has the jurors' attention.

"Just so that you know the whole picture, I must tell you that approximately 12,000 tigers, most of them hybrids, are kept as private pets in backyard enclosures in the U.S. alone. Just in the state of Texas, there are approximately 4,000." He frowns. "Their situation is typically not like the way well-treated zoo animals are kept. Hundreds of these 'backyard tigers,' " Dr. Lucas makes air-quotes, "have attacked and killed or seriously injured humans as a result of the way they were kept, transferred or handled outside of cages." He stops talking for a moment.

Jackie speaks, but the camera stays on Dr. Lucas.

"Dr. Lucas, can you tell us a bit about the qualities of a tiger?"

He is obviously ready for any question she can think of to throw at him. "Certainly. The appearance of the tiger is quite stunning. Truly majestic." He nods his head for emphasis. "They have thick, reddish-orange coats, white bellies, and white and black tails. They are covered with black or dark brown stripes. A bald tiger, if there were such a thing, actually would have striped skin— rather like tattoos. " He smiles, then pauses, looking like he's pulling more tiger facts to the front of his brain.

There is no way the jury can be missing that this man knows everything about tigers. But Jackie keeps pumping interesting facts out of him. Any time he slows down, she throws out another question.

"Generally speaking, a tiger is three and a half feet across at his heavily muscled shoulders, and six to seven feet in length with a three-foot-long tail. The average weight of a female is 300 pounds, and a male is 400 to 450 pounds. However, a male can weigh as much as 600 pounds."

The jury seems riveted, all eyes glued to the television.

"Its talons are two inches to four inches in length on the front feet, but not quite as long on the back feet. The front claws are basically two to four-inch hooks on the outer curve, as sharp as sewing needles at the ends, and with knife-like blades along a bit of the inside curve. The massive forepaws have five claws, in a shape like your winter mitten. A tiger goes after a foe or prey with these paws. Interestingly, the most important use of the front paws isn't to rip into or bat at an opponent. Rather, it's to dig into flesh and secure the tiger's purchase, like with anchors, so that the victim can't escape. The truth is, because of the tiger's strength, proficiency, and versatility, he can basically kill whomever he chooses. Also, a tiger can tolerate almost any domain, and has thrived in 100-degree jungles, as well as in minus 50-degree forests.

"In addition to these qualities, a tiger is quite agile, able to spring twenty feet or so in a single leap." Dr. Lucas motions a quick springing action with his hand. "The tiger normally withdraws his claws to walk and takes three-foot steps. His four canine teeth can bite through extremely dense bone. The combination of all of this allows him to kill animals that are much larger.

"The tiger also has excellent eyesight. His large, deep-green or gold eyes, like your house cat's, appear to glow when reflecting electric light in a dark area. Unlike household cats, tigers enjoy bathing and swimming, and can hunt quite well while also taking a dip. But on terra firma, a tiger hunts using his eyes, ears, and nose. Although his sight and hearing are exceptionally keen, it was debated for some time whether a tiger also uses his sense of smell. He does. However, the tiger rarely needs to rely on smell, since his sight is so…" Dr. Lucas smiles before he finishes the sentence. "Outstanding."

"Finally, a tiger has a number of ways to vocalize. The most famous is the thunderous roar, which means exactly what you would think: *'I'm in charge. I'm warning you! Stay out of my way, you lesser being.'* A low moan is actually the most frequent sound to come out of a tiger. Think of it like the sound of a long human yawn. The tiger uses it in the wild to warn other animals of his arrival. The moan can also signal contentment, the way you might sigh as you sit down on a lounge chair in the sun. In captivity, the moan has been heard as one tiger approaches another with whom he is familiar, or a human that he knows is kind toward him. You also may have heard of chuffing. That sound is a bit like a low version of a human's gargling, or like the sound you make when you clear your throat of phlegm. The tiger creates the sound by keeping his mouth closed, and quickly pushing air out through his nostrils." Dr. Lucas imitates the sound with a quick release of air from his nose. It surprises Kenny that he manages to look dignified while doing it. He continues, "It's a happy sound, which a tiger in captivity frequently makes to greet a human he knows."

Kenny starts to worry that it might be too much information for the attention span of the jurors. But from what she can see, their reaction is just the opposite. Some of the jurors are leaning forward in their seats. Others rest their chins on their hands, eyes glued to the screen. All of them seem to have gotten caught up in Dr. Lucas's enthusiasm about all of the tiger facts.

Jackie says, "Please tell the jury about tiger reproduction and development." Kenny can tell that Dr. Lucas smiles at Jackie, although, since she is off-screen, she can't tell if Jackie smiles back.

"The tiger has a lifespan of ten to fifteen years in the wild and roughly double that, up to twenty-five years, in captivity. Bengals, in particular, are thought to live eight to ten years in the wild, with a fifteen-year maximum, and eighteen to twenty years in captivity, with a maximum of twenty-five years. Of course, their success in captivity is due to safety, food supply, and medical care. The sad truth is, in the wild, approximately half of all tiger cubs don't survive past the age of two. And only forty percent of those reach independence such that they can establish a territory and procreate.

"A tiger reaches sexual maturity between three and four years of age. Females are 'induced ovulators,' which means that they don't release eggs until mating takes place."

Kenny makes a mental note to think more about this later.

"Gestation is 103 days—almost three and a half months. A female can give birth to as many as seven cubs, but the average is between two and four. Until around two months of age, the cubs stay hidden away with the tigress. Then they venture out of the den with her for their first look at the world. She trains them to hunt, and they become independent at it by around eighteen months. They all leave her at two to two-and-a-half years of age and go off to establish their own territories and do their own hunting. She is then ready to have more cubs. A cub continues to grow until it is around five years old." Dr. Lucas's voice slows down, so Jackie comes up with another question.

"And their diet? Can you tell the jury about that?"

Of course he can! This dude is a tiger encyclopedia. Watching Dr. Lucas show off his knowledge and love of tigers is making Kenny very happy. She thinks it's obvious what Jackie is doing. First, she'll absolutely convince the jury that Dr. Lucas lives and breathes tigers. Then, she'll get into his opinion about Ms. Benni being a grudge tiger. The whole process is starting to appeal to her. She'll add trial lawyer to her list of possible careers.

"You may have heard that tigers are carnivores. Their primary food certainly is meat. But experience has shown us that they are technically omnivores. In the wild, they eat mainly deer, wild pigs, water buffalo, antelope and boar, but they've also eaten sloths, bears, dogs, leopards, crocodiles, pythons, monkeys, fish, turtles, frogs, scorpions, tortoises, large lizards and rabbits. A tiger in the wild can eat as much as seventy-five pounds of food in one night. But then, he may not eat again for several days. The simple form of the tiger's stomach and short intestine allow for the easy digestion of the flesh of other animals.

"If, however, a tiger is hungry and none of those meats is available, he will eat fruit, berries, nuts, and, on occasion, cow dung. The truth is, if he is hungry enough, he'll eat grass. And, because the tiger, especially the male, is generally an intensely territorial being, he hunts alone, and does not share what he kills."

Jackie seems to be picking up the pace of throwing in new questions. "What about humans, Dr. Lucas? Are we one of the meats a tiger would pursue?"

Dr. Lucas sighs. "Ah. The man-eaters." He pauses for a moment to think. "What you have to understand is that a tiger will almost never attack a human as a food source unless he cannot satisfy his need to eat in any other way. Typically, a man-eating tiger is old, infirm, seriously injured, or missing teeth to the extent that he cannot satisfy his hunger with his traditional prey. And you must also keep in mind that most tigers who show any evidence of interest in human flesh are eventually captured or killed."

"Are they intelligent animals?" Jackie's voice comes across as sincerely curious.

"Well, let's start with the tangible bit. The tiger's brain is at least sixteen percent larger than that of a lion. Certainly, with a bigger brain, the tiger has the structural capacity to have a higher IQ than other species. And there is no dispute that tigers are quite clever when hunting. They never bolt precipitously after prey. They wait and they watch. Then they wait and watch some more. Still, they are successful only a small percentage of the time because the prey is also alert.

"Consider the tiger's interactions with humans. A common question is: if one encounters a tiger in the wild, is it better to look away or to maintain eye contact? The answer is to look the menacing creature right in the eye—if you can work up the nerve—and slowly back away. You don't want to appear threatening to him. So, when he takes a step, you take a step, he takes a step, you take a step, and so on. You see, stealth is the tiger's primary tool of the trade. He relies on the element of surprise. If your courage remains screwed to the sticking place, you can rob him of that element, and he'll most likely not attack you."

The jurors still seem to be interested in all of the facts spilling out of Dr. Lucas, and they are probably glad they won't be quizzed on it later. The fact that his face is on a TV screen might be helping to keep the jurors absorbed. It's something people are used to doing—staring at an attractive person on a screen for entertainment.

Jackie resumes her questions. "Where are tigers found in natural settings?"

"Today, wild tigers can be found in India, China, Russia, and Southeast Asia. There have never been any in Africa. Bengals, specifically, are found in India, Nepal, Bangladesh and Bhutan. But the vast majority of Bengals call India home."

"Dr. Lucas, please now tell the jury about tigers in captivity."

"Of course. First of all, you should know that tigers are one of the wild animal species that flourish and thrive very well in captivity. Tigers in zoos typically are fed mainly ground beef, and their diet is supplemented with enrichment items each week. They often receive parts of deer, cow femurs and knucklebones, and rabbits to keep their jaws strong and their teeth healthy. They must receive ten to twenty pounds of raw meat each day. Many zookeepers find it beneficial for the animal to fast one day in seven. On that day, it receives raw eggs beaten up in milk, or some other high-protein food. Also, tigresses breed freely in captivity, and breeding efforts with Bengals have been particularly successful.

"So, captivity works out very well for most tigers, especially Bengals, as I have said. But it is a one-way street." Dr. Lucas leans in and speaks emphatically. "Once habituated to zoo conditions, there's no going back. I know of no case of a captive tiger being successfully reintroduced into the wild. Tigers that were born and raised in captivity have no idea how to correctly tackle large prey, even as adults. Well-intentioned people continue to attempt it, but the process puts the animal at a great disadvantage in the wild."

"What is a tiger enclosure like at a typical zoo?" Jackie asks, again sounding like a student asking her professor about something she really wants to know.

"As you would probably imagine, there is a wide range, from vast and well-provisioned with things a tiger finds interesting, to small and wholly inadequate for him to thrive."

"Where does the Warren Family Zoo fit in that range?" *Here it is.* With all the build-up behind her, Jackie is getting to the heart of the case.

"I cannot comment on the entire zoo, as I have focused only on the tiger, Ms. Benni." For the first time, Dr. Lucas takes a long swallow from a glass of water, then clears his throat and continues. "I've reviewed the architectural plans, photographs, videos, and Mrs. Warren's deposition testimony describing the layout. The zoo, as a whole, is not an AZA accredited zoo—nor does it need to be. By the way, AZA simply stands for Association of Zoos and Aquariums. But Mrs. Warren has chosen to try to follow all of the AZA recommendations for the tiger. As a result, Ms. Benni's enclosure is quite large, measuring almost 22,000 square feet.

"It is complex, including a large mature shade tree near its center, and natural grasses throughout. There is a sizable water pond, sloping to a maximum depth of three feet, and also several boulders for architectural interest and to provide a variety of terrains for the animal. The boulders also allow Ms. Benni to withdraw from public view, while still being visible to the zookeepers from their private viewing areas.

"There's a large, elevated wooden exercise platform on one side of the enclosure for Ms. Benni to climb, jump, and play. The platform and ramps are stacked in such a manner that Ms. Benni can always be monitored by the zookeepers. She also has a separate sleeping platform. The substrate in the enclosure is natural soil, which Mrs. Warren replaces in its entirety every two years. The area is cleaned of Ms. Benni's scat every day, and her pool is emptied and cleaned once a week." He smiles. "As I learned as a little chap, much of the art of zookeeping is cleaning up animal poop."

Some of the jurors laugh.

"There is a generous twelve-by-twenty-four-foot shift enclosure where Ms. Benni stays while her exhibit enclosure is being cleaned. Her indoor area, where she can escape the weather, is also roomy, measuring thirty feet square. Its concrete floor has an asphalt coating to soften it, and it is outfitted with another sleeping ledge. Separate from her pool, she has watering stations in the exhibit enclosure, the shift enclosure, and her indoor space." He concludes by nodding his approval.

"Dr. Lucas, please describe any safety features. Specifically, what keeps Ms. Benni inside, and zoo visitors out?"

"All of Ms. Benni's containment area walls are made of welded wire mesh of suitable gauge. The exterior walls are twenty feet high—far in excess of the AZA recommendation of fourteen feet. They are topped with a three-foot overhang of wire mesh—inward facing on the tiger's side at a forty-five-degree angle. Cantilevered supports are also used because the top of the enclosure is open. At the public viewing area, Mrs. Warren has erected a forty-five-inch-high plate of tempered glass, which is situated ten feet from the tiger's enclosure. This is actually better than a wider wall, because parents aren't tempted to set their children on the slim top, and it is less likely a child will try to climb it since there is no place to get a foothold. There are also appropriate warning signs around the tiger's enclosure." Dr. Lucas smiles, and adds, "All of this is very well thought out."

"Please tell the jury about the doors to Ms. Benni's enclosure."

"There are four doors, or sets of double doors, in total. One door is into the shift enclosure, one is to allow Ms. Benni to enter her indoor shelter area, one is for the zookeeper to enter the anteroom of the indoor shelter, and the last is a set of double doors for the zookeeper to enter the large exhibition enclosure which I described in detail earlier. All the doors are controlled by heavy-duty electronic keypads, which are faster to use than old-fashioned metal keys. All of the keypads for the tiger enclosure are coded alike, and the code is different from the one which operates all the other cages at the zoo. There is also an exterior universal lock-down button for emergencies which activates all the locks at the same time. The doors to the shift enclosure and the tiger's indoor area are sliding types. They are also operated by the keypads and have secure and easily checked locks. They can also be reinforced with traditional padlocks, which are present and are used."

Jackie says, "Let's focus on the configuration and safety features of the doors through which Dean Alcott entered Ms. Benni's enclosure on June 24, 2019. Can you please describe that in detail for the jury?" It looks to Kenny like no juror is missing a thing as Jackie gets into the critical facts she needs to prove to save the zoo.

"Certainly. Because I have seen the video recording of Mr. Alcott entering the tiger enclosure, there is no dispute that he entered directly through the zookeeper's double-door access. Of course, before that, he hopped over the forty-five-inch tempered glass viewing-area wall and walked ten feet up to the enclosure. Then he approached the first of the two doors made of welded wire mesh. He had to use his hand to enter the four-digit code into the keypad, which was at chest height adjacent to the first door.

"By the way, this is the code Mr. Alcott learned by looking over Charlie Russell's shoulder as Mr. Russell pressed the buttons on an earlier occasion. Then Mr. Alcott walked through that door, which closed automatically behind him, and turned ninety degrees to walk up to the second door, approximately eight feet beyond the first. He had to, again, enter the four-digit code into the keypad so that he could open the door. That door also automatically closed behind him. All of these features—the use of two doors, each requiring digital unlocking, the ninety-degree turn, and the automatic shutting of the doors—are safety features. No one will be able to enter that enclosure accidentally or mindlessly. Two affirmative demonstrations of the desire to enter are required." The witness emphasizes the last sentence as though he considers it especially important.

"Dr. Lucas, in your opinion, were these appropriate and adequate safety measures for an enclosure containing a Bengal tiger?"

"They certainly were." He speaks slowly and authoritatively. Kenny suspects that Dr. Lucas realizes they are moving into the critical part of his testimony and wants to make sure the jurors pay attention. "All of the safety measures were appropriate, and in the aggregate, were more than adequate. And, of course, all of them worked. Ms. Benni never escaped."

"Once Mr. Alcott had been attacked and sought to exit the enclosure, did the structure impede him at all?"

"No. Zoo employee Charlie Russell said he ran to the enclosure the moment he heard Kenny Warren's scream. The zoo did safety drills every six months. By the way, AZA only requires them once a year. Mr. Russell was through both doors quickly due to the efficient digital locks, and he was able to pull Mr. Alcott through the door closest to the tiger. The door automatically shut, so Ms. Benni was left behind on the other side. It was also a quick matter for Mr. Russell to carry Mr. Alcott the rest of the way through the double-door set-up. Again, this was due to the ease of use of the digital system. Also, although Mr. Alcott wasn't in a position to attempt it, the digital pads would've allowed him to make a speedier exit than would a traditional metal key."

"Let's back up for a moment. Dr. Lucas, let me ask you this. Was it reasonable for Mr. Alcott to have entered

Ms. Benni's enclosure?"

"Of course not. No one should ever be in a tiger enclosure *with* a tiger." Dr. Lucas lowers his chin a bit, then nods as if to underscore what he's about to say.

Jackie says, "You've read all of the deposition transcripts from this case, have you not?"

"Yes. And reread."

"Then you know that all three of the Warren women have, each on a single occasion, and each for a different reason, either briefly entered Ms. Benni's enclosure, or stood in the doorway into her enclosure, while she was present?"

"Yes. I'm aware of that."

"Was it reasonable for any of them to have done that?"

"No." Dr. Lucas frowns.

"Why not?"

"Because a tiger is a wild animal. It cannot be domesticated. No amount of bonding with a cute tiger cub can erase that fact. It is common knowledge that a tiger is a deadly animal. It is never reasonable for anyone to enter a tiger enclosure when the tiger is present."

"Then, how do you explain the fact that Mrs. Warren and both of her daughters were able to do just that, without incident?"

He pauses and purses his lips before he speaks, as though considering how best to explain. "Allow me to offer an analogy. I assume that everyone is familiar with the game of dice."

Most of the jurors nod at the TV screen.

"Let's say you are given a single die. You are told that if you roll a one, two, three, four, or five, you will live. But, if you roll a six, you will die. You could certainly roll a number of ones through fives. But if you keep at it, you will eventually roll a six—and you will die. I hope I make myself clear. They were lucky. They might get lucky again. But it is not reasonable for them to take the chance. Now, let me put it in terms of a true story. You may have heard of a famous Las Vegas tiger act. In 2003, one of the performers was mauled, bitten on the neck, and dragged across the stage during a live performance. Consider this: the seven-year-old tiger that attacked him had been performing in the show with the same man since it was six months old." By raising his eyebrows a smidge, Dr. Lucas seems to ask if the jurors follow.

"Thank you, Dr. Lucas. Now, would you tell the ladies and gentlemen of the jury what a grudge tiger is?" The expert's believability on the next questions will determine the zoo's fate. Kenny bites her lower lip and begins to perspire.

"Of course. A grudge tiger is simply another name for a revenge tiger. It has been well-documented in the scientific literature that certain tigers have taken revenge on humans who have injured them, have attempted to injure them, or have taken some or all of the tiger's kill for themselves. Not all tigers have this propensity. You see, there is really no such thing as *the tiger*. Like humans, every tiger is an individual with its own personality. Perhaps you know someone, a relative even, who holds onto grudges. A personality like this may generally see revenge as his right. Obviously, not all people are like this. It is simply the disposition of some percentage of humans to seek this kind of justice—to court revenge. To hold onto a grudge. This is nothing new, of course. Recall the biblical story of Jacob and

Esau, or the Capulets and the Montagues, the Hatfields and the McCoys, or the Jets and the Sharks, for that matter. It is the same with tigers."

"Can you tell us what you've learned about grudge tigers in the wild?"

"Yes. In the documented grudge tiger cases, the victim of the attack had harmed or attempted to harm the tiger in some way, at some time prior to the attack. There are cases where a hunter had shot and wounded the animal; cases where the hunter had shot at the animal but missed it; and several situations where the hunter had come upon the tiger's kill and commandeered part or all of it for himself. And there was one situation in which a poacher had taken a tiger cub. The result was the same in each. Over time—generally ranging from one day to more than three weeks, but in one case, a whole year—the tiger had watched and waited, tracked and re-tracked, made attempts and backed down to await another day, a better opportunity. Often the tiger passed by other humans, and other humans' lodgings, to get to the object of his revenge. When the tiger attacked, he made it clear the motive had been revenge. You see, the victims were often sliced and diced. Their possessions were scattered. But, generally, these tigers did not eat the flesh of their victims. In addition, almost none of these wild tigers was, or became, a man-eater. They weren't hungry." He pauses for emphasis. "They were angry.

Before all of Dr. Lucas's testimony, Kenny never in her life thought so highly of tigers. From the looks on the jurors' faces, she's sure they are also learning a lot, and they seem to be enjoying it.

"Are there examples of grudge tigers in captivity?"

Dr. Lucas nods. "Indeed. I had the opportunity to get

to know a grudge tiger personally. I was twelve years old and keenly interested in tiger behavior when I first met him. Our zoo took in a five-year-old white tiger called Tony. He'd been raised by a family after they'd purchased him as a cub from an unscrupulous breeder in the north of the country. Tony had grown into a mammoth animal, almost 550 pounds, and the family could no longer afford to feed him, or feel confident that their back-yard enclosure was safe. I was assigned to tend to Tony—to feed him, clean his cage, and maintain the required records on him. I continued with this until I left home for university at age eighteen. Of course, I was supervised in all of this.

"Tony's personality quirk manifested itself right away. The man who delivered Tony was a professional animal transporter. I don't know what happened to Tony between leaving his old home and arriving at our zoo, but every time the man walked by Tony's new enclosure, I saw Tony paw the ground and make a low growling sound, with his ears flattened against his head. When the man finally drove off, Tony calmed down and explored his new environment. It struck me at the time that our new tiger had a bone to pick with the transporter."

Dr. Lucas gives a little nod. "His grudge behavior was not a one-time affair. In the years I was responsible for much of Tony's care, I saw numerous examples of his propensity to hold grudges. I'll give you just a couple of additional examples of what I'm talking about. And I must emphasize, it became clear to me that it wasn't just a behavior, but an integral piece of who Tony was. The next significant event occurred upon the second appearance of our large animal veterinarian at Tony's enclosure. You see, within a month of acquiring Tony, we had him examined by the veterinarian who attended to our animals. The man was, of course, quite familiar with large felids. Tony had been kept quarantined from the other tigers for just over his first month with us, which was standard procedure when we brought a new animal in. It was in the middle of that first month that Tony was scheduled for his initial medical and dental evaluation.

"Unfortunately, our new tiger had never been trained for hand injection, so it was necessary for the veterinarian to shoot a dart into him to administer the chemical anesthetics. As the dart hit Tony, he immediately turned to glare at the doctor. Once Tony was safely unconscious, the veterinarian did a thorough examination. Of course, like your average two-year-old child, Tony had no way to appreciate that the doctor visit was for his good. In fact, he slept through the examination, so his only conscious experience with that veterinarian was getting shot in the rump.

"A younger veterinarian from the same practice did the monthly rounds, so Tony didn't see the man who'd shot him with the dart for a full year. But when that older man arrived at Tony's enclosure—after a year—Tony actually rushed at him. He sprang right into the side of his enclosure." Dr. Lucas holds up one hand, then smashes at it with the other. "You see, he had a long memory when it came to people who injured him.

"The next major incident was a couple of years after that. Tony was in his shift enclosure so I could clean out his large exhibition area, as I did every day. But on this particular day, I'd been told to empty his swimming pool and clean it thoroughly. It needed to completely dry out before being recoated with an epoxy designed to keep it from becoming slippery. Tony kept his eyes on me, as he always did. Once he was transferred back into the large enclosure, he seemed puzzled. He strode up to the dry pool and put one huge paw in after the other. He even lay down briefly on the damp bottom. Then he jumped out and bellowed an earth-shaking roar. I was standing just outside his enclosure, and he had his eyes riveted to me. Of course, I immediately understood that he was angry with me for stealing his bath. He reacted to me this way—ferociously—the next day, and the day after. My parents reassigned me elsewhere, and Tony was calm when a different attendant cleaned his enclosure.

"It was over two weeks later that I was again in his vicinity. I was simply walking by, probably fifteen yards from him, and it happened again. The identical reaction as before, complete with the pawing at the ground and the deep, full-throated roar. It wasn't until another week had passed, and a crew had refinished and re-filled the pool, that I could be near Tony. Things were finally back to the way they'd been before I'd foolishly drained his tub while he could see me." Dr. Lucas shakes his head and smiles ruefully at reliving the episode.

Kenny can't imagine how anyone could possibly still doubt the grudge tiger theory.

"Dr. Lucas, do you have an opinion, to a reasonable degree of scientific certainty, as to whether Ms. Benni is a grudge tiger?"

"I do."

"What is your opinion?"

"It is my opinion, to a reasonable degree of scientific certainty, that Ms. Benni is a grudge tiger." He speaks slowly—authoritatively

"Upon what do you base your conclusion?"

"Everything I've studied points to this conclusion. The testimony of Mrs. Wilcox amply demonstrates that Ms. Benni had the personality and behavior of a grudge tiger from the time she was a cub. The testimony of Mrs. Warren, her daughters, and Mr. Russell confirms that this behavior continued throughout the tiger's life. Thus, it is clear that Ms. Benni is, in fact, a grudge tiger."

"Dr. Lucas, in your expert opinion, to a reasonable degree of scientific certainty, what was the reason Ms. Benni attacked Dean Alcott, two weeks to the day after he aggressively kicked at her head?"

"In my expert opinion, to a reasonable degree of scientific certainty, Ms. Benni was provoked into the attack by the kick toward her head delivered by Mr. Alcott two weeks before."

"What is the basis for your conclusion, Dr. Lucas?"

"We've all seen that Dean Alcott delivered a sharp kick toward the head of Ms. Benni. Because of the fence between the man and the tiger, it would not have injured her. However, Ms. Benni saw that the man was acting aggressively against her. It is also established that, two weeks later, Mr. Alcott let himself in the tiger's enclosure and walked approximately six or seven steps before he heard Kenny Warren scream. For a grudge tiger such as Ms. Benni, the opportunity to avenge herself for the kick was presented, and she gouged her oppressor in retaliation."

Bam!

"Thank you, Dr. Lucas. That concludes my questions."

Kenny feels like she'll explode with happiness that Dr. Lucas did such a great job and said everything needed to win. But he still has to answer Mr. Perdue's questions on cross-examination. In spite of the fact that Jackie pinkie-swore to her that Mr. Perdue didn't lay a finger on him, she knows she'll be nervous until that part is over.

Jackie was standing next to the defense table the whole time, with her eyes glued to the TV screen. She now uses her clicker to press "pause" and says to the judge, "That is the end of the direct examination of Dr. Lucas by the defense. Shall I go ahead and play the cross-examination by Mr. Perdue?"

"Yes. Please do," says Judge Marcus.

Chapter 30

Kenny

Dr. Lucas and the lawyers must have taken a break between Jackie's direct and Hank's cross, because the tape resumes as he is just sitting down. Once the microphone is placed before him, he smiles at someone off-screen. Kenny assumes it's Jackie, since Hank Perdue is present only by speakerphone. A moment later, it's as though a director shouts, "Action!" Hank's voice-without-a-body speaks. It moves a lot more quickly with him asking the questions, since he doesn't seem to want to linger on any one point.

"Dr. Lucas, you say you aren't receiving any compensation for your time testifying here today."

"That's correct."

"But you must've spent many hours if you did, in fact, review all of the witness depositions."

"Certainly." Dr. Lucas nods, his eyes never leaving the camera. "I reviewed the deposition testimony of Dean Alcott, Charlie Russell, Kenny Warren, Marietta Warren, Carolyn Warren, and Eugenia Wilcox."

"What else did you look over to prepare to testify today?"

"The video showing Dean Alcott kick at the tiger's head, the video of Mr. Alcott's actions just before the tiger attack, the plans of the Warren Family Zoo, and local ordinances provided to me by the attorney for the zoo. I also refreshed myself on all of the applicable AZA standards and reviewed my thesis—the section on revenge tigers. And I reviewed many books in my library to confirm my understanding of the grudge tiger stories I relied upon for my conclusions."

"Did you meet with counsel for the zoo before coming in to give your testimony?"

"Yes."

"During that meeting, what did Ms. Bauer say to you?"

"She said I should tell the truth, whether or not I thought it helped the zoo's defense, which of course, I would do without being instructed." Dr. Lucas smiles kindly.

"I see. You also prepared a written report of your findings, did you not?"

"I did."

"And if you take all of this reading and studying and writing and meeting with Ms. Bauer, and add up all of the time you devoted to this thing, how many hours have you put into it?"

"Let me think a moment." He pauses. "I have a rough idea, but I don't want to guess. May I give you a range?"

"Yes. That should work."

"I would estimate that it was forty to fifty hours."

"All without pay?"

"That's right."

Mr. Perdue's voice morphs into a sneer as he asks the next question. "Isn't it true, Dr. Lucas, that you were willing to perform all that work—up to fifty hours of your valuable time—because you have a love of tigers and zoos, and you wanted to make sure that the Warren Family Zoo would win this case?"

Dr. Lucas sits looking ahead but not focusing on the camera—the jury. After a moment or two, his face breaks into a big grin. "I'm gratified that it shows. Yes. I do have a deep affection for the species, and I am a great supporter of zoos which conduct their care of the tigers in as exemplary a fashion as does Mrs. Warren's. Of course, in sharing my knowledge, I must call it as I see it. I won't lie for any man—or tiger, for that matter."

Kenny hears Mr. Perdue sigh. He tries something else. "You've given us quite an education about tigers here today. One of the areas you addressed was tiger behavior. Do you recall that?"

"Yes. I do." Dr. Lucas looks calm and comfortable, like he has absolutely no worry about what Mr. Perdue might ask.

"One of the points you made, Dr. Lucas, is that tigers are very territorial. I believe your words were 'intensely territorial.' "

Dr. Lucas nods.

"So, isn't it just as likely that Ms. Benni attacked Dean simply because he had entered the tiger's territory?"

"No. Your phrase 'just as likely' makes your statement incorrect."

"Well, sir, you testified earlier that it was irresponsible for the three Warren women each to have entered the enclosure."

"It was."

"How could it have been irresponsible for Dean to have entered the tiger's cage when such an invasion of Ms. Benni's territory wasn't sufficient provocation to cause her to attack any of the Warren women?"

"Based on the experiences of the three women, this particular tiger, Ms. Benni, had not considered the brief intrusions into her space to be intolerable. This fact, especially because it happened three times, suggests that Ms. Benni is not particularly territorial. You see, that is an individual characteristic that will vary from animal to animal. I believe the phrase I used earlier was 'generally intensely territorial.' " Dr. Lucas uses his hands to emphasize his words. It's as though answering questions from a person who opposes his views requires this extra effort. "You may recall that what I said was that it is primarily male tigers that are intensely territorial. This fact comes out of the very nature of the tiger, from time immemorial, in the wild. In every territory, there is one dominant male. Other males may seek, and even achieve, dominance in the geographical area, but it is only by killing or severely injuring the reigning male. A female on the other hand, roams between and among the territories of various dominant males, but it is only by the good graces of the male that she does so. When she is in oestrus, that is, at the time she is ready for mating, male tigers will kill each other to be the one with whom she copulates. But once the mating bit is finished, during her pregnancy and even once she has the cubs with her, the territory is not hers. She is permitted to remain there only at the whim of the dominant male."

"Please, Dr. Lucas, simply answer my questions. I did not ask you for another lesson."

"But you did, sir." Dr. Lucas smiles before he continues. "You specifically asked me, based upon the experiences of the Warren women, whether intrusion into Ms. Benni's area, without more, could cause an attack. I am explaining why it would not be reasonable to expect that behavior from this particular animal."

"If this is so, Dr. Lucas, why did you testify that no one should enter a tiger enclosure when the tiger is present?" There is a smirk in the way Mr. Perdue asks.

"Because, while it is more likely than not that this particular tiger, Ms. Benni, will not attack based merely on a human presence, it is still possible that she would. And when horrendous injury, or even death, is a possibility if one enters her enclosure, it is not responsible to take the risk. Even if it is one, or five or ten percent. Shall I give a simple analogy?"

"No. that's not necessary."

It's obvious to Kenny that Mr. Perdue isn't a fan of the expert's analogies.

"Dr. Lucas, let me ask you about the safeguards Mrs. Warren had in place to keep people out of the tiger's enclosure."

"Certainly." Dr. Lucas looks calm and appears to be listening attentively to every word that comes out of Mr. Perdue's mouth.

"Now, Dean Alcott was simply a delivery boy. Correct?"

"As I understand it, he had been delivering animal feed to the Warren Zoo, once every two weeks, for approximately ten years when the accident happened. But I cannot say whether he did other things, as well, as part of his employment with his father's company. Also, 'delivery boy' has a disparaging tenor I won't agree to."

"I understand. But, specifically at the Warren Zoo. His only job was to deliver feed. Isn't that correct?"

"As I understand it, yes."

"Right. And no part of that delivery job ever

required him to make a delivery into the inside of the tiger enclosure. Correct?"

"Yes. That's correct."

"So isn't it true that Charlie Russell, a top person with the zoo, was responsible for allowing Mr. Alcott to see him enter the code to the tiger enclosure, such that Mr. Alcott was then free to walk into Ms. Benni's cage, at will?"

"It is true that Mr. Alcott learned the code, which he knew he wasn't supposed to have, by looking over Mr. Russell's shoulder on the day he joined him inside the enclosure to remove a fallen tree limb. But saying Mr. Russell was responsible for allowing Dean to have the code is rather like blaming a person whose pocket has been picked for having a pocket." Dr. Lucas tilts his head and squints, obviously finding the question foolish.

"But you have to admit it was knowing that code, however he got it, that caused Dean Alcott's grievous injuries!" Mr. Perdue is raising his voice.

"Knowing the code, by stealing it, was one of the numerous *conditions* that existed at the time. It was certainly not the *cause* of Mr. Alcott's injuries." He speaks slowly, apparently to help ignorant Mr. Perdue follow the logic. "Think about it this way. Charlie Russell could've mentioned the code to his own mother. Perhaps it represented a family birthday or some such. But knowing the code would not cause Mr. Russell's mother to enter Ms. Benni's enclosure. So, knowing the code was simply a condition that existed. But in and of itself, that knowledge didn't cause anything."

Mr. Perdue can be heard letting out a shaft of air, probably through his nose.

"Dr. Lucas, you've testified that tigers, that is tigers

that have a vengeful personality, have reacted to humans who have harmed them by remembering them and getting even months or even a year later."

"Yes. They have."

"I've reviewed the books you relied on for your testimony."

"Good. Enlightening sources."

"Indeed. Well, the thing is, Dr. Lucas, one of the authors makes the point that two respected American field biologists who were part of a tiger project indicated that they found the notion of grudge tigers to be hard to believe. They had captured, studied, and released a number of tigers in the wild. Yet they never saw any evidence of a grudge tiger. Isn't that correct, sir?"

"Yes. I'm familiar with that passage in the book."

Kenny prays that Dr. Lucas can deal with this stunner like he did the other questions. Her knee starts to shake.

"So not all tiger experts share your view that grudge tigers are even a thing—even exist?"

"I don't know one way or the other. You see, very few tiger experts have expressed an opinion on grudge tigers. Now, as to the two field biologists, keep in mind that, although the two men sedated the tigers, they did not harm the animals. And they released them right back into their home areas. Is it possible that the tiger makes that distinction? No one knows." Dr. Lucas shrugs. "But there are two explanations. First, as I've said before, not all tigers are grudge tigers. I explained that, of the eight I tended at our family zoo west of London, only one was manifestly a grudge tiger. So, it is quite possible that the two gentlemen simply didn't come across any grudge tigers. Second, I would answer your question the way one of those two men answered it, later in the same passage you rely upon. He was a thoughtful man. He said that what he'd seen tigers do and what they *can* do are two different things. So you see, since Ms. Benni is demonstrably a grudge tiger—since her earliest days—her tolerance for perceived insult is simply much lower than that of other tigers."

"Dr. Lucas, do you know of any others who do not believe there's such a thing as a grudge tiger?"

Kenny thinks it's obvious Mr. Perdue is just fishing.

"Yes. I do."

Kenny can feel Dean's lawyer salivating.

"Please tell the ladies and gentlemen of the jury who these people are."

"Yourself, sir. And, I believe, Dean Alcott."

Some of the jurors laugh out loud. Even though Mr. Perdue is off-camera, Kenny is sure he's grimacing.

"Any others?"

"No. I know of no others who have ever professed such a belief."

Mr. Perdue is being eaten alive by Dr. Lucas. "Dr. Lucas, do you believe that Ms. Benni is a man-eater who should be dealt with accordingly?"

Kenny understood what Mr. Perdue was trying to do with his questions up until this one. But she doesn't have a clue why he chooses to go this direction.

"No."

"How can you be so sure? After all, the monster ripped a slice out of my client's leg—and arm!" Mr. Perdue's voice is raised and shaky at the same time. He actually sounds a little bit crazy to Kenny.

"Ms. Benni is not a man-eater for the simple reason that she's never eaten human flesh. She did not use her teeth on Dean Alcott. The truth is, sir, I believe she showed considerable restraint. She was faced with a man who we know for a fact had aggressively kicked at her head—while she was doing nothing more sinister than resting. We know Ms. Benni has been a grudge tiger for her entire life. Let me just say that when Mr. Alcott entered her enclosure, Ms. Benni accomplished what she wanted to accomplish, and nothing more. She did not bite onto his arm or his leg. She did not drag him like a ragdoll farther into her enclosure." Every word coming from the witness is clear and emphatic, almost urgent. "Can't you understand, sir? Charlie Russell was able to pull Dean Alcott out of the enclosure because Ms. Benni allowed him to. To Ms. Benni, the response was entirely proportional. Further, did you hear Kenny Warren's testimony that immediately after the attack, and I quote, 'Ms. Benni ambled back to the shade, laid herself down, and yawned?' This is not the behavior of a tiger who wants to kill. And it is certainly not the behavior of a man-eater." For the first time, Dr. Lucas speaks passionately, apparently livid at Hank's ridiculous assertion that Ms. Benni is a man-eater. Kenny finds it obvious what Dr. Lucas thinks of the whole situation—Dean's lawsuit is ridiculous.

Hank sighs. "I'm finished."

Kenny has a feeling everyone in the courtroom knows he is.

The judge announces a ninety-minute recess to be followed by closing arguments. Jackie whispers that she has to go into chambers with Hank to argue over a couple of motions and jury instructions. The jury is told they'll be served a late lunch, so Marietta, Kenny, and their mother go downstairs to the basement cafeteria Jackie told them about. The courtroom is only on the second floor, so they take the stairs down. The concrete floor and walls and the fluorescent lighting of the stairway are downright depressing, and the cafeteria reminds Kenny of the ones in hospitals, sterile and completely unappetizing. They stay together in the salad line, rather than face decisions among the other options. The benefit of the salads is that they give the women something to pick at while they don't eat.

When Carolyn asks what they thought of the trial, Kenny says, "I tried to think of it as just 'a trial,' since I never got to sit through one of those before. But it was all so personal that I was pretty much just keeping score."

"You mean from the jurors' point of view or your own?" asks her mother.

"Totally the jurors. We have a really good view of their faces. Like when Dean was testifying, they were really into him, but when Mrs. Wilcox and Dr. Lucas testified, it was like they forgot about Dean and ate up the information about Ms. Benni being a grudge tiger."

"I think we're going to win," Marietta says, who then knocks on the fake wood table.

"I, for one, live in dread of Hank's closing argument," Carolyn says. "Particularly, the list of damages which Jackie told us he'll write on a dry-erase board for the jury—especially the grand total of $3.8 million dollars—if they believe the story about the modeling career." She shakes her head and lets out a long sigh.

"Don't think about that," Kenny says. "If he loses, which he will, it doesn't matter what numbers are on that board."

Her mother looks at her. "So you agree with your sister that we'll win?"

"Duh! Of course we'll win. Think about it. Jackie proved that Ms. Benni is a grudge tiger. And the jury saw the video of Dean kicking hard at her head two weeks before Ms. Benni got him back. Jackie says the statute is our only risk, and provocation is a complete defense to it. Honestly, Mom, how can we not win?"

Kenny and Marietta try to get their mother to see what is perfectly clear to them. There is nothing Mr. Perdue can say in his closing argument that has the power to change the evidence. They have to win because it's the only logical verdict.

Closing arguments begin about twenty minutes after they get back to their table in the courtroom. Mr. Perdue goes first. He's smarmy-nice and smiles at the jurors a lot. He really lays it on about Dean's injury, his medical bills, and his partial disability. And he outdoes himself moaning about the tragedy of Dean not being able to pursue his life-long dream of a modeling career. It's interesting to Kenny that he says very little about the two videos or the grudge tiger testimony. His point seems to be that, while it might be theoretically possible that Ms. Benni is a grudge tiger who attacked Dean because of the little tap to her head, the chances of it certainly do not rise to the required legal level of being "more probably true than not." Kenny actually expected Mr. Perdue to lie a lot and throw darts at her mother, like he did in his opening statement, but she supposes he knows that approach won't work anymore, now that the jury has seen and heard the evidence. He puts a dollar value on each of Dean's losses and writes it all down on a giant dry-erase board. The total is $3.8 million, and that's what he asks the jury to award Dean.

Jackie stands before the jury with no notes and no dry-erase board. Her voice is calm and friendly.

"Dean Alcott is here, asking you to award him millions of dollars from Carolyn Warren, a woman who has provided the family fun and the education of the Warren Family Zoo to the community for ten years. She and her daughters, Marietta and Kenny, and the zoo's lead maintenance man, Charlie Russell, told you a lot about what it takes to keep up the grounds and all the lovely exotic animals. As she testified, this is Mrs. Warren's passion—to offer joy to local families in an attractive and safe environment. She has always been especially cautious with Ms. Benni because she knows tigers are, and always will be, dangerous animals.

"She installed safety systems and redundant safety systems to keep Ms. Benni inside, and the public outside of the cage. You've seen the pictures and heard the testimony: the twenty-foot height of the walls of the tiger's enclosure—far above the toughest requirements, the AZA standards; the inward-facing, cantilevered top of the enclosure; the forty-five inch tempered glass barrier wall which keeps guests at least ten feet from the cage; and the sophisticated digital entry system. Only Charlie Russell and the three Warren women were to have the code to the digital locks on Ms. Benni's enclosure. Mrs. Warren made sure it was designed so that only those who have the code can enter, so that nobody can end up on the tiger side of the cage unintentionally. A person would have to press the code on the first door, wait for it to lock behind him, and then enter the code on the second door. No one ever got into Ms. Benni's cage by mistake.

"There is no allegation that anyone ever jumped over the forty-five-inch protective barrier wall—no one except Dean Alcott, that is. There is no allegation that any guest was ever surprised to find himself inside Ms. Benni's cage—only Dean Alcott felt free to steal the code and let himself in. Did Ms. Benni ever escape from her enclosure? No. Never. Did any visitor to the zoo ever sustain injury by getting too close to the tiger? No. never. This incident happened because, and only because, Dean Alcott intentionally unlocked a door with a digital code he essentially stole from Charlie Russell, and then intentionally unlocked a second door with the same code to get into Ms. Benni's enclosure while he knew full-well the tiger was present.

"But it's worse than that. Two weeks before the accident, he deliberately kicked at Ms. Benni's head in an aggressive way. Kenny Warren testified that Mr. Alcott hauled off and tried to wallop Ms. Benni in the head with his steel toe boot. But you don't have to take her word for it, do you? You've all seen the video of his assault on Ms. Benni. What had the tiger done to deserve this? She had lain down for a nap in the sun, and she had the audacity to rest her head against the fence.

"Unfortunately for Mr. Alcott, in the words of Eugenia Wilcox, the woman who had raised the cub for the first two years of her life, he picked 'the wrong tiger' to kick at. Is Ms. Benni a grudge tiger? Mrs. Wilcox told you how prominent this aspect of her personality was from the time she was a tiny cub to the day she was taken to the Warren Family Zoo. Carolyn Warren, Marietta Warren and Kenny Warren told you how it was so clear to all of them that Ms. Benni holds grudges that they call a family member who seems to be holding on to her anger a 'grudge tiger.'

"And then Dr. Nigel Lucas gave us a primer on tigers in general, in the wild and in captivity, some of which have been confirmed to be revenge tigers. He explained in great detail all of the reasons why it is true, to a reasonable degree of scientific certainty, that Ms. Benni is a grudge tiger. Dr. Lucas also testified that, to the same degree of scientific certainty, Ms. Benni attacked Mr. Alcott *because* he provoked her just two weeks earlier.

"The instructions Judge Marcus will read to you explain that, if Dean Alcott provoked the tiger attack, he loses under the Animal Control Act. It doesn't matter whether or not he knew that Ms. Benni is a grudge tiger, and it doesn't matter whether or not he intended to provoke her. The question is simply whether, from the tiger's point of view, she attacked as a result of a provocation by Dean Alcott. Ms. Benni clearly did. Therefore, under Illinois law, you must find in favor of Mrs. Warren and against Dean Alcott.

"Now, Mr. Alcott is a very pleasant young man. He is obviously a very handsome person. There is no question he was badly hurt, he will need future medical attention, and he will have two scars. Any decent person feels sympathy for him. He also says he wanted to be a model, although he hasn't taken any steps toward that goal and doesn't know any details about that profession. He never mentioned it to Marietta, although they spoke roughly every two weeks for a decade. But perhaps he did have such a desire. All of this matters to our natural sympathy for him.

"But it doesn't have any bearing, under the law, on the question of whether Carolyn Warren must pay him money for what happened. Think back to the day when I had the opportunity to ask you questions before you were selected to be a juror in this case. I asked each of you if you would follow the law, even if you disagree with it. You, each of you, promised to do so—even if you personally feel the law is wrong. Our system will only work if the law means something, and it is your legal duty here and now to uphold it.

"The truth is, this is really a simple case. Carolyn Warren must be found not guilty if Ms. Benni attacked Dean Alcott *because* he provoked the tiger. Perhaps with some other tiger, the provocation would've been forgotten. But Ms. Benni isn't some other tiger. She is herself, a tiger with a strong need for retribution. Not only did elderly Mrs. Wilcox, and the three Warren women, and Charlie Russell prove this. Dr. Lucas, who has studied tigers his entire life, proved it—scientifically. Did Dean Alcott's lawyer bring in an expert witness to testify differently? No. Nor did he disprove it in any other way. Oh, Mr. Perdue cross-examined Dr. Lucas, all right. What did we learn from that exchange? Mainly that Dr. Lucas, and I quote, 'won't lie for any man…or tiger.'

"Mrs. Warren asks just one thing—the same thing that Judge Marcus will instruct you to do—make your decision based on the law. If you do so, you will find Carolyn Warren, individually and d/b/a The Warren Family Zoo not guilty. Thank you."

Kenny loves Jackie's argument, and honestly can't see how her mom can lose. Now, she's sure she understands why Jackie didn't go after the modeling career thing more. It's a distraction. Her mother can't afford to lose, with or without the additional dollars for that. Jackie has to get a not guilty verdict.

Mr. Perdue gets to stand back up and have the last word. Jackie told them this is actually fair because the plaintiff has the burden of proof, and it's supposed to be a heavy burden. He basically makes another grab for sympathy and doesn't say a word about grudge tigers in general, or Ms. Benni, or provocation. It's fascinating to Kenny that Mr. Perdue always raises his voice to try to emphasize his important points. But Jackie slows her pace and lowers her volume. Kenny prefers her approach but realizes it doesn't matter a bit what she thinks.

Because it is past four thirty p.m. when the closing arguments are finished, the judge asks the jurors to come back the next day, Friday, to be instructed on the law and to begin their deliberations. She needs her courtroom in the morning, so they're all told to return at noon. Jackie takes the Warrens into a small conference room to talk about how they all feel it went. Carolyn says she's pleased, but not convinced of victory, but Marietta and Kenny say they are.

"My daughters think I've already won, Jackie. But I really need to know your assessment."

"I feel good about it. We got all of our evidence in on our grudge tiger defense. I'm confident we've proven both that the kicking was an aggressive provocation by Dean, and that Ms. Benni acted in response to it two weeks later."

"So Mom will win?" Kenny asks.

"Of course she will," Marietta says.

"She probably will," Jackie says.

"Why only 'probably'?" asks Carolyn. "I'd like to know my odds numerically. Based on your experience, what do you think the chances are that I'll get a not guilty?"

"All things considered, I believe we'll probably get the not guilty verdict we're hoping for. Our chances are excellent," says Jackie.

"But not a hundred percent?" says Mom.

"Carolyn, I wish there were such a thing. But on a rare occasion, a sure-fire winner can go sideways in front of a rogue jury. If you want a number, I'll say you have an eighty percent chance to win. And that's only because eighty percent is the highest I'll ever go—and I've never done it before today." Jackie smiles. "Like I said, I feel good about it."

Chapter 31

Hank

Hank says good night to Dean and heads home, feeling miserable—again. He's going to lose. It's obvious to anyone who has been paying attention. So, great. His only hope is that the jurors haven't been paying attention. To a tiger case?

It's his own fault. He's done nothing but fumble throughout the damn case. He never should have let himself get so far behind on his files. Fortunately, the repercussions of one of his mistakes were eliminated. Hank doesn't need to be all that concerned about his failure to read the defendant's amended pleading before he produced Dean for his deposition. That was pretty much legal malpractice on his part. But it's missing one of the elements—damages. Dean redeemed himself— themselves—with his testimony, saying the kick had been so gentle, such a non-event, that he simply forgot about it. The kid is pretty sharp. Hank has no idea why he did so poorly in school.

Of course, Hank knew from the start he'd lose the negligence count and is glad he withdrew it since it's obvious that Dean was more than 50% at fault for what happened—to put it mildly. One of his larger mistakes was not realizing that Jackie would put so much work into defending the count he brought under the statute—

her whole provocation defense thing. She did her homework and he didn't do his, but it must've been pure luck that Mrs. Wilcox and Dr. Lucas are such charmers. The jury ate it up. The pathetic truth is, they convinced Hank, too. Ms. Benni is obviously a grudge tiger, a type of Panthera Tigris that has been thoroughly studied by scientists who care about such things. He doubts he could've prevailed even if he had hired a whore scientist to say there's no such thing as a grudge tiger. No. His biggest mistake wasn't that he didn't hire a tiger expert. It was that he didn't prepare Dean for how badly the trial could go.

There is no way Hank can let the jury decide the case. He'll lose an "any idiot" trial and become the laughingstock of the county. Not only that, but if Dean gets a big goose egg from the jury, after Hank pretty much assured him that he'd win, those green eyes might start to see dollar signs in a malpractice suit against him.

The jury will start deliberating at noon the next day. Hank has to persuade Jackie to get her client to put the $500,000 insurance money back on the table, and he has to convince Dean to take it. He doesn't know which will be harder, since they both will be virtually impossible. He'll appear pathetically desperate if he pursues either result too soon. No. He needs to wait until the jury has been out deliberating for at least an hour or so before approaching Dean or Jackie. On Friday, he'll just keep an eye on his watch. At the right moment, he'll tell Dean they need to talk, and he'll sit down with his client in one of the quiet alcoves just outside the courtroom to test his powers of persuasion on a young man who is probably brighter than people think. Hank's hope is that he's actually right about the kid's brains. If Dean really is smart, he'll also know they are about to hear a verdict of "not guilty."

Chapter 32

Kenny

Carolyn drives Marietta and Kenny home on Thursday evening, where they all grab quick sandwiches, and head for their respective rooms. Kenny falls into her bed, too wiped out to read or even stream a show. Although she's basically a washrag from exhaustion, she can't fall asleep. After staring at the ceiling for what feels like a couple of hours, she glances at her wall clock, which says it's almost two a.m. Apparently, she did drift off now and again, but at this point she's simply not sleepy, so she gives up. She throws her white hoodie over her pajamas, tiptoes down the hall, and finds her footing on the least creaky parts of the stairs.

Once Kenny makes it to the kitchen and knows she won't disturb her mother or Marietta, she slips into her flip flops which sit among the shoes lined up at the back door. She wanders onto the back porch and sits on the lowest step. The night air is balmy and sweet, so she shrugs off the jacket. The sky seems ablaze with stars. As she gazes at them, she's carried back to the time when her father taught her about the constellations—asterisms, actually—and the Greek and Roman myths. She wishes she were a wiser person, in a Virgo kind of way, and could have a clear idea of what's coming.

The next day they'll all find out whether they can go on with their usual lives—what she now realizes are enchanted lives. Her right knee bounces rapidly up and down, and she can't control it. Also, the more she worries, the more her chest hurts. She wonders if a sixteen-year-old can have a heart attack. Then she realizes it's the same thought she had the day Ms. Benni attacked Dean, and her mother sent her running for sheets.

All the nervousness suddenly vanishes when a flash of light near the entrance to Ms. Benni's enclosure seizes her attention. She grabs her sweatshirt as she stands and pulls it on as she slowly makes her way toward the light. By the time she reaches the willows, she can tell there is someone with a small flashlight fiddling with something at the outside gate to Ms. Benni's cage. The tiger isn't making a sound, so Kenny can't really tell where she is in her pen. Although Kenny hasn't the faintest idea what's happening, she quietly sidles to the point in the willows closest to the cage. By instinct, Kenny slips through the gate on the picket fence and bolts for the post with the emergency lock-down button. Posts like this one are scattered throughout the zoo, the way the brochures say they are placed all over college campuses for student safety. Kenny knows she has to hit the two digits of the emergency code and then press the red button in the center. Her hand trembles as she enters the code then mashes the button with her open palm. As far as she knows, no one at the zoo has ever had to use the system before, except for safety drills. The post is located between the backyard and the far side of Ms. Benni's cage, so Kenny can't see the intruder as she activates all of the locks in the zoo, but she knows there's no way for him to override what she did.

That's when she realizes she doesn't have her phone with her to call 9-1-1. The moon lights up the yard enough that the person will probably see her if she sprints for the house. So, she takes a deep breath and walks with completely false bravado toward whoever is at the gate. At about twenty-five feet away she can make out red hair and a pale face. The man is locked between the two doors to Ms. Benni's enclosure, captured by the lock-down.

She approaches to within ten feet of him, and she thinks she manages a steady voice. "Hi, Jimmy."

He looks shocked. His mouth literally falls open. "Who's there?" He sounds terrified, and she realizes she probably looks like a spectral figure with her white top and pale pajamas in the moonlight. "Is that you, Kenny? What are you doing here?"

"I live here, Jimmy. The question is, what are *you* doing here?"

"I'm trapped!" He is still entering the 4-digit code, maniacally, over and over. He says, "The code doesn't work!"

"True. The zoo is in emergency lock-down. You can stop trying the code. It won't do anything."

"What?"

"I have you locked between the two doors. Think of it this way…you've been taken prisoner."

"What do you want?"

"What do *I* want? Jimmy? That's a seriously stupid question. What the hell are you doing in there?"

His face contorts as if he's working to think of a believable lie, but no words come out.

"Listen, Jimmy." Kenny sinks her right hand into her jacket pocket to simulate grabbing a phone. "I'm about one second away from calling 9-1-1. Tell me the truth or I'll call the cops right now."

"Shit."

"That's not an answer." She turns away from him and play-acts pulling out a phone.

"No. Please, Kenny. I'll tell you."

She surprises herself with her pretend self-confidence. "Nice try. I don't want your worthless promise to tell me. I want the next words that come out of your mouth to be an explanation of what you're doing and why."

"Okay. Okay. I was going to open the doors so the tiger could get out."

"What! That's insane. Someone could've been killed."

"I guess so."

"But why would you do such a thing?"

"Because Dean's about to lose the trial. So I figured if the jury hears that the tiger from here is on the loose, they'll be more likely to go against the zoo."

"You're crazy." She thinks for a moment, then adds, "Does Dean know about this?"

"Nah."

"Then how did you get the code?"

"Oh, I've had it for a while. One time when Dean was drunk and I wasn't, I asked him for it."

"Why?"

"I thought it might come in handy someday." He pauses. "It did."

"Yeah. Really handy. It got you stuck in a cage at a zoo." She shakes her head. "Jesus, Jimmy. You'll probably go to jail for this. Why did you think this was a good idea?"

"Well, the thing is, Dean's in bad shape. He can't work. He can't do much of anything. I want to make sure he gets like millions of dollars from the trial."

"Even if people get killed by a tiger?"

"The cops would probably kill the tiger before that could happen."

"And you're okay with Ms. Benni being murdered so you can help Dean take over my mom's zoo?"

"He's my best friend."

"And you're an asshole. By the way, it wouldn't have worked."

"What do you mean?"

"It's set up so both doors can't be open at the same time. So you couldn't have just opened them up and left. You would've had to stand outside the last door, in Ms. Benni's path, to open it."

"Oh. I didn't know that."

"Obviously."

"You know what, Jimmy? All of a sudden, I'm really sleepy. I'm going to bed."

"But you'll let me out first, right?"

Kenny looks over into Ms. Benni's cage and sees she is lying on her platform, eyes riveted to Jimmy. "I'll see you later." Kenny starts to walk away, then pauses and turns back to look at Jimmy. "And don't bother to drop your mess onto Dean. He has no idea how to release you. Good night, Jimmy."

"Damn it, Kenny! Don't leave me here!"

She keeps walking. When she gets back to her bedroom, she really is sleepy. She knows Jimmy is perfectly safe in his little cage, so she has no qualms about forgetting him for a few hours. She sets her alarm for five a.m. so she can deal with him before Charlie and the other employees start their workdays at five-thirty.

When Kenny's alarm goes off, she jumps up, washes her face, brushes her teeth, then puts her hair into a quick ponytail. She steps into a pair of shorts, pulls on a sweatshirt, and grabs her phone. Then she hurries downstairs and through the yard, the willows, and the gate to Ms. Benni's pen. Jimmy is curled up in a ball in one of the corners farthest away from Ms. Benni, who still has her gaze laser-focused on him. Jimmy looks like he's shaking. Whether he is or not, she doesn't feel any sympathy for him. She stands maybe ten feet from him and slowly stretches her arms over her head. "Sleep well, Jimmy?"

"Shit no, I didn't sleep well. Are you kidding?"

"Okay. Here's what's going to happen. I'm going to record your confession on my phone. You just need to explain everything you did last night, and why you did it. Then you'll make a promise—also on the recording— to never set foot on our property again. Not the zoo, not our house, or any of our acres in the back. Never again."

"Yeah. Fine. Whatever. Let's get going."

She starts recording, and Jimmy gives a passably coherent version of what he told her the night before. And he makes the promises, exactly as she asked. Of course, she has to send the video to someone so Jimmy won't get any ideas about trying to take her phone. So, she emails it to Marietta and Becca with a note to save it to a hard drive. Jimmy grimaces when she tells him she sent it to a couple of friends, so she knows she was right to think he might lunge for her phone. When she gets to the same post as the night before, she enters the "all clear" code, which releases the universal lock-down. She walks back to where Jimmy is, still between the two doors. "Now you can enter the code and the door will open."

"Are you taking the video to the cops?"

"Not now. Maybe someday, if you ever trespass again."

"Why aren't you?"

"I guess I'd rather have it hanging over your head, the way losing the zoo has been hanging over my mom's head." The steel mesh door opens and Jimmy pops out like a jack-in-the-box. Kenny doesn't see a car around, so he must've walked the four miles from his house to the zoo. He bolts in that direction.

Kenny does feel a little guilty for making poor Ms. Benni stay up all night being a watch-tiger, so when she sits down for breakfast, she asks her mother if she'll feed Ms. Benni a little early and give her an extra treat. Fortunately, Carolyn is so distracted by the fact that this is likely going to be the day they'll hear the verdict that she doesn't even ask why. She just says, "Certainly, Kenny."

Chapter 33

Carolyn

On Friday, after the jurors listen to the instructions from Judge Marcus, they are escorted to their room to deliberate. Jackie, Marietta, Kenny, and Carolyn are sitting around the defendant's table. All of the Warren women are trying to concentrate on the novels they brought to pass the excruciating minutes, and Jackie is working on a brief for another case. It's been about an hour and a half since the jury went out. Hank approaches their table, pulls Jackie aside, and walks with her to his table, where they have a five-minute conversation. Carolyn watches Jackie do a lot of listening and almost no talking.

Jackie returns to the Warrens and tells Carolyn that Dean is agreeing to accept the insurance money to settle the case, and she needs to call Helen right away to get her approval to put the money back on the table. She excuses herself and walks to the back of the courtroom and out the door to make her call. Carolyn suspends her reaction, awaiting more explanation from Jackie. When Jackie returns, she tells them Helen is willing to pay the $500,000 to settle the case, but only if it is what Carolyn wants to do. Jackie explains that Helen feels Carolyn has been through a lot, so she wants to leave it up to her whether she would prefer to hold out for the expected not guilty verdict. Carolyn's daughters implore her to let the jury vindicate the zoo, since they are both certain she'll win. Jackie said she's given the best odds she's ever given. Obviously, even Hank expects the zoo to win. Still, Carolyn's not so sure, so she asks Jackie how much time she has to decide.

"You have plenty of time. It will take the jury a couple hours just to get through all of the instructions, choose a foreperson, and begin to review the evidence. Take your time, Carolyn. This is a big decision."

"I'd like to take a walk," she says to Jackie. She would love to drive to the cemetery near her home to talk with her husband to try to figure out what he would do, because on his good days, Tom always did the right thing. But there isn't time.

"That's a great idea." Jackie tells her there's a small memorial garden behind the hospital, just two blocks away. It's the site of an annual remembrance of the babies who never made it home from the hospital. Jackie says there are a couple of benches, lots of trees, and usually no people. Carolyn is too distracted to stop to ask how Jackie knows about it.

Carolyn's mind swirls as she makes her way to the garden. It's impossible to ignore that everyone, including Hank, thinks she'll win, and she's always trusted her lawyer's judgment before. Marietta and Kenny are begging her to refuse to give Dean anything—not even the insurance money. Kenny even announced she was certain her father would never have agreed to give Dean Alcott a penny they didn't have to, but how could her daughter know this? Carolyn wishes Helen would've decided without her input. She's sure the insurance adjuster thinks she's doing her a favor by leaving it up to her, but she is truly torn.

She arrives to find just what she hoped for, an oasis of natural beauty and peace, and she sits down on a concrete bench. There is no one around.

What should I do, Tom? You always knew what was best.

And in case you do see everything now, I have to apologize for my feelings for Charlie. You've only been gone for two years, and I'm embarrassed to say my affection for our dear friend is making me feel like a schoolgirl. Although we brought him in as an employee, Charlie has always acted more like a trusted partner, hasn't he? You and I often spoke of how much we respected and admired him. Then when he lost his beloved Eloise, I believe we both grew quite close to him.

Now, I think he reminds me of you in how gentle and kind he is. But he's also himself, and I can't seem to stop my feelings for him, although I've really tried. None of this is an excuse, darling. It's just that if things ever do go anywhere between me and Charlie, I hope you can be happy for me. And I like to think I'd have been happy for you if you had been the one to survive, and then discovered a chance at love again.

I've come to talk with you about whether I should settle the lawsuit with the insurance money.

Marietta insists I hold out for a not guilty verdict for vindication. Kenny says you wouldn't give Dean a penny we don't owe him. You know very well that I don't have the soul of a gambler. Everyone seems to think we'll win. But I don't think I could bear to lose the case, and our precious zoo, if I let the jury decide and it goes badly. I'm afraid it would feel like losing you a second time. We built our zoo together, brick by brick, animal by animal, improvement by improvement, didn't we, sweetheart?

Well, I think I've figured it out...just by talking to you. I have to make sure I keep the zoo— because it's all I have left of us. Compared with that, vindication is worth nothing to me. I miss you so much that it's almost unbearable some days. I'll do everything in my power to hold onto what we built together as long as I live. I'll love you forever, Tom.

****

When she walks back into the courtroom, the jury is still out. Jackie hurries toward her. "What have you decided, Carolyn?"

"We should offer the insurance money—all of it."

Jackie stares at her "You sure?"

"Yes. I couldn't be surer."

Jackie gives her a quick hug, then hurries to Hank with the news. They speak, out of Carolyn's hearing, for a minute or two. Hank approaches Dean and whispers back and forth with him for a couple of minutes. Then Jackie and Hank walk together through the door near the judge's bench and into the back hallway that leads to her chambers.

After a few minutes, the bailiff walks into the courtroom from the same hallway and straight to the jury room, which is on the other side of the courtroom, opposite the area where the twelve of them sat during the trial. Marietta and Kenny, who had run to the restroom, walk into the courtroom at the same moment Judge Marcus, Jackie, and Hank return from chambers. The two lawyers take positions at their respective tables, and the judge sits down on the bench, reviewing some paperwork and not looking up. Marietta and Kenny join their mother at the defense table.

Marietta whispers, "What's happening?"

"Wait. You didn't offer the insurance money?" says Kenny.

Carolyn motions for them to take their seats. "I did."

"But Mom..." Kenny says.

Carolyn shakes her head. "No, Kenny. This is my decision. I have my reasons. It's all over."

The bailiff calls for order in the court as the jurors file out of the deliberation room and back into the jury box. Once they are all seated, Judge Marcus informs them that the case has been resolved by settlement and that their work was instrumental in concluding the case. She thanks them for their service and says they are free to go.

A number of the jurors look over at Carolyn as they make their way out of the courtroom, but she can't read their expressions and doesn't really have the energy to try. She remains seated with her girls as Hank shakes hands with Jackie. He then walks over to their table and shakes hands with each of them and wishes them all the best. He says it was his pleasure to meet them and that he enjoyed working on such an interesting case. Carolyn sees Jackie turn to look for Dean, but he is already passing through the courtroom door.

Once the room is almost empty, Jackie sits on the corner of the defense table and asks if any of the women has a question.

"So, it's all over—just like that?" asks Kenny.

"Yes. Anti-climactic, isn't it?" says Jackie.

"I'll say."

Marietta says, "Does Mom have to do anything else?"

"Hank will draw up the settlement papers this

afternoon or tomorrow. As soon as I receive them from him, I'll bring them by for you to sign, Carolyn."

"All right," she says.

"You ladies ought to go out and celebrate. The nightmare's over. I wish I could join you, but I'm way behind on my other files, so I need to head back to my office."

"That's okay," Marietta says. "I don't really feel like celebrating. I just feel like getting some sleep."

"Me too," says Kenny. "It's weird to be moving at like a hundred miles an hour, and suddenly just run into a wall."

Jackie laughs. "I always feel like that after trials. It takes a little time to decompress."

Carolyn sighs. "I know that settling disappointed all of you. I think we would all feel like celebrating if this had ended in a 'not guilty' rather than a settlement. I'm sorry to have robbed you of that. We've all been through a lot." She pauses. "I feel like I've learned quite a bit. And Jackie, we couldn't have made it through this without you."

"Yeah. Thanks, Jackie," says Kenny. "Thanks especially for London."

"You were wonderful," Marietta says.

"Entirely my pleasure."

After a long pause, Carolyn says, "Girls, I want you to know that I feel the same let-down you do. But I wouldn't do this differently for anything. I'm not feeling like celebrating either, but I am relieved. Very relieved. Shall we go home?"

Kenny hugs her mother. "I love you, Mom."

Marietta says, "Me too," and also gives Carolyn a long hug.

Jackie steps up and says, "Carolyn, you're a very strong person. It's been an honor to represent you." Then she also hugs her, quite tenderly. Carolyn can no longer hold back a trickle of tears. Marietta hands her a tissue, and Carolyn regains her composure. As Jackie is gathering up her papers and Carolyn is reaching for her purse, the bailiff approaches them. He says the judge wants to see Jackie and Ms. Watson in chambers. Then he walks to the back of the room, presumably to find Ms. Watson.

Kenny says, "What's going on, Jackie? Who's Ms. Watson?"

Jackie smiles at Kenny. "Ms. Watson is an assistant state's attorney in the civil division. She's been here every day, monitoring the case. So, I assume the judge wants to tell us something about our pending motion to dismiss the state's attorney's case against Carolyn and the zoo."

During the trial of Dean's case, Carolyn almost forgot about the other lurking threat. She and her daughters sit back down as Jackie and the young woman lawyer wearing a navy skirt suit and sensible flats leave the room with the bailiff. Carolyn has seen her before and assumed she was just another spectator, since there were so many of them sitting in the back pews. She is too nervous to talk, and it appears that her daughters feel the same way. After about ten minutes, both women return to the courtroom, without the bailiff. Ms. Watson doesn't look at them but walks on through the room and out the door. They are the last souls remaining. Jackie says, "Judge Marcus told us she'll be working on her ruling this afternoon and will stay until she finishes it. She said the parties can access it on-line any time after 6 p.m."

"Do you still think we'll win?" asks Marietta.

"We should. But, like I mentioned before, she'll probably give the state leave to file an amended complaint. Listen, I know you are all exhausted. And I really need to go back to the office. I'll call you from there as soon as I have her ruling."

"We'll be waiting," Carolyn says. They all walk out together and hug again as Jackie leaves them at their car.

Since her daughters have both fallen silent staring out the car windows, Carolyn tries to make sense of it all as she drives. Of course, losing Ms. Benni wouldn't be as devastating as losing everything. But Carolyn has adored that tiger since she and Tom first glimpsed her at the Wilcox's *Animal Kingdom*. It wouldn't be hard to find a home for Ms. Benni outside of Illinois, so it's the prospect of having to part with her, not being responsible for her being put down, that still stalks Carolyn. One last hurdle as punishment for—what exactly? For daring to run a zoo? For the audacity to include a tiger as an exhibit? For the foolishness of allowing a strong, young man to make deliveries for his father? What she's learned from the trial is simple—she's vulnerable. Things she'd been ever so careful to prevent have happened and could well have destroyed everything she spent her life building. She struggles to find some meaning beyond raw vulnerability.

One positive is that settling the case immediately eased the months-long constriction in her chest. After that ordeal, the threat of losing dear Ms. Benni causes more of a profound sadness than active anxiety. Carolyn kids herself that the upshot may simply be that she should keep paying her insurance premiums on time. Maybe she should offer to shoot a commercial for

Benevolent. She shakes her head and tries to focus.

As tears stream down her cheeks, she wonders if the real lesson is that it's the very vulnerability she laments, that enriches life. It's undeniable that confronting the possible loss of her zoo made her appreciate it all the more. Tom used to say, "*Siempre adelante*, Carolyn." So that's what she'll do—always move forward. She's grown closer to her daughters through the ordeal, and at a time when they otherwise would've been straining for more independence. And she's watched as they grew closer with each other. She takes a very deep breath and allows herself the luxury of a smile. It's been a long time coming.

Chapter 34

Kenny

When they get home, Carolyn goes to her room for a nap and Marietta says she'll lie down with a glass of wine and her poetry book. After Kenny changes into shorts and a t-shirt, she wanders around, alternating between staring at the kitchen clock and staring at the dining room table. So much has happened, and a lot of it around that very table. Memories of the family meetings with Jackie keep popping in her head. In the kitchen, her eyes hop from the clock to the wall phone. She knows Jackie will call the landline since that's the phone Carolyn prefers to use. And, as much as Jackie and Kenny like each other, of course she'll make her call to Carolyn, since it's her zoo and her Ms. Benni. That thought makes Kenny burst into tears at the idea that her mother could be forced to sell their tiger. She remembers that the state's attorney said in his papers that he wants to put Ms. Benni down if her family can't find a home for her outside of Illinois, but she knows her mother would do whatever it takes to find someone responsible to take Ms. Benni.

Kenny wipes her face on her arm and steps out onto the back porch. It's almost ninety degrees and humid, but she didn't notice the steaminess earlier in the day. She thinks about how hot Ms. Benni must be and walks down into the yard, through the hedge of willows and the gate on the picket fence, and on toward the back side of the tiger enclosure. Since it's coming up on closing time, there are only a couple of people on the visitors' side. At first, Kenny doesn't see Ms. Benni at all, and she gasps that it's some kind of premonition. Then the animal's beautiful mammoth head rises out of her pond, her fur raked and flattened from the water. When she steps out and shakes her body, the high-flying water droplets catch the sun and shimmer with iridescence, a thousand tiny sparklers. Ms. Benni pauses, looks around, then gracefully lifts and sets down each paw, seeming deliberate and intentional, like a Clydesdale horse in a parade. Kenny has never seen Ms. Benni look so proud and in control—or maybe she hasn't watched her nearly enough. When she looks directly at Kenny with her piercing green eyes, and then chuffs, Kenny get chills. Of course, she realized years ago that Ms. Benni knows who they are, but it's been ages since their precious tiger chuffed at her.

Ms. Benni finds a spot in the sun, just beyond the reach of the shade from her tree and spreads herself out. Her belly is on the ground, legs straight out, and her head rests on the grass. At that moment Kenny loves her with the intense feeling you have for someone you're losing. She knows it well from what happened with her father. She doesn't just love Ms. Benni—she loves the whole zoo, and she realizes she needs to work to be really present when she spends time with their beloved animals. Kenny is the luckiest girl in the world to be growing up as a zookeeper, and she promises herself never again to take it for granted. She hooks her two little fingers together and makes a pinkie swear with herself.

Of course, it's a promise she knows she'll probably break—over and over again—but it's one that she will always remind herself of. She sits in the grass and revels in watching Ms. Benni.

Jackie never seems to be too worried about the state's attorney's case, but Kenny wishes she'd asked her to explain why. She does trust Jackie's judgment on legal things. After all, she did make it possible for Dean and Mr. Perdue to agree to take just the insurance money. Kenny is trying to get over the way her mother decided to offer it to them, when the zoo was about to win the trial. But Jackie's handling of the case is obviously the reason those guys knew they were about to lose, took the $500,000, and skedaddled. It's just that Kenny feels so close to Ms. Benni after all of this that she'd be devastated if the judge were to order her mother to sell her. The truth is, Kenny can't really even imagine it. She thinks there are some things our minds just say "no" to— *"Don't go there."*

Whatever the news is about the judge dismissing the current complaint, it seems the case will go on. The state's attorney will get to fix it if he wrote the complaint up wrong. She'll ask Jackie to explain why she doesn't think Mr. Babdick will win at the end and prays Jackie will be convincing so she can dial down her worrying.

Her phone says it's five minutes to six o'clock, so she hurries back to the house. Her mother and Marietta are already sitting at the kitchen table, quietly waiting. Kenny pulls up a chair to join them, but she doesn't speak either. It's like they are all afraid of jinxing the message Jackie will have for them. It's almost 6:20 p.m. when the phone rings, and they all three jump.

Carolyn hurries to answer. "Hello?" She pauses.

"Yes. The girls are here with me... Oh, no. That's quite all right. Of course, you had to take the time to read the judge's ruling." Carolyn looks at her daughters. "May I put you on the speaker, Jackie?"

Jackie says, "Can everyone hear me?"

"Yes," Carolyn and Marietta say at the same time.

Kenny says, "Hi, Jackie."

"Hi, Kenny. Marietta. Carolyn, how is everyone holding up?"

Carolyn says, "Okay. But I think we're all about to burst with worry. Can you just tell us the bottom line first?"

"Of course. The bottom line is that Judge Marcus sees no basis whatsoever for the state's complaint. She's awarded you costs and fees."

Kenny says, "But is she going to let them file an amended complaint, like you said?"

"That's the surprising part. She made it very clear that she does not want to hear from the state again on this matter."

"Wow," Marietta says.

"Can the state appeal?" asks Mom.

"They could. But the chances they'd attempt it are slim to none, and Slim just left town." Jackie laughs. "Sorry. It's just something one of the judges here likes to say."

"That's wonderful news," Carolyn says.

"Would you like to hear my favorite paragraph?"

"Duh!" Kenny says, then laughs.

"Here goes: *In conclusion, the state of Illinois has wasted taxpayer money filing an entirely frivolous complaint against Carolyn Warren, individually and d/b/a The Warren Family Zoo. The state's complaint fails to state a cause of action, as a matter of law. More taxpayer money was wasted on the state's nonsensical and legally incomprehensible memorandum in opposition to Mrs. Warren's motion to dismiss. I will not opine on what goal could have inspired such unprofessional and inexcusable filings. But let me be clear. I will not have the good citizens of this county, like Mrs. Warren, subjected to what is little more than harassment. The case is dismissed with prejudice, all costs and fees to be assessed against the state. Counsel for Mrs. Warren shall submit a fee petition within fourteen days."*

"So, we won." Marietta is a master of understatement.

"Yes," Jackie says. "I'd say so."

"Was it because of what the judge heard at the trial?" Kenny asks.

"It shouldn't have been. The facts aren't supposed to be weighed in a motion to dismiss. It's just a question of whether the state alleged enough to state a cause of action. Of course, the judge had learned a lot about what really happened during the trial. And she's just human."

"Was the ruling correct?" Kenny feels she has to know.

"Let's just say the state has nowhere to go with this, in the long run because Ms. Benni has never been a threat to the public. So even if they challenged the ruling and won, it would be a pyrrhic victory. And they have to be aware of the 'taxpayer money' aspect, which Judge Marcus hammered in her opinion."

"So it's over for good."

"Yes, Kenny. I believe it is."

"Should you call the newspaper and let them

know?"

"Never poke a tiger, Kenny."

"What?"

"Like I said, the state's attorney never had a valid case against your mom because it's a fact Ms. Benni has never been a threat to the community. But if I were to blab about the judge's order, I just might infuriate Mr. Babcock."

"So?"

"He has lots of ways to make a citizen's life hell."

"Oh. No more hell," Carolyn says. "We'll all keep our silence."

"Right. Of course, it is a matter of public record, so the papers will get it on their own. But not through any of us. Okay, Marietta? Kenny?"

"Absolutely," Marietta says.

"My lips are sealed, too. Pinkie-swear."

They all thank Jackie again. Although hugely relieved, their fatigue has only increased from the stress of waiting for the phone call. Carolyn and Marietta say they just need to rest for a bit, and return to their rooms. Kenny makes some microwave popcorn and fills a tall glass with crushed ice and a cola. She knows she'll need to stream a movie to unwind.

Kenny had remembered to text Becca right away as soon as they got out of the courtroom after the settlement, and she texted her to explain why she'd sent the video of Jimmy in the cage. Now Kenny texts her again with the good news about the judge's order before she heads up to her room with the popcorn. Becca sends back a happy face emoji and three hearts.

The two friends would've gone out to a movie to celebrate, but Becca is still grounded, in spite of the reprieve for the London trip. So Kenny gets herself all set up in her bed, with her food stash on her nightstand and her laptop nestled atop her sheets. Her phone rings.

"Hi, Kenny. It's Barb."

She can't place the voice. "Barb."

"Barb Hale from freshman English."

She is one of the last people on earth Kenny expected to hear from. "Oh, hi, Barb. How're you doing?"

"I'm fine. My dad made me call you because he was on the jury."

Kenny has never met Barb's father—she barely knows Barb. She had no idea a classmate's father was on the jury. "Really?"

"Yeah. He wants you to ask your lawyer something. He says her name is Ms. Bauer."

"Okay."

"He wants to know if he's allowed to talk to her."

"No problem. Hang on and I'll shoot Jackie a quick text."

"Okay, I'll hold."

Kenny sends a message to Jackie and the response comes right away. "Barb?"

"Yeah?"

"Jackie says he's allowed to talk about the trial with her or anybody else—now that it's all over."

"Good. My dad says he'd like to stop by her office on Monday morning. He got the address from their website. He has to be at work at nine a.m. so he'll drop by at eight, if that works for her."

"Let me check."

Again, the return text comes through immediately. "She says that'll be fine."

"Cool. Thanks, Kenny. Maybe we'll have a class together."

"That'd be great."

"See ya."

"Bye, Barb."

Kenny wonders what Mr. Hale will have to say about the trial. But there is no way she'll upset her mother or Marietta unless Jackie tells her on Monday that there's something they need to know. Kenny leans back against her pillow, pulls the movie set in London back up, and presses "play."

Chapter 35

Jackie

Monday morning is hectic. Jackie meets with Mr. Hale for a half hour, then has to scramble to get her documents together for a nine a.m. status hearing on a case she hasn't worked on in a couple of months. When she gets back to her office, she sees that the settlement papers in *Alcott vs. Warren* were delivered, already signed by Dean.

Jackie is finally able to get away at lunch time to visit the Warrens and get Carolyn's signature. She calls first to be sure Carolyn will be in. When all the Warren women meet her at the front door, it hits her how much she'll miss the zoo, Carolyn, Marietta, and especially Kenny. As she steps through the front door, she says, "Say, could we all sit down for a minute? I have something to tell you." She's already heading for the dining table by force of habit. They all take their usual seats.

Kenny says, "Jackie, you can't keep that smile off your face, can you?"

"No. That's why I don't play poker." She laughs. "You'll all be smiling when you hear what I have to tell you."

"We could use something to smile about. My girls are down about not letting the jury give us a not guilty,"

Carolyn says.

"No, we're not," says Kenny. Her mother stares at her. "Okay, we're a little bummed about it."

"So, what's the news, Jackie?" Carolyn says.

Jackie suspected that Kenny didn't tell the others about the contact by Mr. Hale, so she says simply, "One of the jurors stopped by my office this morning."

"Really?" Carolyn says. "Are they allowed to do that?"

"They are. It was one of the men. He said he was on his way to work and didn't have much time. But he wanted me to know what the jury thought of the case."

"Oh, my," Carolyn says.

"Mr. Hale told me that all eight of the women wanted to find the zoo guilty under the statute."

"But what about our 'provocation' defense?" asks Kenny.

The three women are staring at her intently. "Apparently, they did agree that Dean kicked at Ms. Benni—"

"No duh," says Kenny, "since we have a video of it."

"Right. And they believed all of you, Charlie, Mrs. Wilcox, and Dr. Lucas that Ms. Benni is a grudge tiger."

"Good," Carolyn says. "I thought Dr. Lucas was very persuasive."

"Then what didn't they believe?" asks Marietta.

"They refused to believe that it was the kick to Ms. Benni's head that led to the attack. It seems, according to this man, that the women were bound and determined to give 'that poor sweet boy' some money."

"Yikes!" says Kenny.

"Yeah. The women had convinced the other three

men and were working on the last one—Mr. Hale—
when we settled. He wasn't sure how long he could hold
out. Most of them were arguing with him and yelling at
him. One tried to sweet-talk him. Well, they were all
over the poor guy. He felt so much pressure that he was
starting to doubt himself."

"Wow," Marietta says.

"Did he say how much they wanted to give Dean?"
Carolyn asks.

"Oh, yes. That was the first thing they all decided—
as in, unanimously. They believed everything Dean said
about the modeling career. If they found the zoo guilty,
they'd already agreed on the number."

The three women stare at her. Kenny says, "How
much, Jackie?"

"Three point eight million."

Carolyn gasps.

Kenny says, "Oh, my God!" then leans over and
hugs her mother. "You were right. You saved the zoo!"
She shakes her head slightly and adds, "I'm so sorry I've
been pouting all weekend about Dean getting the
insurance money."

Marietta says, "I don't know how I could've been so
stupid. Of course the jury ate it up. Everyone loves
Dean."

"Yes. It seems you're right," Jackie says.

Turning to her mother, Marietta says, "I'm sorry too.
You're amazing, Mom. You were the only one who saw
it coming—thank goodness you stuck to your guns."

"Well, I had it wrong, too," Jackie says. "And it's
my job to see it coming."

Carolyn puts both hands down on the table. "Please.
Stop congratulating me! I didn't see it coming either. I

thought we were going to win, too."

Kenny says, "Then why did you decide to offer the insurance money?"

"Because, girls, I thought there must be some chance—however slight—that we'd lose. And Jackie, I don't play poker either."

"Well, I'm certainly glad you don't." As Jackie rises from the table, she laughs. "With the judge's ruling on Friday evening, and now this, I'd say we all have something to celebrate. May I take you all out to dinner tonight? Somewhere splendid and expensive."

Carolyn looks up sharply and says, "No." Then she laughs. "*I'll* take us out to dinner. As I mentioned when we first met, Jackie, I'm not a turnip yet."

* * * *

Jackie isn't nearly as sanguine about narrowly squeaking by a financial disaster for her client as she lets on during her meeting with the Warrens. The moment Mr. Hale walked out of her office, she started to second-guess herself. It appears that she not only convinced the Warrens, Dean, and Hank that she was about to win the trial—she also convinced herself. But any decent trial lawyer would've known that the verdict easily could've gone either way. And not due to a rogue jury defying the court's instructions, as she intimated to Carolyn and her daughters.

It's on the drive back to her office from her meeting with the Warrens that she forces herself to think through the whole thing dispassionately—much easier to do with the stress of the trial behind her.

If they hadn't settled, and the jury had awarded Dean the three point eight million, she would've filed a post-trial motion for judgment notwithstanding the verdict or a new trial, basically arguing the verdict was not in keeping with the evidence, so that no reasonable jury would've found against the zoo. But her motion would've been denied. Correctly.

The question for the jury was simply whether it was more probably true than not that Ms. Benni attacked because of the kick at her head. If Hank had just made a more compelling argument, Jackie would've recognized her vulnerability. Anyway, it feels better to blame him for her failure of judgment. He should've stressed three things more forcefully. 1. That even if the jurors believed Ms. Benni is a grudge tiger *and* that Dean kicked her in the head two weeks earlier, there was no conclusive proof that this combination caused the attack. 2. That this was bolstered by Dr. Lucas's own testimony that in spite of the fact that Ms. Benni did not attack the Warren women for their incursions into her enclosure, they were foolish to have tried it, and risk serious injury if they try it again. 3. That, therefore, Dr. Lucas conceded that the mere intrusion into the cage *can* result in an attack. The bottom line is that the attack could've been a direct result of the grudge, or could've been a direct result of the intrusion. The jury was free to weigh the two possibilities, and its conclusion it was more likely the latter was well within its discretion. Judge Marcus never would have overturned such a verdict, and neither would an appellate court.

They were able to settle because she convinced Hank and Dean that the zoo was about to win. But she didn't convince the jury. And she should've realized that could well be the result—even if Dean had been an ugly troll of a boy rather than a Greek god. So, all-in-all, the settlement was a lucky break.

Jackie takes a deep breath, and lets out a long, slow sigh. She'd brought Carolyn perilously close to ruin with her overly optimistic estimate of eighty percent chance to win. It was only her client's sensible decision to settle that saved them both. She knows this is exactly the kind of reality that could plunge her into more second-guessing, rumination, and even paralysis. She recognizes it because of the similarity to her immersion in despair from her loss of Sam and Gloria. What had Nigel said? That she could get her life back. She can let things eat at her—or not. She supposes he's right that it really is a choice. She'll find a good therapist.

****

The next day, Jackie receives a text from Kenny telling her that her mom emailed Nigel to thank him and to let him and Jamie know how everything turned out. Carolyn also told Nigel that Dean never would have accepted the insurance money had it not been for his persuasive expert testimony. And she invited them both to visit the zoo if they ever find themselves in the states. Jamie then texted Kenny, "Confidentially, I'll make sure we come. Pinkie-swear." Jackie had long since written off her expert witness as a romantic partner because he is, after all, in England. So, she surprises herself by how pleased she is that she'll be able to see Nigel again. She catches herself whistling as she walks down the corridors of her offices.

****

A few days pass and she can no longer resist the temptation to make a call. "Hi, Hank. I assume you received Helen's settlement check."

"It came in yesterday. Thanks for checking up on it."

"Sure. Would you tell Dean something for me?"

"Maybe."

"Tell him I never believed the stuff about his modeling vocation."

"No. I won't tell him that."

"Then just tell him this. Tell him I think he should pursue a career as a salesman. I'm serious, Hank. Tell him I think he'd be a huge success."

Chapter 36

Kenny

In the first month of school, only three girls, all seniors, mention the trial. They don't seem to know about her Dean-stalking, or maybe they just don't care.

One says, "I can't believe Dean sued your mom because he let himself into your tiger cage. What a dick!"

The second says, "I'm glad you guys didn't lose the trial. My little brothers are absolutely nuts over your zoo."

Then Barb Hale sees Kenny at her locker, grabs her arm and pulls her close. She whispers, "My dad told me what happened. I'm so glad your lawyer was smart enough to settle." She gives Kenny a big smile and walks on.

Kenny realizes she's pretty stupid for a smart girl. She should've known that even the meanest girls would be too wrapped up in their own senior-year dramas to give a thought to hers. She vaguely remembers Marietta said this might happen.

In another month she's totally back on track studying colleges and scholarship opportunities. One afternoon, she jumps off the school bus and makes her usual beeline to their mailbox, expecting more materials from colleges. Among them, she finds a tan envelope with a foreign-looking stamp and smudged return information. Since it's addressed to her mother *and* her, Kenny feels fine about ripping it open.

Dear Mrs. Warren and Kenny,

My father insisted I prepare a proper letter and send it to you the old-fashioned way. He and I very much enjoyed meeting you, Kenny, and your friend Becca, and Jackie. We were both delighted to hear how the trial was resolved, and hope that things have calmed down for all of you and returned to normal. I write because I will have a four-week break from university beginning on Christmas Eve. My father and I are hoping it will be convenient for us to visit you for whatever week in January would work best for you.

We completely understand if it is not doable for any reason. My father is writing separately to Jackie with the same proposal. I really hope a visit will be possible. In any event, I have to ask. I pinkie-swore to do so.

Yours fondly,

Jamie

P.S. Please respond by text or email since I'm dying to know your answer…

A word about the author...

Judith Fournie Helms grew up in southern Illinois, and attended college and law school in Chicago. She became a founding partner of a law firm based in Chicago with offices on both coasts, and was recognized by her peers as a "Super Lawyer" and a "Leading Lawyer." Retired from the practice of law, Judith writes novels and short stories at her home in Virginia where she lives with her husband. She is the author of the 2018 novel, 'The Toronto Embryo,' the 2025 novel, 'Statures of No Limitations,' and the 2025 novel, 'Blue Ridge to Bolivia.' www.judithhelms.com

Thank you for purchasing
this publication of The Wild Rose Press, Inc.

For questions or more information
contact us at
info@thewildrosepress.com.

The Wild Rose Press, Inc.
www.thewildrosepress.com